Elena Zhuravleva

The Temptation of the Midnight Bird: Last Turn

Table of Contents

4

The Temptation of the Midnight Bird: Last Turn

A Novel

Chapter 1

The forest hummed and sighed dully, making guttural sounds, as if somewhere in its depths a one-eyed hunchback was brewing his magic potion, stirring it with a long-handled spoon. The temperature in the cauldron was climbing by the minute, air bubbles rose from the bottom, making their way through the thick oily film on the surface, forming small craters, through which a foul smell escaped. The pressure under this film slowly kept on rising, making it appear the cauldron could explode any minute, but the evil potion-brewing hunchback threw wood onto the fire again and again.

Life in the forest froze. A lonely night bird suddenly shook its wings, and began to thrash about, wail, and take to the air unexpectedly, hitting the trees and wounding itself with prickly branches. After her, a young, inexperienced crow cawed stupidly, but an owl hooted an admonishment, and everything fell silent again. Neither birds, nor mice, nor any other forest animal dared raise their voices and interrupt the heavy leaden expectation. The pine forest, filled with warm fragrant air, changed gradually; the soft light dissolved into the creeping swirling darkness, filling every corner, every clearing and path and pushing the light up into the sky. And in the silence that followed, one could hear him move.

And suddenly a crazed wind, like a wild horse that had been kept on a leash for many days, broke loose and let out all its anger on the forest. The huge pines shuddered, but resisted, and then the wind, which seemed to have been entangled in the treetops and lost all its force after the unsuccessful first attack, rushed into battle again, spiraling everything that came its way. Tearing off leaves with violent force, crumbling dry branches and bending to the ground those loners who dared to grow on the edges, without the protection and patronage of their mighty brethren. It whooshed around the neighborhood and fell silent, as if suddenly losing interest in this forest. Those who still hoped that the storm would pass began to relax. However, after only a few seconds, the wind soared into the dark skies and, tearing the night clouds to shreds, revealed the dazzling beauty of the moon to the world. Like a jealous husband bursting into his wife's bedroom and tearing off her bedspread, it hoped to find a lover in her bed. But she, alone, innocent and beautiful, shone high above the world, and then, out of shame at what he had done, the jealous bastard began to destroy everything around. Mighty pines hummed and groaned, begging for mercy and to let them be, while smaller trees simply prostrated themselves, expressing complete submission to its superiority. Heavy clouds filled to the brim with moisture flew to aid the wind, and everything around rumbled, spun; jets of ice poured down, flooding everything in their path, forcing those who had not yet obeyed their instinct to hide to immediately seek refuge, lightning flashed every minute, and thunder exploded deafeningly like cannon volleys.

Lisa was instantly soaked to the skin; she looked around helplessly in search of shelter – she had already gone quite far from any human habitation, and the storm had emerged so suddenly. Opening her eyes wide in the coming darkness, trying to see something, anything, and then squinting from the fiery flashes, she saw nothing but the black trunks of huge pines. Knowing that a storm like this was very dangerous, and she needed to take cover somewhere, she kept frantically searching, but there was nowhere to hide – there was no nearby shelter, only tall pine trees with their crowns somewhere high, and they could not save her from the downpour.

Her dress stuck to her body, becoming one with it, and Lisa felt naked, like the moon, which had been exposed by the wind not long ago. Trying to somehow hide from the cold rain, Lisa first wrapped her arms around her shoulders, because her small backpack, more of a stylish bag, did not cover her back at all. The rain was too strong and cold. Lisa had raised her hands to her face in a vain attempt to protect herself from it, but wet hair was glued to her neck, sneaking into her mouth, and the rain wouldn't let her see.

Lisa had to remember where she had come from. This was not a wild forest, this was the city park, or rather the part of it where well-groomed alleys ended and only barely noticeable paths and narrow glades remained, leading into the thicket. And she was here for a reason. She had a goal and a specific task.

"Calm down! Don't panic! It's just rain," she told herself.

The park entrance was behind her, because she had been following one of the alleys and never changed course. Everything was as she had been told. All she had to do was go back to the place where she made a turn into this clearing and look for shelter somewhere in the park. With so many coffee shops and gazebos around, she had nothing to worry about. This thought warmed Lisa a little but did not give her strength. All she wanted now was to just curl up into a ball like an animal and wait out the storm under some tree, among strong roots peeking out of the ground. Not a great hideout, per se, and it wouldn't stop the cold rain; also, she could simply freeze lying on the bare ground. No, she had to move, had to run! Lisa turned around and dashed in the opposite direction. Not really seeing anything in the dark, she immediately caught her foot on a pine root and fell, landing hard on her hands and knees. Scrambling up, she tried running again, but the wet grass stuck to her legs, winding round them, not letting go of its prey. She could only wander hopelessly, looking for another root or boulder in the lightning flashes. Another step and Lisa slipped on the slippery mash and tumbled down, grazing her elbows, back, and shoulders.

Was there a ravine here before? Or was she lost? Which way was the park?

Fortunately, Lisa only had to get out of a shallow pit, which she had mistaken for a ravine, on all fours, grabbing at grass and roots, tearing off her nails. She lost her footing a few times, fell on the lumpy ground on her face and slid down, but still crawled back to her bag, which flew off her back sometime during yet another failed attempt to escape.

Running in a storm was not a good idea, she suddenly remembered reading that somewhere. You could bait out lightning, and hiding under trees was not an option, because lightning very often strikes the highest ones. So, she had to keep going...

Suddenly, a new sound reached her through the wind; somewhere close a woman was crying—no, she was sobbing and wailing and calling for help. Lisa froze and strained her ears, trying to focus, to hear where the sounds were coming from, no easy task thanks to the overlapping thunderclaps. No, she didn't know that voice. Looked like someone was in an even worse situation than her. But how could she help? Lisa removed the backpack, which had become twice as heavy because of, well, being soaked through, and at first, couldn't untie the knot on the ornate curled rope. Lisa's fingers were numb from the cold and would not bend. The rope slipped and the knot tightened even more. Only after biting into it with her teeth was Lisa able to stretch the knot and find the phone inside the bag. The screen flashed with such a familiar, pleasant light, as if winking, "Don't be afraid, I'm with you, I'm your reliable friend, I'll always come to the rescue." But it was an empty promise – there was no connection. And what should she have expected in such a thunderstorm? Just call the rescue service and say, "Hey, I'm here, somewhere in the dark forest and someone is calling for help. So, hurry up, help. And while you're at it, get me out of this hell?" Stupid.

Lisa shoved the useless phone back inside her bag and listened carefully, trying to hear the woman's voice again through the roaring thunder, but couldn't.

"Maybe I imagined it," Lisa thought hopefully. She had to get out and fast, so she ordered herself to breathe in and out, keeping her head low so as not to choke on water, forcing herself to concentrate on finding the clearing, looking for it in flashes of lightning. And then she heard that voice again. The woman was screaming desperately, calling for help. At the worst possible moment, Lisa, for some reason, remembered the forest fairies, who, like sirens, lured sailors into the sea, using deception to trap people who got lost in the woods.

What if it really were a fairy or some other forest creature, mythical or real? But it meant nothing now, in the pouring rain, so if Lisa succumbed to the spell and ran to help the woman, could there be anyone out there? Anything. Yes, anything, and pictures, each scarier than the one before, began flashing before her eyes – deep pit traps hiding under seemingly harmless dry branches, and in the pit, a huge man-eating spider, or branches of bushes suddenly turning into snakes and slowly suffocating people, or something black, furry, horrendous... At that moment, indeed, something black and furry moved towards her. Shrieking so that all the forest dwellers, who had been hiding from the storm in their secret lairs, probably heard her, Lisa made a ridiculous jump to the side and took off running, no longer thinking about the grass grabbing at her feet, or about the lightning, which always hit a moving target. Fear gave her incredible speed, and she ran in a frenzy, at random, only to get somewhere else.

The furry, black monster was catching up with her. Lisa was panting, constantly slipping and, only by some miracle, staying on her feet. She felt its hot, stinking breath on the back of her head; finally, exhausted, she turned around and immediately tripped, fell on her back, and the monster jumped on her chest...

Chapter 2

Lisa slowly opened her eyes. The furry monster did not disappear, its narrowed yellow eyes staring into her face, endless contempt flowing from them. The white whiskers around its mouth bristled, tense lips twitched, partially exposing the sharp teeth. The monster's claws dug into her shirt, scratching at her skin. The monster sat on her chest with its body half-turned and seemed ready to run in an unknown direction.

"Well, that's enough! Enough, I said! Get out of here, or she'll wake up, and you'll be flying around as if you had a fan on your back," someone's raspy voice reached Lisa through heavy oblivion.

She opened her eyes wider, barely forcing her eyelids open, and found a huge smoky-gray cat on her chest.

"Scram, I said," the same rough voice shouted at the cat, and Lisa recognized her neighbor who lived in the house on the other side of their small quiet street.

"Am I at home? How did I get here? How did *you* get here?"

she whispered through swollen lips.

"Oh, you're awake," the now familiar voice rasped. "My Lord sneaked into your house, and I was looking for him... that's how I ended up here..." Lisa knew from the neighbor's downcast eyes that she was lying.

"And how did you open my door?"

"Honey, your lock can be picked with a pin. You should change it. There have been some lowlifes around here lately just scurrying about... And with your lifestyle..."

Martha, that was the neighbor's name, started giving a boring lecture on how bad it was for a young woman to live alone, avoid neighbors and have no friends... Added something about them being not made of stone and understanding that she had reasons to live like this... That she was young, beautiful, got her whole life ahead of her...

"Stop, Martha, just...stop! I've already asked you to stay out of my life."

"Yes, and I would do that, but with your way of living..."

"What do you even know about my life? And actually, I live however the hell I want. I'm quite happy. Is that clear?"

"I can see that," the old woman continued to grumble.

Only now, when she tried to get up and put the uninvited guest out the door, Lisa felt pain, pain all over her body at once – in her legs, shoulders, neck, arms. She threw the blanket aside and saw a big bloody gouge stretching up from her knee. Lisa checked another part of her body, where it hurt just as bad – her left arm – and saw a significant bruise, growing and spreading right before her eyes. Her whole body was covered with bruises and abrasions of various sizes and shapes, as if she had been stoned, and then lashed.

"That's what I'm talking about," Lisa heard the same old rasp again. "What happened to you, my dear?"

Following a hunch, Lisa reached for her backpack. There was a small mirror in her makeup bag, but she remembered the big one in the bathroom and tried to get out of bed. She felt dizzy, the room began spinning, and she had to sit down.

Surprisingly, the old hag made no comments on her unsuccessful attempt and only shook her head. Nothing but vague mumbling came from her side.

On the second try, Lisa managed to get up. Barely holding back a groan, she went to the bathroom, stopped halfway and, turning her head to her neighbor, said firmly, "Yes, you're right! I went to the highway, to the ring road to turn tricks. I always do it. A client beat me up. No! Actually! I was beaten up by my pimp for not being able to please a client! No! Wrong again! Here's a better one. I bit him! Why? He wanted to fuck me in the ass, and I didn't. Are you satisfied? Then get lost! And tell everyone who is concerned about my fate, all the gossips with their big bleeding hearts, that I am a whore!"

The neighbor did not respond to her monologue.

At first, Lisa did not believe what she saw in the mirror: pale greenish skin, sunken cheeks, dark circles under her eyes and a huge abrasion, as if she were dragged face down on rocky ground.

Great! Just great!

Lisa turned on the tap, lowered her head, putting the left side of her face under the stream to wash the scratch. The searing pain made her recoil. Then, she just got into the shower, as she was, in a dirty tattered shirt. The cold water was instantly sobering, so she had to make it warmer. Lisa poured a handful of shampoo on her head, furiously lathering her hair and trying to wash away the fear she had experienced along with the dirt. Afterward, she removed the shirt, letting her body feel the life-giving power of water.

At some point, Lisa remembered that she was not alone and slammed the bathroom door.

"I thought you were dead. You haven't been out for so long. So, I came to check on you, and Lord was eager to see you," she still heard over the noise of the water.

Lisa didn't like the neighbor's cat, Lord. One time, she'd come home and found him sleeping on the keyboard of her computer. The cat got into the house through a half-closed window, stomped all over the keyboard, and then, apparently exhausted, lay down to rest. As a result, all the settings were screwed, a million tasks were running at the same time, and some lines with code appeared constantly... In short, it was impossible to work. The computer tech had a look at it and just asked, "Did you Skype with the devil himself?"

Since then, Lisa had been carefully to lock her windows and doors. But how did Martha get into the house today? And how did

Lisa get home by herself? It looked like she passed out as soon as she was through the door.

The old neighbor amplified the sound of her squeaky voice box and, surprisingly, easily shouted over the water.

Lisa didn't answer her, standing there as water flowed through her hair, over her shoulders, down her back, washing away the dirt and filth and everything else she had been through tonight.

"And why are you all beaten up?" Martha kept asking.

"Will you just go? It doesn't concern you! And I've already explained everything to you."

"Well, as you wish."

And Martha left, carrying the squirming cat under her arm.

"It's been so long since you've been outside," Martha said. So long... how long exactly? So, it didn't happen last night? Was she unconscious or was it some kind of lethargic sleep? Or was her neighbor lying to make her feel ashamed? She shouldn't have sent old Martha away.

Somehow wiping her body with a bath towel, Lisa took an antiseptic from the first aid kit, wincing and crying out in pain, and began to treat her wounds. When the healing torture was over, she rummaged in the closet, found an old, washed out, stretched shirt and put it on.

Throwing a handful of beans into the coffee maker, she pressed the button like she always did. The machine shook, as it always did, screeched threateningly, as if reminding her that it was time to take it to a repair shop, but then it buzzed smoothly, peacefully, and the usual morning aroma floated through the kitchen, reminding her better than any alarm clock that a new day had come.

Lisa poured some coffee into a cup and took the first sip, the same sip that millions of people around the world started their day with. These few minutes of bliss replaced morning prayer for many – let this day be calm, successful, let it pass without shocks and let all hopes come true.

The coffee was very good. Lisa even narrowed her eyes with pleasure. She brought this pack home from the last presentation of the new brand. No wonder they had been going on about this little-known, not yet widely promoted, but very good grade of coffee. Many firms sin, initially producing an excellent product that becomes much worse when it goes into wide distribution, but this coffee was not there yet, and for now, she could simply enjoy a great drink.

And then her eyes saw it – a simple white envelope laying on the table near the front door where she usually left her keys. Lisa shifted her gaze to the trash can; a few days ago, one of these letters ended up there too. Actually, no one had written to her for a long time, and she only checked the mailbox for the plethora of flyers and booklets that stuffed the box until there were too many of them for the old box to not fall apart. Knowing that such things unnerved her vigilant neighbors, Lisa emptied it from time to time. Last time, she found a letter without the sender's address or name among all the junk. She immediately threw this letter into the trash along with the other advertising literature, believing that it most likely contained a pitiful request to transfer money to the account of some "terminally ill" person. Recently, the world had grown tired of all things online, which was first caused by the Internet, then by a virus; now, it was trying to get back to normal, and such requests that came through social media or e-mail were simply cleaned out like junk. Scammers remembered the good old-fashioned way of communicating their ideas - text on paper, simple and relatable. More expensive? But, as the record had shown, it was more effective.

And yet, some vague feeling of anxiety made Lisa take the letter out of the trash and open it. There were only a few lines of text.

"If you think that the past cannot be changed, then you are mistaken. Every day you wake up and remember what causes you unbearable pain, despite all the years that have passed, and ask yourself, 'Why did I do this then, and could I have done it differently?' And more importantly – is it possible to change it? What if you could? Are you ready to try?"

Instructions on what to do and where to go followed the message:

1) Go to the city park;

2) At the very end, turn into the third alley, which will lead you to a place where you will receive further instructions.

The insolence of the sender made her laugh. Well, of course! Now she's going to drop everything and hurry into the woods for more instructions! Who was this even supposed to be for?

Lisa laughed again, imagining herself on a bus to the public park and then looking for some clearing in the forest to get instructions. Although the letter's authors did have a basic understanding of psychology, she'd give them that. Perhaps every adult had a situation in their life that they would like to change, to relive... And many people do live with an inescapable sense of guilt for what they have done, for the pain they caused to a loved one... Sometimes this pain is so unbearable that a person drowns their sorrows with alcohol or drugs... And in some cases, they are unable to cope... and just kill themselves...

"That's enough!" She cut herself off. She's not going to the park to look for some clearing...

Was it just a stupid prank? Could someone truly fall for something so silly? Go to the park, turn into a clearing and find who knows what? She wouldn't have gone if it hadn't been for a strange incident a few days before the letter: in the supermarket where she always went shopping for groceries and necessary household goods, someone called her, "Laura, is that you? Laura, hi! You've changed, but I recognized you anyway. How are you, Laura?"

Lisa turned at the voice – some woman, a total stranger, with her arms open, was walking towards her and smiling. *She must have mistaken me for someone else*, Lisa thought, but the woman came closer and began hugging her, kissing her on the cheeks, while sighing and looking at Lisa, as if trying to discover what had changed about her body and what had remained the same.

"You're wrong," Lisa cut her off, "I'm not Laura."

"No, Laura, why don't you recognize me?" the stranger's face became resentful, "It's me, Sophie, your best friend."

"No," Lisa backed away from this strange woman who claimed to be her friend, "I do not know you. You mistook me for someone else. I do not have a friend with that name."

And Lisa ran for the exit, and then the bus stop, without buying anything.

All the way home, her own words rang in her head, "I don't have a friend with that name." And it was true. Sophie was friends with her younger sister Laura, a wonderful little girl with curly blond hair and soft warm palms – beautiful as a doll that you'd want to kiss all the time. Unlike many children, Lisa immediately accepted and loved her younger sister when her parents brought her from the hospital. Over time, Laura became a real beauty – a thin, slender figure, blond waves of hair falling over her shoulders and sky-blue eyes that looked at the world with childish delight and surprise, as if she was always waiting for gifts from it. A kind and sweet girl, whom that very world had treated so badly.

But Lisa didn't look like her at all, and the woman who called her by her sister's name in the store looked nothing like Laura's friend Sophie.

Her sister, her little sister, had disappeared, and they still didn't know where she was, if she was even alive. The search revealed nothing, although they had been looking for Laura for a long time.

The police assumed that she had been murdered, or rather, her boyfriend, an adult man whom she had been recently seeing, had murdered her. People who knew about their relationship claimed that they often fought and Alexander, the boyfriend, wasn't all that gentle and kind with her. She could have just run away from him and hidden somewhere. The police also searched for him, and they found the man – dead, in his apartment, but no evidence was discovered pointing to the killer or the motive of the crime, and the investigation reached a dead end. Could Laura have offed Alexander? Of course, they thought about that, but knowing how Alexander was killed – a strong blow to the head with a heavy object, and comparing that method to Laura's fragile physique, the detectives on the case concluded that she could not have done it. And yet there were still too many questions with no answers.

Time passed, hope faded, but the pain was never gone. Sometimes, when playing with someone's children, Lisa purposely took a child by the hand, as if hoping that by touching that little palm, she would feel Laura's warm touch. She wanted so badly for Laura to be found and for them to meet, for her sister to run to her, wrapping her arms around her neck. And so they would stand, just holding each other for a long time, sharing warmth and breathing in dear smells.

That's why she went to the forest, despite the absurdity of the offer in the letter, and then got scared and ran away because of a stupid thunderstorm, cutting off, perhaps, the only thread that could lead her to her sister.

And now there was a similar white envelope on the table by

the door. No longer in the mailbox outside, but in her house.

Maybe it was Martha who took the letter? But then, Martha would have brought in all the other junk. She would never have thrown it away without sorting it and putting it in special bags. So, not Martha.

Lisa went to the table and carefully touched the letter with two fingers. Only her name was written on the envelope. No return address, just like in the first case. So, it wasn't the mailman either. But while putting a letter in a mailbox is not that difficult, who could bring it into the house? Maybe it was Martha after all, and Lisa was sorry again for telling the neighbor to leave. No matter, she's going to leave this for later. And now she just tore open the envelope and took out the same white sheet of paper with the text typed on a computer. A hail of reproaches rained down on her seconds later: why did she run away from the forest – a thunderstorm, no problem. Why didn't she follow the woman's voice? If she wanted to know the truth, then she must consistently follow the instructions.

Yes, yes! Precisely! Lisa remembered – in the first letter they emphasized that it was necessary to pay attention to anything unusual. That voice in the forest was unusual, and it was calling for her. And Lisa, as if in a daydream, heard those sounds, pleading, calling. And she also heard the thunder and the piercing rain, drowning out everything except that voice. But that voice in the forest, calling for help... Lisa was ready to run to where it was coming from, but it was someone else's voice, not like her sister's.

Lisa paced to the couch and sat down.

What did all this mean? The woman in the supermarket and these letters? If they wanted to harm her –for example, to kidnap her for ransom, then the time she spent in the forest would have been quite enough. If they wanted to kill her, then even more so. And why even kidnap or kill her? She never had much money, and she didn't have the time to make any mortal enemies. If it was just a prank, then who planned it and why?

Lisa read the letter again. They forgave her for now and promised to send further instructions in the near future.

And then she heard a vibrating sound – her phone. Still working? Back in the woods, there was no coverage, she recalled, while hobbling to her backpack, thrown on the floor by the couch.

And now it was back. The phone was working and messages about missed calls popped on the screen. A couple of calls from an old acquaintance, with whom she occasionally met for coffee. The rest were all from her boss, Daniel. Lisa and Danny had become friends while working together in the same newsroom, at one time their ways parted, and then, they started working in the same office again, only now he was her boss, and she was still a reporter. Danny was a good editor, she'd give him that. Despite him being young and not having much experience, he knew the value and capabilities of each employee and did not overwork Lisa with the minutiae that was inevitable in small editorial offices where everyone had to replace one another. But a beautiful report from a presentation of a new product, or an exhibition, after which the organizers placed ads in their online publication? Something like that Danny would entrust only to her. For this, Lisa got a good bump. And, of course, Lisa did reports on the most resonant events of their city. Danny knew perfectly well her ability to get people talking, to give them all the opportunity to speak out and thus show the different sides of a situation. True, there weren't that many such events in their city, but Danny sent her on business trips to such incidents, despite the still very limited budget of their young outlet.

Turning on the voice message, Lisa heard Danny's uneven voice.

"Where are you? I've been calling and calling. We have an emergency – some terrorist has seized a bus with people and is threatening to blow it up. The bus is now on Freedom Square. If you're not dead yet (Danny sneezed loudly at this point), then go there immediately."

A terrorist hijacked a bus full of people? In their peaceful, boring city? Such things occurred in other cities and countries, but not here. Everything went dark before Lisa's eyes. She was terrified.

"Okay, calm down! Remember, you are a professional, forget about emotions!" she told herself. "The bus is on Freedom Square, so get there."

Lisa looked doubtfully at her skinned leg, at her wounded arm... let's say she could still cover these with clothes, but her face... No makeup could conceal that...

After putting her phone on the charger and letting it get some juice, she found several messages about the hijacking of the bus. There wasn't much, just bits of information, but it all came down to the following:

"A stranger took a bus full of hostages and notified the law enforcement of his demands. Negotiations are underway while the hijacker is being kept on the phone."

"According to the chief of the local police department, the man published a post on social media, in which he expressed his dissatisfaction with the existing system. The attacker has not put forward any specified requirements and demands."

"The police are negotiating and trying to restrict civilian access to the central part of the city. Residents and guests are being asked to be understanding and for their own safety not to approach the scene of the crime."

Damn it! This was big! Lisa was barely keeping down her annoyance. Journalists from all over the country would come here, and she couldn't even move! She had frustrated tears in her eyes – so stupid, so untimely, she fell for some silly prank and went to the forest and now some asshole must be quietly laughing at her.

Lisa once again examined herself critically – no, she couldn't go to the scene, so she would have to tell Danny no, but surprising herself, she texted him, "I'll do that report."

She sent the text and then laughed at herself. Where could she go in this state? Besides, her leg had begun to hurt even more. And her arm and whole body ached in the worst way. No, she was no fighter today. Too much pain and discomfort, she just needed to go to bed. It would be nice to change the forest-mud smeared sheets, but Lisa had no strength left for this, so she took a painkiller with the remains of cold coffee, plopped on the couch, and fell into a deep sleep.

The phone woke her up. Half asleep, not understanding what was happening for several minutes, she just stared at the unknown number on the screen. She had absolutely no desire to talk to anyone. It was dark outside, so it was already evening or perhaps night, and only the light of the streetlamp lit up her room.

The phone kept ringing, so eventually she picked up the call. And at that very moment, it stopped. Lisa cursed and was about to get back under the covers when she suddenly remembered that she had given Danny a completely irresponsible promise to do a report. Sleepiness was gone. She jumped up with the intention of immediately going to Freedom Square. Since it was dark outside, she could simply put on a long-sleeved shirt, loose jeans, a baseball cap and sunglasses. Sunglasses at night? Perhaps no one would recognize her, and she could avoid all the questions like how her injuries happened or who had caused them. Or an even more direct inquiry, "Who beat the shit out of you?" And she wasn't going to tell anyone about that ridiculous trip to the forest.

After using a few band-aids on the graze to stop her clothes from disturbing the wound even more, wincing and moaning, Lisa carefully got into her favorite pair of loose jeans. She tried moving.

Everything looked normal, she could move around with ease. Another pill would take care of the pain.

Having found the latest information about the hostage situation on her phone, she calmed down a little. Nothing particularly terrible had happened so far, so she hadn't missed much action.

"According to the police, there are about thirty hostages on the bus, among them a pregnant woman and children. Special forces have arrived at the scene. They are trying to negotiate with the hijacker and make him surrender. The terrorist promised to present his demands to the country's top leadership in the near future."

This usually happened in such situations: the perpetrator stalled for time, whipping up tension and drawing as much attention to himself as possible. The law enforcement officers were waiting for his demands and, at the same time, hoped that he would run out of steam and then either start releasing the hostages one by one or lose his nerve, making a mistake that would allow for a tactical entry.

There were several more messages from Danny, asking for at least some information from the scene. Good thing he didn't call, assuming that Lisa would be in the immediate vicinity of the bus. And she had shamelessly slept for several hours. This had never happened to her before – work was work, it was necessary and indisputable. Today was the first time she'd broken that rule.

Throwing aside the still wet, stylish backpack and turning on the light in the hallway, Lisa found an old, worn duffel bag in the closet from the days of school trips to the woods with the whole class.

She put her phone, a bottle of water from the refrigerator, and a pack of painkillers in that bag. Suddenly feeling hungry, Lisa took a pan of spaghetti leftovers from a couple of days ago from the fridge and began to eat, scooping the pasta out of the pan with her hands and swallowing after barely chewing. Emptying the pan and finally getting full, she took a deep breath, then put the pan in the sink and washed her hands. It would be nice to have something to drink. There was juice in the fridge, but the lid on the jar was suspiciously swollen, and Lisa did not dare to drink it. God! She would like some compote of fresh fruit, but at the bottom of the compote jar she found only some limp berries. Coffee, of course, was always an option, but there was no time for it anymore. Lisa knew that she could not hold out on this for long, but it should be enough to have a look at the scene, ask colleagues, and make a deal with some journalists she knew to share some of the material from the past hours. How she would explain the cut on her face if they noticed, Lisa did not consider. She also didn't give much thought to the fact that the darkness outside the windows was already beginning to recede, and dawn was coming soon. How long had she been asleep? But Danny would still get his report. She had never let him down yet. Besides, she really needed the money. Recently, Lisa had to get by with small earnings; of course, in a time of crisis, everyone had problems with work, but this wasn't much of a consolation. Although a report on a hostage situation, or even a series of reports, would be very handy.

She had already hobbled to the door when her phone rang again. Lisa shook her head – Danny had chosen to call her in the end.

She'd have to lie to him for now; she couldn't tell him that she just overslept. However, it wasn't Danny, just some metallic voice.

"In ten minutes, a car will drive up to your house. Get in it. And don't ask the driver any questions."

Her first thought was to tell the jokers to go to hell and get to Freedom Square as planned. These crooks were becoming too cocky, weren't they? Like a fool, she'd been running through the woods in a thunderstorm, and now, she was all bruised and hurt, afraid of people seeing her. No, she wouldn't fall for their tricks anymore! No time for stupid pranks! To hell with them all!

That's what she was going to do, but as if in response to her thoughts, the same metallic voice said, "If you don't go now, you'll never know the truth. You want to know it, don't you?"

And Laura's face with huge, tearful eyes popped up before her eyes. The same face she'd had when she came to Lisa when someone hurt her. Her older sister was Laura's only defender after the death of their parents. She was Laura's mother and father, her family.

Chapter 3

A car with tinted windows rustled across the gravel and stopped at her porch, turning off its headlights. Lisa watched it through the window, hiding behind the curtain.

Should she call the police? It was unlikely that they would arrive any time soon. Today, the attention of all law enforcement was on Freedom Square, and even if they came, how would she explain the bruises and scratch marks on her face and body? What would she tell them? Hey, it was a prank that ended in me going to the forest, and now they are calling again, but I don't want to go anywhere anymore? They'd definitely ask her why she went there in the first place. Tell them about her personal tragedy and possible connection to the caller? Definitely not! She suffered enough when everything happened. Back then she was thoroughly questioned by the police about her relationship with her sister, how often they fought, especially recently. They'd asked how she felt about her sister having a relationship with an older man... So many questions, one after another, repeating and returning to the beginning of the day when her sister went missing.

At first, after Laura's disappearance, everyone pitied Lisa, comforted her as much as possible, even assigned a therapist, but then it all changed – Laura was still gone, and Alexander was dead, so who was there to feel sorry for? Whom to suspect? That's when Lisa became a suspect, although she was not formally charged. It all went on for quite a long time. But since no evidence was found against her, they let her go.

Lisa had finally snapped. She got drunk in a bar and caused a scene, accusing the bartender of introducing young Laura to his friend, and because of that, Laura was gone.

Lisa was screaming her head off and the entire street could probably hear her. She'd just lost it and didn't care at all what people would think of her. Her little sister, her dearest princess, had disappeared, and no one could find her. What if she's still alive and tied up, locked up in some dungeon and calling for help? Or lying dead in a ditch somewhere? And her small hands were clutching the lumps of dirt that she was covered with...

Lisa was immediately flooded with memories.

"This is the end, the end! Don't you get it? It's over, it's all in the past! I don't need you. I'm sorry for being harsh, but you don't understand. I've tried to tell you many times that I don't love you anymore... I'm sorry it happened, it happens when people... yes, when people were happy together, and then something happened, something broke... No, don't say anything, just, just... Life is such a complicated thing... you don't need to listen to tired tropes. Now we'll break up, we'll just go our separate ways and that's it... don't ask why, I don't know the answer and no one does... This is how life works, it's stupid, cruel...

No, I asked you – don't come near me and don't ask! And, oh God, don't you dare cry... I didn't deserve this... I'm sorry, forgive me if you can. Don't come near and don't try to kneel down, I'm starting to feel like the worst possible bastard, but what did I do? I've simply fallen out of love with you... Please don't tear my heart out, don't cry... I decided to be honest with you and tell you everything as is."

But Laura, her beautiful little princess, still got down on her knees and crawled to him, begging him not to leave her, begging him to stay with her at least one more day.

"Do you want me to be gentle with you?" Alexander grabbed her and dragged her to the bed, then took a rope, pulled her hands together and tied them to the nickel-plated headboard, and then hit her hard, then again and again...

And she also remembered picking up a heavy bottle of sparkling wine from the floor...

No, Lisa wouldn't be calling the police.

If she wasn't abducted and killed the first time in the forest, although it could have been done quite easily, it was unlikely that the strangers planned on doing that now. But then what was their purpose? What did they want from her?

Her phone rang again, and the voice said, "Another thirty seconds and the car will leave."

Fine, let it leave, and you will go work on that report, the voice of reason whispered to her, but in spite of it, Lisa grabbed her backpack and yanked open the door. A cold wind immediately wrapped its claws around her. She thought about going back and grabbing a jacket, but there was no time left. The back door of the car opened as if by itself as she approached. Lisa pulled it towards her, looking into the dimly lit interior. The back seat and the seat next to the driver were empty, and the driver himself did not even turn his head in her direction.

The car began to inch forward as soon as she got in. The light from the streetlamps gradually faded, dissolving into the oncoming dawn. The black silhouettes of trees became more and more distinct against the brightening sky, the rare car rushed past and, judging by the way how each whooshed outside the windows, Lisa realized that the car she was in was also gaining speed. Quite quickly, leaving behind the deserted, at this hour, streets of the city, the car drove out onto the freeway. Lisa realized that the windows that seemed at first only slightly tinted had somehow suddenly become even more light-proof, and she could no longer see where she was being taken. She tried getting to the driver but was met with another obstacle – a glass partition rose, separating the driver's seat from the back of the car.

Lisa tried to open the right door first, then the left, stupidly and desperately pulling the handles, leaning with her whole body. Useless. She was securely isolated from the outside world.

Well, of course, now some kind of gas would be let into the car, and she would either be killed immediately or put to sleep. Lisa even thought that she heard a faint hiss come from below the armrest. Her first thought was to cover her face with something. But the car was completely empty, and the jacket, which she had remembered only after it was too late, remained hanging in the closet.

The phone rang again. Lisa almost tore the rope on her backpack in her frantic grab for the phone. The same imperturbable metallic voice said, "Don't be scared. No one is going to kill you. The windows are blacked out so that you can't see where we take you. If you don't like our conditions, we will take you back right away."

Lisa's heart was pounding, just like in the forest when some night bird suddenly shook its wings and then began to thrash about, hitting the trees and wounding itself with branches. She felt a lump in her throat and wanted only one thing – to get outside. She just had to say, "Yes, I want to go home. Take me home."

She took out the bottle of water from her backpack and, without looking up, drank it all to the very last drop. She looked at the phone with hatred and wheezed out, "Let's move on."

The car picked up speed, then slowed down a few more times, turning to the right, then to the left and then racing off again. She had already stopped counting the number of turns in the hope of memorizing the road and was just waiting for what was next. Sometimes the car braked too suddenly, and Lisa would think the airbag would go off now, so she tried to squeeze into the back, clinging to the upholstery. Lisa had already been in a car accident once, and she still remembered the terrible loud explosion of the airbag, and herself stunned, sprinkled with talcum powder from head to toe. Back then she was sitting in the back and got off with only a fright, and the passenger in the front seat had his nose broken from the airbag. It was not at all like in the movies – smoothly, using slow motion; no it was sudden, bright and painful.

The phone rang briefly – another message from Danny. In it, Danny thanked her for the report from Freedom Square, saying that her exclusive arrived at the right time. He was also worried, asking if everything was all right with her and telling her not to get into trouble. Ah, and a special thanks for a great picture of the "crying guy."

Her report? But she didn't send any report. She wasn't at the scene at all! Danny must have gotten something wrong. Perhaps one of the free journalists sent him his report in the hopes of getting it published and earning some money.

Lisa opened their website. Yes, here it was, her name under the report from Freedom Square and the introductory text confirmed Danny's words.

"Our reporter directly from the scene.

At about three in the morning, shots were heard in Freedom Square, where the hostage drama is unfolding.

Bullet marks appeared on the windows of the bus. There were also screams, but then everything went quiet. Just a few minutes later, the terrorist contacted the law enforcement officers and, finally, after several hours of tense silence, when he wasn't answering the calls of the negotiators, voiced his demands.

The perpetrator demanded that the country's top politicians record a video where they recognize themselves as "terrorists," whose crimes are directed against people. If the demands were not met, he threatened to blow up the bus and another bomb planted in a place with a constant crowd of people.

Meanwhile, a man tried to break through to the bus, saying that his pregnant wife was among the hostages. They stopped him and now he is with therapists.

The police pushed the people at the scene further away from the bus, and once again asked them not to film what was happening and not broadcast it on the Internet, since the suspect could see their actions.

Law enforcement officers have not yet confirmed the information about the second explosive device, allegedly planted in a crowded place and which the criminal can control remotely. At least for now, its location is unknown.

The attacker allegedly refused to talk to his wife, who arrived as soon as his name was made public.

The only concession on his part was an agreement to take some bottles of water for the hostages.

Our reporter at the scene managed to talk to the terrorist's son, who came with his mother but allegedly did not want to meet with his father. He said that he and his father had basically a normal relationship, and he did not expect anything like that from him. It seems that today really divided this man's life into 'before' and 'after.' And his future depends on how the current events will unfold."

Under the report, in addition to general pictures of a bus standing in the middle of a deserted square, close-ups with bullet holes on the windows, there was also a photo of the terrorist's son: the boy hid his face, his head low, arms crossed; he was crying.

There was also a section about the terrorist's identity, but there were no signs or factors that would push him to a crime – an ordinary employee at a car rental company who graduated from college with honors, in good standing at his company, friendly and calm, according to colleagues, normal family – a wife and a son.

What's going on? Lisa didn't send any report. She didn't even go to the crime scene. She was so confused. Did one of the journalists send their material but accidentally put her name? No, that wasn't likely. Competent editors would not allow that mistake in their paper. Did Danny lose his patience waiting for a report from her and publish someone else's text under her name, having previously agreed with the author to pay for their story generously? But then why would he send her a thank-you message? Something wasn't adding up in this puzzle. Lisa was about to call Danny and tell him everything but stopped – she had to figure it out by herself.

She was brought out of her thoughts and back to reality by another stop. This time they seemed to have arrived at their destination. Lisa held the phone up, expecting that another call would follow with new instructions on where to go next. However, contrary to her predictions, one of the windows became transparent again, and a structure, surrounded by a metal fence made to look like twigs intertwined with flowers, appeared before her eyes. Behind the fence was a three-story building standing at a distance and a stadium. An ordinary school stadium. From where they stopped, on a parallel street separated by a long flowerbed stretching along the entire road, they had a perfect view of the driveway and cars stopping one by one near the gate. Children in school uniforms with backpacks emerged from the cars. Sometimes parents also came out, kissed their children, and quickly said some parting words. Then, the cars drove off, giving their spots to the next ones.

It was a school. Just a school. Every district in her city, and the entire country had them. Why had she been brought here? Lisa pressed on the door handle, but the door still wouldn't budge. Then, she began staring into the faces of the children. Perhaps they wanted to show her one of them. What for? She'd probably understand when she saw it. But the cars came and went one by one, and nothing happened. *And what if there will be a terrorist attack here too?* She thought suddenly. What kind of life was this? Quite recently, last month, the main news on the Internet, television, and other media was an explosive device planted in an urn. Only by a lucky chance was no one injured. And no one, absolutely no one had claimed responsibility for this explosion. Before that, someone left a bomb on the bridge over which international buses ran, and tourists strolled along the sidewalk, taking pictures against picturesque hills and the calm majestic surface of the lake. Yes, all this happened in other cities, many miles away, but it all happened in today's life!

Why do people do this? Don't they know that in most cases, terrorists are simply killed? Surely, they understood this. Why does life become so desperately unbearable for someone that choosing suicide by cop is the only way out? And if they manage to escape somehow, then how can they live with the knowledge that they killed someone's relatives, friends, perhaps left children without parents...

Suddenly, she caught something familiar about the next father's body, while he whispered something in his child's ear, kissed him and pushed him ever so slightly towards the school building. His hair too – shoulder-length waves tucked behind his ears. He pulled back one stray strand with a familiar gesture. The way he straightened up and put his hands in his pants pocket was also familiar. She had seen it many times. The affectionate kiss was the only new thing about him. Lisa thought her mind was playing tricks on her – that person was not capable of affection... All this lasted only a few seconds. Someone from behind leaned on the horn, and the man quickly returned to the car and drove away. Lisa glued herself to the window, turning her head at an impossible angle, trying to see his face or at least the license plate, but then her window began to darken again.

Alexander was alive? Then who was found in his apartment? No! This can't be happening! He was killed, and his death was confirmed by a medical examiner. What the hell was going on?

Lisa began desperately pounding her fists against the partition, demanding that she be released immediately, but the driver, like a robot, did not even turn around. The car started moving away from the school, still picking up speed, then braking, winding across streets she didn't know. All this time Lisa, desperate to reach the driver, helplessly raised her hands up, then grabbed the phone, but the number from which they called her was unavailable. The car stopped after some time. The door lock clicked softly, and Lisa realized she could finally leave. Very carefully, not knowing what to expect, she opened the door a crack and saw the porch of her house. Next to the porch was her neighbor, Martha, holding the same squirming cat in her arms. When Lord finally managed to slither out of her hands, he climbed onto Martha's shoulder and buried his face in her ear.

"He's probably whispering some nasty things about me," Lisa thought.

Martha was the last person Lisa wanted to see right now, especially while coming out of a Volvo. Then, she noticed the police car parked outside her house and an officer nearby.

Lisa turned cold. They must have been here for her. Perhaps they found some evidence linking her to Alexander's murder and came to arrest her. The terrible secret that she had been keeping all these years would come out and her good name, her talent as a journalist, all of it would be gone. But then again, Alexander was alive, she just saw him with a child! He's alive, so she didn't kill him! Yes, she picked up a heavy bottle... and then... and then something happened that she didn't remember. But it didn't happen that way, did it? Or maybe it did? But why didn't she remember what came after? She'd never had memory problems before!

On the other hand, she tried murdering a man, which was also a criminal offense.

Or maybe Alexander was behind the stupid prank, she thought. He was a creative person. He wrote scripts for television and action-packed plots were his forte. But why? If he wanted to report her now, why had he been silent for so long? And where was the evidence? Maybe he had the footage. The operator probably gave him the recording.

Most importantly, where was Laura?

She had to get out of the car. Lisa, already crushed by the oncoming accusations, stepped on the ground, took two steps forward, and stopped. Her legs felt like rubber. The Volvo immediately left. Seeing her, the cop got his ass off the hood of the car and went to meet her. Lisa could already envision herself being turned around, pushed onto the car and handcuffed, and she also pictured a crowd of journalists, her colleagues, taking shots and footage of the killer for their articles with a hail of questions flying from all sides. That's how it goes. In their quiet city, two such significant events at once – a terrorist attack and the arrest of a murderer who had been hiding her crime for many years. Everything became blurry before Lisa's eyes. Her legs went limp. She was going to faint. God, what a shame! But Martha grabbed her by the shoulders, as if she was holding a friend, and kept her from an inevitable fall.

"Your door was open, and my Lord jumped into the house. I didn't dare to go in at first, remembering that you kicked me out, and called the police," she whispered.

Then Martha waved to the officer and shouted, "It's fine. She just forgot to close the door."

The cop wanted to approach but got distracted by his radio, so he waved back to Martha, quickly got into his car and drove away. Lisa was left alone with a neighbor, who, of course, had read the letter that was left on the table.

"Just don't start with the ring road. You read the letter, didn't you?"

Martha lowered her eyes.

Paying no more attention to the neighbor, Lisa entered her

house and slammed the front door. *Screw you all...* She'd been worried all these years that her secret would be revealed, and now she didn't care. *Bring it on! Prison, and shame... let it all be!* She didn't want to be afraid anymore. Of course, she should have immediately confessed to the police that she was in the abandoned house that day, that she saw something that shocked her, and that she'd killed Alexander, who was hurting Laura. For many years, she'd been asking in her thoughts for forgiveness from both Laura and Alexander for his death. But didn't he deserve to die?

And now the day of reckoning had come. For so many years, she tried to go back and redo that day. What if she had just screamed or stopped the scumbag some other way? It would work, of course, but not for long. He would still find Laura and beat her or worse, and she would crawl to him on her knees again and again.

Anger got the best of Lisa, and she had done what she did. If it were possible to change everything, maybe then Laura would not have disappeared... Maybe...

But today everything changed; she saw Alexander alive. Which meant she had nothing to be afraid of anymore! Unless Alexander accused her of attempted murder. And another thing: who showed it to her and why?

Thoughts were racing in her head, the same questions constantly rising with no answers to give. Her head was splitting. Lisa needed to be alone and think about all of it.

Chapter 4

Lisa threw her backpack into a corner. She removed only her shoes before she fell on the couch in her outside clothes. She could see it before her eyes. Alexander kissing that child, gently pushing him to the school. So, he's alive and has a kid? And if there is a child, then there must be a wife. Could it be her missing sister? What if they just decided to run away together – run from Lisa to be exact? There were so many cases in modern history when victims continued to live with their abusers and, yes, even gave birth to their children. It suddenly occurred to Lisa that maybe she was too overprotective of her sister, to the point where it became too much for Laura. Could it be? After the death of their parents – father from poisonous paint vapors in an accident at the factory where he worked, and soon after that, mother from a heart attack – Lisa couldn't come to terms with their death. She'd loved them so much. Remembering the events of those days, Lisa always stopped herself at this very moment. No, a mother could not love her husband that much, so much that she could not cope with grief and follow him. And Lisa could never forgive her mother for that – for leaving them all alone!

Good thing that by that time, Lisa was already quite independent, and relatives helped in any way they could, including taking custody of her younger sister. They had to move into an old house inherited from their grandfather because the bank took their parents' house. But at least they did not become homeless. Of course, the money was tight, and the lawsuit for their father dragged on and on. The owners of the company where he worked tried to fault their father and the other workers for their injuries. Lisa had to transfer to extramural studies and start working. Again, relatives helped – Uncle Mark got her a job working as a police reporter for the city newspaper where she saw everything, going on urgent calls and family disputes, and fights, and murders. She was well acquainted with the police officer who was waiting for her at the house. Perhaps that's why he left so quickly after recognizing Lisa. No! He left because his radio went off, she recalled, and most likely, something had changed with the situation on Freedom Square.

She grabbed her phone and found a news website.

The terrorist had released two hostages, and now, wiping away tears, both an elderly woman and a pregnant woman of thirty-five were saying that the terrorist was, in fact, a wonderful person – he did not hurt them, offering heart drops to the old woman and a bucket to all the hostages for their needs. He also calmed them down, said that everyone would be fine if they behaved and did as they were told.

Yes, they just need to give him an Oscar! Or a gold medal! In a competition among terrorists, he would definitely take first place! That's just how amazing of a terrorist he is, a real darling.

Lisa was about to write a sarcastic comment under the article, when she suddenly noticed that this information was taken from their website and, following the link, saw a new report, again signed with her last name.

This was all too much! She didn't know what was driving

Danny, although his motives were probably quite clear: all papers covered what was happening on Freedom Square, and their special correspondent had simply disappeared. Yet, there was a limit to everything. He could have at least warned her. And what did his thank-you message mean? Maybe she didn't understand, and he was just being ironic?

Lisa stopped herself from calling Danny again. What would she say in her defense? With all that was happening now on Freedom Square, where frightened hostages were waiting for death, her problems looked so small and insignificant. She was also afraid of the question: what for you, a journalist, was more important than the people captured by a terrorist? Why did you go somewhere again on the orders of some stranger?

Lisa's head was throbbing with pressure and the puzzle pieces did not want to fall into place. The best way to sort things out was to talk to someone. She brushed aside the decision to call Emma, her only remaining friend. Emma didn't know how to keep secrets. Trusting her was like standing in the square and telling the whole story through a loudspeaker. No, she needed someone else. During her voluntary isolation, not wanting to let anyone into her life to avoid intrusive behavior, Lisa reduced the number of contacts to the necessary minimum – only for work or when necessary for transport to the store. She simply didn't believe in genuine sympathy and desire to share her burden. Nobody cared about anyone. Every person was looking for a benefit for themselves in another, even if it was just the realization that they came out unscathed, while someone else got into trouble. They could just cross themselves, sending their gratitude to God.

And then Lisa saw Martha through the window, waving around a gnarled stick, trying to drive her Lord, who had climbed the tree for some unknown reason, from a branch. Most likely, he was scared off by the neighbor's dog that sometimes unexpectedly rushed at the fence separating their plots with loud barking. Of course, calling the rescue service today was unrealistic at best. All eyes were on the hijacked bus and the rescue teams were also probably there.

Grunting and jumping, Martha called the cat with all sorts of affectionate words, but to no avail. Despite his impressive name, Lord screamed like a commoner drunkard at a fair and did not want to come down. Attempts to drive the cat away with the stick were also unsuccessful, and now Martha, it seemed, was going to climb the tree herself to rescue her pet. She lifted her leg and leaned on the branch, miraculously pulled herself up, clinging to the trunk, and put her other foot on a higher branch. Lord immediately moved up the tree. Martha was already grabbing the next branch with her hands, but then the dry branch under her feet cracked, and she was on the ground.

Lisa remembered the words of an old, experienced man who worked as a night watchman in the building where their office was located: "Stop panicking over cats screaming in the trees! If they want to eat, they will get down themselves! Well, has anyone ever seen a corpse or a skeleton of a cat in a tree that failed to make it back down?"

Nevertheless, Lisa took a light portable ladder and carried it to the wailing Martha. Extending her hand, she helped Martha up from the ground, then put the ladder against the tree and quickly got up. A couple of minutes later, the hissing and scratching cat was handed over to its happy owner.

While Martha was kissing and soothing her pet, Lisa was examining the new wounds on her hands left by the claws of cute Lord. One scratch more, one less, what difference did it make now?

"Let's go to my place. We need to disinfect that," Martha suggested. "Lord is very clean, but he was on a dirty tree..."

Without looking back, she went to her porch, carrying away the evil furry creature. Lisa dragged herself along behind her.

Chapter 5

Pouring freshly brewed fragrant tea into the cups, Martha also brought a homemade cake from the kitchen, covered with powdered sugar like it were frost. Opening the cabinet door, she looked at the line of mismatched bottles for a few minutes and closed it again.

Meanwhile, Lisa was examining her surroundings. Martha's living room, contrary to expectation, was quite different from what old ladies' living rooms usually were – no embroidered napkins, lace tablecloths, souvenirs on shelves and pictures. Little furniture but an entire wall-long sliding door wardrobe with some of the shelves open. Only books and photo albums on the shelves, and at the bottom, an old radio and a stack of records in worn envelopes. On a small table by the window sat a porcelain Chinese vase with several branches of soft lilac and purple hydrangeas. A couple of paintings hung on the wall. They were abstract, but not kitsch, just nice paintings.

Giving the surprised Lisa the opportunity to thoroughly examine her living room, Martha put a piece of cake with raisins and chocolate on her plate and pushed a cup of tea with some oriental flavor closer. Lisa devoured the cake immediately.

"More?" Martha asked.

Lisa just nodded.

"You know what? Let me bring you some homemade patties," and without waiting for Lisa's consent, Martha went into the kitchen and soon returned with four patties strewn with herbs. There was also a large slice of fresh white bread on the plate.

That's weird, Lisa thought, eating the patties. *The furniture is not appropriate for an old lady at all, and the food is homemade, fresh. Even the bread seems to be baked at home.*

She had never been to Martha's house before. Lisa and Laura moved to this street after the death of their parents. They used to live in another part of the city before that, and after coming here, the sisters did not make friends with the neighbors. Over the years, while the house was empty, many of the old residents, those whom they remembered from visits to their grandfather, were no longer alive.

Having eaten her fill and even soaked the bread in the gravy from the patties, Lisa leaned back on the couch. It would be so great to just close her eyes and doze off like she did after her mother's dinners when she came home as a girl after playing all day and threw herself on her mother's food. Then, through the oncoming sleep, she watched as her mother quietly took away the dirty dishes and covered her girl, her little troublemaker, with a soft blanket. Lisa often fell asleep like that, on the couch, and did not understand at all in the morning how she got to her bed. Her younger sister, Laura, could hardly be imagined without her pink pajamas, hair wrapped in large curlers, washed with scented soap and sprinkled with fragrant toilet water.

Lisa snapped out of happy memories, realizing that now she was just visiting a neighbor who was being too intrusive in her attempts to get into her life.

"If you don't want to say anything, so be it," the elderly woman lightly touched Lisa's hand. "Just get some sleep. I'll fetch you a blanket."

"Don't!" Lisa shouted and added in a quieter voice, "I don't need a blanket. That would be too much. I'm just... I'm confused... You see..."

Martha silently looked at her, and with light movements swept away some invisible crumbs from the table.

"Fine," Lisa leaned away from the couch, straightening her back like she did as a kid during her music lessons, and realized that she was not ready to tell a stranger about what had been tormenting her for all these years.

But Martha was not going to back down either. She stared at Lisa from under lowered, heavy eyelids, waiting to hear more. She did not rush Lisa, did not ask questions, just waited.

"You know, I think I'll go," Lisa started to get up, but the old woman lifted her hand from the smooth surface of the table and touched her hand again.

"Well, all right," Lisa sat down and, not knowing where to start, paused and then mumbled, already regretting coming here and her sudden impulse to share her pain with someone she barely knew. "Here it goes. Imagine a person, a young woman, who did something terrible and has been blaming herself for it for years. It was the most important part of her life. And suddenly it turns out that she didn't even do anything wrong... But still nothing is clear... She should be happy, but something is wrong... And now she wants to know..."

Lisa fell silent, suddenly realizing that yes, this was her goal. She wanted to know what happened that day.

"Have you talked to anyone about this?" Martha asked, probably realizing that she would not hear the rest just like that.

"No, I can't talk about it at all... I've only told bits to Emma, but just that I really wanted to see my sister alive, to see her at any cost."

"Who else? Try to remember," Martha insisted.

"Who else? Yes, this one time... I got drunk at a Christmas party at work and just talked and talked, but then, we all got so wasted we didn't remember anything at all the next day. I don't think anyone heard my confession... we were all very drunk."

"And you don't even suspect who's been sending you these letters?"

"No. And most importantly – why? Why did I have to go to the forest?"

"And where did you go last time?" Martha kept interrogating her.

"You know, I should probably go," Lisa jumped up. She realized that she would have to tell Martha's everything and begged inwardly, *Oh, God! I'm not ready. Help me!*

It was as if someone in heaven heard her fervent plea. An entire group of cats tumbled into the room, flinging themselves around, screaming, growling, tearing each other with their claws.

Martha immediately rushed to separate her pets, but a cat fight is no joke, and these cats were dead set on clearing up some very important matter. At first, Lisa was shocked. She did not expect to see that many animals at her neighbor's place. Only Lord usually sneaked into her home. But then she joined Martha, grabbing the animals, some by the hind legs, some by the withers, and pulled the red, black, striped pets in different directions. Those whom they managed to separate from the main pile, Lisa threw aside, but they immediately rushed back into the fight. And from this muscled tangle of fury, shreds of fur, fluff and splashes of blood flew. The stylish carpet with an abstract pattern on the floor turned into a shapeless, crumpled pile of rags.

It was all in vain, but then Martha brought a bucket of water and splashed it into the fighting ball of menace. The cats scattered in different directions, still hissing and snarling viciously, but calmed a bit. With slaps and kicks, Martha dispersed them, sending some into the kitchen, locking others in the pantry, throwing one into the bedroom, and putting the last one out the door. Only then did she sink into a chair, exhausted. The bucket was lying in a wet puddle in the middle of the room, rolling.

"I'm sorry," Martha whispered.

"No, I'm the one who's sorry," and Lisa slipped out the door.

Chapter 6

Her phone rang as she was about to enter Freedom Square. Lisa glanced at the caller ID and decided not to take it. First, she had to figure out what was going on and then apologize to Danny.

She no longer wanted to dance to the blackmailers' tune. They obviously wanted something from her, so she decided to do everything according to plan: first to Freedom Square – to do her job, and then – personal business.

A small bus with a warped blue-white stripe all over the body was still standing in the center of the abandoned square. The same bullet-riddled windows with curtains. The area was cordoned off with police tape. Onlookers and journalists had long been pushed back to the adjacent streets, blocked by special forces vehicles. Behind the cars, on the other side of the square, Lisa noticed some reporters with their equipment. They wouldn't let them get closer, fearing that the terrorist, as promised, would start shooting.

Lisa looked up at the windows and balconies of the houses surrounding the square, but as expected, there were snipers hiding everywhere. This meant she couldn't possibly get there. Damn, if she had come sooner, she would have surely found a way to climb higher, find a place where she could get a better view.

Lisa went around the square along the adjacent streets. It would be nice to quietly join her colleagues, listen to their theories, gossip, find out about the terrorist's new demands, because usually someone had insider information and could throw their colleagues a bone. Sometimes, it was just speculation or conjecture, but the owner of such information would see themselves as mighty and seem so to the hungry crowd of journalists nosing around such places. The significance of the event attracted a large number of journalists from all over the country, including the central media. With so many strangers, Lisa was hoping to remain unrecognized and avoid questions about the state of her face. She hid the other injuries on her body under a long-sleeved shirt and a pair of jeans. A baseball cap and big sunglasses completed the disguise. Only glancing at her ID, the police officer, someone she knew, let Lisa through to the other journalists without question.

The phone rang again, and this time, Lisa took the call. Without waiting for the voice, she hissed, "What? Do I have to go somewhere again? What happens if I don't go? You wanted to show me that Alexander is alive? Great! Thank you! I'm just so happy! Now leave me alone and let me do my job."

They clearly did not expect her to push back like that and just hung up.

After talking with a cameraman, she knew that there was no news from the terrorist and everyone was waiting for his next step, Lisa calmed down a little. She asked other journalists and quickly drafted out a report for Danny, mostly saying that nothing new had happened yet, then sent it.

The blue sky that had turned whitish from the heat was gradually clouding over, shadows floating over the deserted square strewn with glass fragments, making this frightening emptiness even scarier. The disturbing silence was broken only by the sounds of paper cups, driven by a draft, across the cobblestones.

There was no way to see what was happening inside the bus from such a distance. Special forces drove the journalists into an alley, and from there, the view was, well, quite bad. The group coordinator very convincingly asked the journalists not to film or broadcast them, thereby giving the terrorist the opportunity to see what they were doing.

Judging by the relaxed poses of men in camouflage, Lisa realized that no one was going to storm the bus any time soon. Both the law enforcement officers and the terrorist were waiting it out.

"You're free. It's easy for you to wait, but what's it like for them?" Lisa thought with unexpected anger. To spend so much time with some armed bastard... when they didn't even know how things would turn out, and who knows how adequate this desperate man was – could he really blow himself up along with the bus? Lisa did not believe the stories of the two released hostages about a kind terrorist – the people who got back their freedom were simply immensely happy and ready to forgive even the man who held them at gunpoint, even the one who humiliated them and subjected them to psychological torture.

When her phone rang again and the annoying number appeared on the screen, Lisa just turned it off and left the square. She walked to the stop, waited for the right bus and went to where everything had begun.

Chapter 7

She did not immediately recognize the old, dilapidated house among the ruins in the area intended for demolition. It had been dangerous to come here lately. A lot of Asian migrants had settled in the city, and, unable to find work and normal homes, they lived here, in houses with no electricity and running water. The city authorities tried to evict these troublemakers several times but did not dare to take drastic measures, fearing accusations of cruelty and inhumanity towards people in need. No one knew what to do with these people who had gone wild from hopelessness. It was impossible to simply put them on a plane and send them to their historical homelands. Most came from countries at war, which meant they could be killed if they returned, and under international laws, such deportation was considered a crime.

Lisa tried the front door handle; however, despite the seeming shabbiness, the lock held firmly. She looked around the house, found a window with broken glass and, trying to stay in the shade, got close to it. The clouds had already completely covered the sky, thunder rumbled somewhere in the distance. It looked like it was going to rain soon, but not just rain – quite a thunderstorm was brewing.

Pulling herself up on the windowsill, Lisa climbed inside and landed on the dirty floor. There were some rags, shards of glass, remains of old broken furniture everywhere. Lisa looked around, realizing she was in that same room. Stepping carefully, she went through the open door into the hallway, then reached to the staircase and began making her way up, choosing the more reliable steps. Eventually, Lisa got to the top floor, stopped, and listened. From afar came sounds of music, someone's screams, loud laughter... People here were having a feast today, but was it only today? For some reason, she thought that they had a superstitious fear: if they stopped shouting loudly, playing their music, yelling offensive speeches, they would simply disappear.

A few more steps towards the closed door. Lisa knew that door. Here she stopped, took a deep breath and pulled the handle. Unexpectedly, the door opened easily. The hinges didn't even creak, as if the owners had never left this apartment. Stepping over some junk at the door, Lisa walked inside. Everything in the room remained as before – a small table with dirty plates and mouse droppings by the shuttered window. There was a bed by the wall with torn wallpaper that had come off in places. An old bed with an iron-clad frame and a chrome back, a thick cotton mattress casually covered with an old blanket in a duvet cover, once bordered with lace, now dirty and torn.

This is where it all happened. She'd entered the room like she did now and saw it happen.

"This is the end, the end! Don't you get it? It's over, it's all in the past! I don't need you, I'm sorry for being harsh, but you don't understand, I've tried to tell you many times that I don't love you anymore..."

Lisa again saw Laura, just like before; as if on command, she knelt down and crawled to Alexander, wearing only a nightgown on thin shoulder straps made of transparent fabric, hiding nothing – not her small bulging still very childish breasts, not the graceful curves of her young body, not the strong round hips. Her little sister picked her gown up higher so as not to get tangled in her knees, and crawled and crawled to Alexander...

Lisa's eyes went dark again, as they had then.

Inhale and exhale, again and again.

Lisa looked around for a heavy bottle of sparkling wine. There was no bottle now. Someone took it, but definitely not the forensic team. If they had, she would have been serving her prison sentence. Everything remained the same here.

There was a rustle from behind. Lisa froze. She'd heard the

same rustle the first time she'd been here but had not paid attention to it.

Lisa straightened up and turned around. No one seemed to be there, but the door swayed slightly on well-oiled hinges. Was there a draft or was someone watching her?

Her first thought was to run away from here. How would she explain her presence in an abandoned house? If she was being watched by the locals who had noticed her, despite all precautions, then why were they being so quiet? It wasn't like them. They would have already swooped in a pack like wolves, and it was unlikely that she would have been able to get out of here unharmed.

Then who?

Lisa, unexpectedly for herself, rushed to the entrance and kicked the door, because someone was hiding behind it. A scream and a familiar voice.

"Careful, God!"

First a disheveled gray head appeared from behind the door and then Martha herself.

"Jesus, Martha, you almost scared me to death. What are you doing here?"

"You almost killed me. Good thing I held the door with my hands. Otherwise, you would have smashed my head."

"What the hell? Are you following me?" Lisa was so enraged she couldn't breathe properly.

"Be quiet," Martha hissed. "Do you want all the locals to come here?" She continued, lowering her voice, "Yes, I'm watching you. I can see what's going on with you. You're ready to do the most reckless thing right now, and I don't want you to."

"Why do you care so much?" Lisa asked, having regained the ability to speak but still exhausted.

"Just because, no particular reason..."

Lisa stood with her hands at her sides. A vivid memory that caused a surge of emotions was suddenly cut short due to the appearance of an old woman poking her nose everywhere, because she didn't want Lisa to do something reckless. Lisa wanted to yell at her, to take all her anger out on Martha. She could barely restrain herself.

Martha started to move towards her, but Lisa stopped her with a gesture.

"Can you repeat how you followed me?"

"What? Repeat? What for?" Martha didn't understand.

"Don't ask. Just do it."

Martha was still looking at Lisa blankly.

"When exactly did you see me?"

"I was following you from the start, just staying a little behind."

"Did you follow me to Freedom Square, too?"

"I did," Martha said shortly.

"Why didn't I see you? Were you in your car?"

"Well, yes."

"And they let you in?" Lisa couldn't believe it.

"I didn't have to go to the square per se. I parked a little earlier, where all the public transport stops are, because you would have returned there anyway, sooner or later."

"What if I was stuck there for a long time?"

"No, I don't think so. Your thoughts were elsewhere."

"Can you read minds too?"

Martha just spread out her arms like a first grader caught cheating.

"Let's repeat everything."

"What do you mean by everything?" again, Martha played dumb.

But Lisa, without explaining anything more, returned to the front door, carefully entered and stood in her former spot.

Finally realizing what Lisa wanted from her, Martha fussily, as if again afraid of incurring the wrath of her neighbor, repeated her steps. And again, Lisa heard the sound of the door moving.

"So that night I wasn't alone here, there was someone else..."

And Martha, tensing her whole body and stretching her head

forward so as not to miss a single word, stared at Lisa. Careful footsteps and the same rustle behind the door made her turn around, and then they both fell to the dirty floor, and from all sides, splinters and plaster began falling on them from bullets hitting wooden shutters and furniture. Someone was firing at them. Both Lisa and Martha, without a word, crawled to the bed, using the cotton mattress as a shield. It could hardly save them from bullets, but their gut was telling them that this was the only way. And after the shooting, a flash of lightning lit up the dim room and thunder broke out.

This stormy summer justified its name one hundred percent. After several days of horrible drought, another thunderstorm hit the city, which had repeatedly caused power outages. Straining her ears, Lisa tried to catch the sound of the stranger's footsteps, determining their direction. Martha rolled herself into a ball, closed her eyes and covered her ears with her palms, shuddering violently at every thunderclap. Now the shooter would look around and easily find them under the bed... The seconds dragged on for an incredibly long time, stretching into an endless chain... With another flash of lightning, the shadow in the doorway moved.

That's it. This is the end, Lisa thought. Out of the corner of her eye, she saw Martha crouching, and for some reason, she remembered the terrorist on the bus at Freedom Square offering heart drops to his victims.

Then she heard footsteps. The shooter tried to make little noise, but it was impossible. He stepped on some glass, and it cracked in between the explosions of thunder under his heavy boot.

Lisa's eyes frantically searched the room for some miraculous way out of here, but the door to another room was pinned shut by a bookcase, and they would be shot before they reached it. Her gaze stopped on a large piece of glass lying not far from the bed. She figured if she could grab it and stick it in the shooter's leg, it would give them a few seconds to get to the front door, but for that to happen, Lisa had to really hurt him to distract him long enough. Which was highly unlikely. Of course, there was almost no hope, but there was no other way out either, so Lisa waited for a pause between the flashes, pulled her hand from under the bed, expecting every second that the unknown assailant would notice and step on her fingers. She felt the smooth glass surface with sharp edges and carefully, so as not to disturb the trash around it, took the shard. Then she tried calculating her steps for the attack, because she wouldn't have a chance for a second go. And she realized – no. Hitting him from her position would not do anything, she would not be able to swing properly, which meant she had to crawl out from under the bed, throw herself at him and let it play out. She had to act immediately, before the shooter searched the room and realized that the bed was the only possible hiding place for two unarmed women.

Lisa pushed Martha and she suddenly opened her eyes, like a child who was told that the monster was gone and she was no longer in danger.

"On my signal, run to the door," Lisa whispered.

Martha shook her head in disagreement, but Lisa was no longer looking at her. She could, of course, aim for the knee if she could reach it – that would definitely slow the asshole down, but for how long?

Meanwhile, the footsteps were getting closer. Old worn-out riveted boots, such as Lisa had seen in a military store and which could easily beat them to death, were standing very close to the bed. The position was extremely unfavorable for Lisa. She would not be able to attack him from there as he did not leave even a small distance. Now he'd order them to climb out, and then it was either hit or miss.

Abruptly, Lisa saw the boots turn and head towards the door. What was that? He couldn't not know where they were hiding. Then she heard a strange sound and saw how the shadow of the attacker seemed to squat down by the door.

Ah! That's how it's gonna be! He'd decided to shoot them, but first get a better angle to be sure.

It was too late to jump him. Besides, Martha's grip on her leg felt like a ton of bricks. Stupid Martha, her savior Martha. *Had to be here*, Lisa thought angrily, and then she heard the strange and absolutely inappropriate noise of stifled sobs. The shooter was sitting on the doorstep and crying. *What?*

For a while, stunned Lisa listened to these sounds; no, she was not mistaken, the man who was just shooting at them was now sobbing, sobbing and rubbing the tears with his fists. That's what she saw in the next flash of lightning.

Suddenly Martha, trembling like a mouse targeted by a cat, crawled out from under the bed with a cry, "You bastard! Scumbag!"

Lisa pulled her back, trying to shut her mouth, because the shooter would come to his senses and they would die, but Martha kicked, pushing Lisa away, and kept shouting insults. Her fear was gone and now she was no longer a mouse, but a fierce cat, ready to tear everyone to shreds.

Then they heard the footsteps of a man running away, already outside the door, on the stairs.

Both women immediately rushed to the staircase, trying to get out of this trap as soon as possible. They just needed to get outside...

At the last minute, Lisa grabbed Martha and pushed her towards the stairs leading to the attic. And without choosing between sturdier and looser steps, they went up. Once Lisa's foot fell through a broken plank and she hung, clutching at a piece of the railing with her hands, the stairs creaked and sank and could collapse any second, carrying her with them.

Martha made it to the attic first. Grabbing Lisa by the hair, she pulled her up. Lisa almost howled from pain but found Martha's hand, which was surprisingly strong. The stairs somehow withstood her weight and, pulling herself up, Lisa also climbed through the hole to the attic. Then they ran, bumping into rusty metal pipes, brick partitions, old junk. They stumbled, fell, got up, and ran again, spitting out dust that got into their mouths.

"There must be an exit to another building somewhere. Martha, where did you leave your car?"

"Let me get my bearings," Martha straightened up, listening

to external noise. However, all the sounds were drowned in the roar of the raging thunderstorm.

"Remember, Martha, please," Lisa pleaded.

"We were in the second building, and I left the car a block away." She thought a little longer and then pointed in the direction from which they had just come. They would have to go back.

"No, we can't." The shots could be heard even through the thunder, which meant that the locals may have already been there. "Let's try to go down this ladder."

But here, too, they heard voices of people approaching.

Lisa opened the window leading to the fire escape, and the cold immediately blew in from outside. The rain was still pouring, but the voices from the stairwell left them no choice. Lisa waved to Martha and began climbing down the wet, slippery ladder, clinging to the rusty metal.

Martha, still hesitant, looked outside. Lisa shook her fist at her, silently screaming and spitting out the rainwater.

Turning around with a visible effort, the old woman also followed her down. At the very bottom, they had to jump because the ladder did not reach the ground. Lisa landed safely, and Martha got stuck again, too afraid to let go, and then Lisa jumped up and literally pulled her down.

Looking around and hugging the walls when lightning flashes of the restless thunderstorm lit up the sky again, they reached the first building. Then, Martha confidently led Lisa along the old houses to where she had left her car.

Chapter 8

At first, they took turns showering with hot water. Then Lisa, at Martha's behest, settled on the large bed, not at all suitable for a lonely old woman. The rain had already stopped, but there was no electricity, as always after such a storm.

Martha boiled some water on the gas stove, brewed some tea Lisa had enjoyed previously, brought two crystal glasses and a bottle of pear liqueur, and they warmed up with it, drinking the tea afterwards. There were also some leftover patties and soft veal steaks in Martha's fridge, which came in handy for two hungry women. Lisa enjoyed the delicious food and the comfort of this house, the liquor relaxed and confused her thoughts, enveloping them in a pleasant, sweet fog.

"Tell me one more time, and try to remember who else knows about this. Who have you been talking to lately?"

Lisa, once again, sipped the amazing fragrant tea, narrowing her eyes with pleasure. She was so tired that she didn't want to remember or discuss anything, she did not even wish to move her arms or legs. Only her jaws moved, and as soon as she chewed and swallowed, she again sent more food down her throat.

When this nightmare ends, I too will fry an entire pan of these amazing homemade patties, Lisa promised herself and, so that

Martha would leave her alone, she muttered, "I rarely speak with anyone now, if only out of necessity."

"And still?"

"Just Emma then," Lisa thought about it and then continued, "She also talked to me about forgiveness. Something about me needing to forgive and then I would feel better... And also asking for forgiveness from someone I hurt... And some other fancy nonsense like that..."

"Fancy?" Martha asked.

"Well, yes. There's a sea of all sorts of gurus online who have one recipe for all occasions – forgiveness... If only it were that simple..."

And with these words Lisa fell into a deep sleep.

The next morning, she woke up with a headache and at first, could not figure out where she was until Martha came into the bedroom, dressed, neatly combed, and smelling of fresh apple pie.

"Get up already, sleepyhead. Have breakfast and let's go."

"Go where?" Lisa asked, surprised.

"We'll go talk to your friend."

"Which one?"

"The one you told me everything about while drunk."

"You're crazy! Emma is such a blabbermouth, and if she didn't tell everyone then, then come on, let's remind her... and now she won't miss the chance to dish the dirt," Lisa turned away, pulling the blanket over her head.

"Exactly!" Martha said, "Why didn't chatty Emma tell anyone?"

"Well, maybe she forgot."

"Your story is not something easily forgotten, especially for a woman who likes to talk."

Lisa sat up, outraged by Martha's relentlessness,

"And what am I going to tell her? Aren't you the one playing stupid tricks?"

"Judging by the fact that they wanted to kill you yesterday, it's not a trick."

"Me? Or us both?"

"I think it's probably just you. I happened to be there by accident and, I believe, that was a nasty surprise for the someone who was after you."

Lisa remembered the horror she had experienced yesterday, the sounds of gunshots, fountains of old plaster flying in all directions... and then the shooter crying...

"Why do you think he was crying?"

"That's what bothers me," Martha raised one hand and shook it, as if trying to awaken some ideas by literally shaking the air.

"Well, yes, if he had just shot us, you would have been much less interested in it," Lisa tried to make a joke but failed.

Martha grabbed the red cat, who quietly slipped into the bedroom, by the scruff of the neck and threw him out the door.

"Get up. Let's have tea and discuss our plan of action. I made apple pie."

Lisa looked at her neighbor in disbelief. Just yesterday, this limping, grumbling and incredibly annoying old lady was to be pitied, but today, she was completely different. Martha was collected, fit, with a sparkle in her eyes, as if last night with its difficult events had breathed new life into her.

Martha seemed to have found a purpose. It's probably horrible to be old and lonely, even if you have a garden by the house, a beautiful lawn, and beloved pets.

Well, let her help if she wants, Lisa thought. *She already knows everything, and two heads are better than one, as everyone knows.*

Why not? Someone was helping her with the reports, and that was not bad at all.

When I understand who is doing this, I will tear their head off even if it's Danny's idea, Lisa promised herself. *He could have told me he hired another person.*

Besides, why were those reports signed with her name? Strange and inexplicable. *You could have just asked Danny*, the voice of reason objected. But Lisa wasn't listening.

And what was happening with the hostages? Lisa blushed with shame. People were in such trouble, and she, a journalist, was sleeping peacefully.

Lisa reached for her phone, opened a news website and jumped up as if scalded. The terrorist was told that if he didn't release the hostages soon, the special forces team would storm the bus, and this information was leaked to the press. After that, another update: he decided to give himself up, and it was going to happen very soon.

Putting on her still wet jeans, shirt, and baseball cap, Lisa hurried to the door.

"Martha, I'll take your car! That terrorist is going to surrender!"

She grabbed the keys hanging on a hook by the door and ran outside.

"Goodness gracious!" Martha just threw up her hands, "Do you even have a driver's license?"

Lisa drove the car through the streets, ignoring the traffic lights since the roads were empty, only seeing rare cars and pedestrians. However, she could not get to the square. The whole city seemed to have gathered here to watch the show, which promised to be very entertaining, because nobody knew what this desperate man could do. At the entrance to Freedom Square, the streets were crowded with cars. People left their vehicles just off the road and tried to break through the roadblock to no avail. She also failed to get through; her ID was drying at Martha's after yesterday's downpour, and accredited journalists were given special passes. She had no choice but to watch the live broadcast from her phone.

At first, nothing seemed to be happening, the same bus with bullet-riddled windows and glass on the pavement and ringing silence, only occasionally interrupted by the muffled commands of special forces. But then, with a sudden metallic sound, the bus door opened, then that tense silence again, and the first hostage appeared in the doorway – a woman who put a plastic bag in front of her as a shield, apparently the shopping she'd done before getting on this bus. Her posture, unsteady gait and the bags before her all screamed "don't shoot!"

The woman stepped onto the pavement, and the next hostage appeared behind her. Men in camouflage, ducking and moving quickly from one car to another, ran up to the first woman and, grabbing her by the shoulders, led her away to the waiting ambulances. Soon, everyone who got out was also there.

A seemingly endless silence fell again. The sun was still mercilessly scorching, and not even a tiny cloud flew over this place. After a few painful minutes, a man in a windbreaker appeared with a bag in one hand and a phone in the other.

There was a loud order to immediately put the bag and phone on the ground and kneel.

The terrorist hesitated and still obeyed the first part of the command, carefully lowering the bag, but then suddenly opened the jacket, under which was an entire belt of explosives.

"Back up! Everyone back up!" Special ops shouted, and everyone who managed to break through to meet their loved ones now was running back, away from the bus. Those who watched this scene unfold from afar, from behind the cars, froze, waiting for anything to happen. In the uncomfortable ringing silence, only the clear commands were heard.

"God, I wish it would end soon!" Lisa blurted, not taking her eyes off the phone, as thousands of people following the events prayed for the same.

The terrorist stood with his arms wide apart, holding a finger over the button on his phone; another moment and the square, along with everything that was here, could have been blown to shreds by the explosion.

Suddenly, a teenage boy jumped out from behind the roadblock and ran to the terrorist yelling, "Dad! Dad! Don't do this! No! I'm sorry! So sorry!"

The special ops officer caught the boy and dragged him back to the safe zone. But his desperate cry lingered over the square. The terrorist seemed to be hesitating... And the whole city was whispering after the boy.

"Don't do this! Don't do it!"

The terrorist first put his phone on the ground, unbuckled his belt and lowered it down to his knees, but he did not fall to the ground until he was knocked down by the special forces.

Then, Lisa heard a scream.

"Move away! Now! Back! Back! No filming!"

She realized that the cameraman, whose report she was watching now, trying to show the events as best as possible, got too close to the terrorist.

As he retreated, the camera obediently switched to the faces of people around the square; despite the obvious danger, people were stretching their necks and raising their phones high, hoping to capture the most dramatic moments. Correspondents with TV cameras, microphones, tripods also got caught on video. Lisa saw familiar faces – the wide-open eyes of Sophie from the City Bulletin, a very young girl who had recently become a journalist and had not yet learned what professional cynicism was. Shocked, she forgot about her job and just watched. Omnipresent and always first at the scene, Evan was talking quickly on the phone, moving a little to the side. He wasn't filming either, although Lisa knew that his article would come out with the brightest, most impressive photo material. And his eternal rival, the black-eyed handsome Sergio. The way the special ops soldiers would throw the terrorist on the ground and how people in riot gear would carefully approach the bag and the explosive belt.

"All this happened before many times," Lisa thought, "Terrorism has become a part of our life..."

She repeated this thought to Martha, when she called, but the latter cut her off.

"Why are you wailing like some old hag? Why won't you also cry about the tragic fate of all mankind? We live, we flutter, but all the same, we all meet our end. How old are you? Yes, terrorism has become an everyday phenomenon, and it will continue to be so until some genius comes up with a way to sterilize the brains of those who love blowing things up. Let's say a person goes through the metal detector at the airport, and at the same time, his brain is being scanned and cleared of all thought and intention to commit a terrorist act. Impossible, you say? Remember that not so long ago you, had to go to the post office to send a simple letter to a friend, buy an envelope, a stamp, some paper... and the letter would reach the destination only days later. And now? Just press a couple of buttons on the phone and it's done."

Martha sounded unusually harsh. Lisa even felt as if her neighbor had thrown a glass of water in her face.

"You're right," Lisa replied, slightly hurt. "Is that all, or do you have something else to tell me?"

"They were showing on TV just now..."

"I know what was on TV," this time, Lisa cut her off and was about to end the call.

"Wait. My friend committed suicide..."

And Martha fell silent.

"How did it happen?" Lisa asked in a completely different voice.

"Took some sleeping pills."

"Then maybe..."

"No," Martha interrupted, "Not her... She was always against all kinds of drugs. Never drank anything before sleep, except for mint tea and warm milk..."

Lisa wanted to say that people change, their habits change, but she didn't say anything.

"She married a very successful, rich man, at least the haters said so. At first, everything was great. For several years, they were quite the happy couple, and then something happened... They began to fight... and before that..." Martha hesitated, not wanting to utter the terrible word "suicide," "And before she... They had a terrible fight."

"And now the husband is suspect number one," Lisa finished for her.

Martha lost it. She burst out sobbing, saying that she didn't believe it was a suicide. She knew this girl well. She went to college with Martha's daughter Helene. "We didn't talk much lately because... different cities ... but she could not do it ... she couldn't have..."

Lisa didn't even try to calm Martha down. Realizing that she needed to let it all out, cry out her grief, she only sighed and listened. Then, she found information about the suicide of a millionaire's wife, a famous philanthropist from some noble family, which Lisa did not remember – what difference does it make? Martha did not mention in her story that, according to the husband, his wife seemed to have been blackmailed.

"Of course, he's just protecting himself, so he said she was being blackmailed," Martha would say, and she was not the only one.

One tragic event had barely ended and now a new one, and the whole community of journalists, and crowds of onlookers would rush out of the city, where the comfortable villas of the rich were, surrounded by gardens, overlooking the beautiful lake. Lisa decided to do something else.

"I think I should go to the office and talk to Danny. To hell with the bruises. I'll say that I fell down the stairs when I wanted to get to the attic or something."

Her mood changed for the worse the minute she remembered the attic. Yesterday's events needed an immediate explanation. After all, she could just call the office and not go, but Lisa wanted to get there, because she didn't want to go back home – not just didn't want to but was too afraid to. She clearly remembered how the man who shot at them was crying, but those tears did not mean there would be no second attempt. Only this time, the killer could come to her house.

Martha's next call brought her back to reality. Martha said in a different, more cheerful voice, "I'm sorry for dumping my grief on you. The police, of course, will figure it out... Let's really keep an eye on your friend Emma. If she knew, why didn't she tell anyone? Is that like her?"

Chapter 9

They noticed Emma coming out of the office. While sitting in an old Volkswagen, Lisa raged inwardly. Why did she yield to Martha's demands? Besides, it was strange to sit in a car parked outside her office and not go in. It was weird watching her colleagues from outside.

Then again, while sitting in ambush, she learned something new about her colleagues. The first was their accountant, an exemplary mother of three children and a role model in general, whose coffee cup was always sterile like an operating theater, unlike most employees' things. She left the office, and after casting a furtive glance around her surroundings, quickly walked down the street, and then suddenly dived into the half-open door of a Mitsubishi parked nearby. She didn't remain long before emerging, brushing herself off, straightening her hair and freshening up her lipstick on the go. After a while, the chief manager of the commercial department of their office came out of the same car, a respectable, middle-aged man. A family man. He also straightened his trousers, checked his fly and, looking in the rearview mirror, carefully wiped his lips with a napkin.

"What... What were they doing there?" Lisa was confused.

"Having an important business meeting," Martha shrugged her shoulders, completely unperturbed.

"So they... In their workplace ... well, almost workplace..."

Martha turned to the window, hiding a smile.

From time to time, employees came out one by one and walked to the corner of the building, very businesslike, disappearing for a while, only to reemerge ten minutes later.

"Where are they going all the time? As far as I remember, there is no coffee shop or shops there, and there is a kitchen with a coffee machine in the office, and vending machines with water, chocolates and sandwiches in the lobby."

"There's something more interesting there," Martha's mouth stretched into a smile.

"Well, what is it?"

"There's a small stadium there."

"Are they training?" Lisa doubted her own words.

"Well, yes. A ten-minute jog about once an hour?"

Looking at Lisa's astonished face, Martha burst out laughing.

"Oh, come on..." Lisa shrugged her shoulders, feeling stupid.

"You have a non-smoking office, am I right?"

Lisa nodded.

"And all employees lead a healthy lifestyle, do yoga, some are vegetarians or vegans, do not use disposable bags when buying groceries in supermarkets? Environmental concerns one of the leading regular columns of your newspaper..."

"Well, yes. What's wrong with that?" Lisa interrupted her.

"Nothing. But people still need to smoke. So, they run into the bushes behind the stadium. Don't you want to join them?"

"I quit a long time ago."

"I would take a couple of drags," Martha sniffed the air, while her nostrils fluttered, like a real addict.

When Danny rushed out the door, Lisa almost ran to him, but Martha held her back. Danny was fighting off a courier who had recently delivered their mail.

The man was screaming. "You promised! I won't let you down! You have to believe me!"

But Danny turned a deaf ear to his pleas, got into the office car and the driver immediately stepped on it.

Lisa just shrugged her shoulders in response to her neighbor's unspoken question. You never knew what the editor-in-chief could have said. Maybe the boy was raving about journalism, and Danny promised to take him on as an intern.

They saw Emma close to noon. After leaving the office, she also looked around, and only after moving away, did she take out her phone and speak hotly into it. Lisa started the car, but driving at a slow speed behind a pedestrian and not attracting attention was hopeless, so Martha stepped in.

"Stay here," she said to Lisa and, hunched over, limping and dragging her foot, got close to Emma, who was too engaged in her phone conversation to notice.

They reached the pedestrian crossing and Martha grabbed Emma's arm not even having to pretend much. There was nothing left for Emma to do but help the old woman to the other side of the street.

"Got it!" Martha said in a loud whisper when she was back in the car. "She was very nervous. Said she didn't want to be a part of it anymore... But they said something, and in the end, she agreed to see it through and that's it, she's out."

Martha's eyes shone, her cheeks were flushed, as if after a walk in the cold, and she almost jumped with joy.

"So what?" Lisa wasn't as convinced. "She could have been talking about anyone."

"No!" Martha was insistent, "Trust me, this is it. I have a nose for such things. We need to check it still! She made an appointment to meet today at 7 pm on the terrace of the Gloria café. Great place, by the way! They have bacon and rum flavored ice cream. The only place in the city that serves it." And Martha rolled her eyes, expressing the greatest possible pleasure on her face.

Lisa looked doubtfully at her neighbor. Martha was still an old woman, probably with high blood pressure. Maybe she shouldn't have dragged her into all this. Then again, you couldn't say for sure who had dragged whom.

A funny smiley face flashed on her phone. Lisa had turned off the sound when they went to follow Emma, and she seemed to have already missed several calls.

Danny called, thanked her for another, very heartfelt report and asked about her health. After he received a message from her that she wasn't well, he was ready to order a report to another journalist, but she did a good job – she did not let him down, as always. Still, he told her to go rest, stay in bed for a couple of days – because fever was not a good thing.

Lisa took the phone away from her ear, looked at Martha and repeated the words of the editor-in-chief aloud. Praise was always nice to hear, but Lisa was ashamed. She had just described in detail everything she saw on her phone screen and immediately sent it from the scene. But she didn't send any message about being unwell to Danny. All of a sudden, she saw Danny standing next to their car. The partners did not notice his return, and now he was talking just steps away. If he turned, she would have no place to hide in the small, cramped car. Lisa shrunk her head into her shoulders, pulling her baseball cap lower over her eyes. What a mess! And Danny just stood there. A little longer and he would inevitably turn at least to make a remark to the driver of someone else's car parked so close to the entrance to the editorial office. But Martha came to the rescue again. Groaning and calling all the saints to witness, she crawled out of the car and, limping on both legs this time, headed for Danny.

"Oh, hello! I know you! You're a journalist! Exactly what I was looking for. I'll tell you everything now, listen. My neighbor developed this terrible habit of letting his rabbits into my garden at night... of course, I have nothing against rabbits, but there are rules... He thinks – I can perfectly imagine what he thinks to himself – an old, blind woman will never see the rabbits in the dark... she will think – these are hedgehogs, such long-eared hedgehogs that eat grass, but everyone knows that hedgehogs do not eat grass. They are predators, they eat all kinds of spiders and beetles, a viper, if it's off guard. They can catch and eat an entire snake..."

Danny didn't wait for the end of the "old crazy complainer's" rant. She was clearly one of those who constantly came by the office in the hope of attracting journalists' attention, because the police no longer reacted to them. Instead, he made for the door to save himself by getting under the protection of strong men in black uniforms with the badge "Security." Martha grumbled and raised her hands for show, returned to the car, and they hurriedly drove off to a safe distance.

"God! Almost got caught," Lisa removed her baseball cap and wiped the sweat from her face.

"Did you see me there?" Martha demanded her share of glory.

"You were amazing!"

There was still time until seven, and the women decided to have a snack in a restaurant.

"Oh! I know a place not far from here, in the old part of the city," Martha brightened up again. "They have the most amazing pork knuckle, so delicious!" she rolled her eyes upward.

This time, Lisa looked at her with more alarm. Should someone at that age eat pork with all that cholesterol? But Martha did not want to listen to any objections and her Volkswagen obediently drove towards the old city.

They stopped near a small old building. The first floor was occupied by a restaurant, completely decorated, from the sign on the street to the walls inside, with a variety of images of pigs, cheerful and sad and winking mischievously. At the entrance, a fat piggy sculpted from white stone with long eyelashes and a glass of wine clenched in a hoof sprawled in an imposing pose.

At least there are no live pigs in the restaurant hall, like in some establishments specializing in eco food, Lisa thought. *Although, is it normal to take care of a pig, love it, call it by name, then kill it for sausage?*

They took a table by the window, and Lisa turned the napkin holder with the grinning face of another pig away from her. A mouth-watering smell was coming from the kitchen, but still, when their order was brought, she cautiously cut off a piece of something floating in gravy and served in a soup plate. It turned out to be very good – pork cooked in fragrant herbs and cream. At first, Lisa thought seeing such a greasy dish that she was going to be sick. However, after trying it, she ate everything and even thought about having more.

"Come on, eat," Martha encouraged her, "You need to gain some weight. You're all skin and bones..."

"Go on, tell me that it's time for me to do something with my life, get married..."

"Doing something with your life – what do you mean by this?

Getting married and having a bunch of kids is not your thing. And that would require a lot of money."

"I have a friend," Lisa recalled Evan, the photojournalist, "His wife is expecting either their fifth or sixth child... So, he takes any job, always the first, always on the front line. Nervous, fussy, bald, with a beer belly, kind of unkempt, always sweating in any weather, but he won't ever give up a possible cash grab."

"You know, I think having many kids is not a bad idea. At least you won't be alone when you get old."

Lisa looked at Martha questioningly.

"No, no, I'm not talking about myself. I have a daughter. She loves and spoils me so much. It's just you know... a thought."

When the food was eaten (no seconds), they ordered coffee and dessert. For dessert, Martha chose two slices for herself – chocolate cake with whipped cream and nut cake with butter cream. Lisa once again did not comment on Martha's very high-calorie choice and ordered a sponge shell with fruit. The coffee and dessert were also amazing.

After eating every last crumb, Martha leaned back from the table and threw her hands on the back of the soft couch.

"I love me some delicious food," she purred contentedly. "An hour-long nap to digest everything would be great, since we have business tonight," she finished like a detective from an old movie.

Chapter 10

They went to where Emma was supposed to have her rendezvous to look around, see if they could approach unnoticed and eavesdrop on her conversation. Lisa was still very skeptical about Emma being a part of this: it was all too convenient for them to have immediately found Emma, and Martha to overhear her conversation and get the information they needed. Like magic. However, she chose not to argue with her neighbor.

Their fears of a lack of safe approach were justified. The cafe's terrace was too open, the tables were quite far from one another, and the plan – just to sit down at the next table - was no good. Lisa rejected the option to let Martha play an old cripple once more. Emma could recognize her. No, they would have to adapt to the circumstances. They sat at one of the tables, partially isolated from the main terrace by a large Ficus in a tub, and began waiting.

At the appointed time, Emma appeared. She flew into the terrace and sat down at a table in the most open part of the terrace, leaving Lisa and Martha no chance to be covert. Nervously grabbing the menu brought by the waiter, Emma buried herself in it, seemingly studying it carefully, but all the time, looking around. Finally, she ordered, while impatiently tapping her foot in a stylish shoe and glancing at her phone on the table.

"The worst scenario is if they call her now and move the meeting to another place. She will leave in a hurry and then we will have to catch up with her, and that could lead to us being found out,"

Martha summed up the disappointing outcome.

Lisa just shook her head.

At least a quarter of an hour of tense waiting passed. Emma was still there: a couple of times she picked up her phone, answering some calls, but apparently, they were unrelated to today's meeting.

"Did we get burned? Did they see us?" Martha's face shrank from disappointment, outlining the deep wrinkles even more.

Another fifteen minutes gone. Emma did not move. Lisa and Martha had each finished two cups of coffee and had ordered two more. Too much caffeine made Lisa's heart pound, echoing somewhere in her throat, but Martha looked as if nothing had happened, resembling a wild cat hiding behind a bush, waiting out its prey. Finally, a man joined Emma. Despite the heat, he was wearing a hoodie, dark glasses and long shorts. Emma started up. Without responding to his greeting, she leaned to him and immediately began to speak, nervously and hotly.

Lisa listened, stretching her neck and alternately her right and left ear in their direction. She realized that from such a distance they would not hear anything, but still. What if they got lucky? In doing so, she missed the moment when Martha disappeared. Looking around in bewilderment, she saw a puppy running among the tables, followed by a boy. God who knows where it came from. It was as if they were playing a game. The boy threw small pieces of sausage to the puppy, and it quickly grabbed them, hid behind the leg of another table, and ate them. The boy crept up to the pet, intending to catch it, but the puppy slipped away. It didn't get far, however, waiting for the next treat. The people in the cafe chuckled watching the two, the women raising their feet when the puppy hid under their table.

"Quickly give me your phone," Martha said, appearing as if out of nowhere.

Lisa looked at her in surprise, but Martha grabbed the ringing phone and touched the Accept button, then pressed the phone to her ear and gestured to Lisa to join her. The sound was somehow hollow and booming at the same time, but still all the words were clear.

"... are you really going to leave everything and not finish the job?" they caught the barely audible voice of the stranger.

"...I can't do it anymore. I don't want to..."

"... do you feel sorry for her?"

There was a pause, then Emma continued.

"It's cruel."

"But she has to go through forgiveness. She killed a man, and you will help her."

"It doesn't look like help. We didn't agree to this..." it was Emma's voice again.

At this point, the conversation was interrupted by the waiter who came up to ask what Emma's friend would be ordering. He had to, however, obey the stranger's casual gesture, which meant he wanted nothing, and walked away.

"You must understand that I will have no other choice but to share with your family and with your friends a very juicy story."

"You won't do it! It's not fair!" Emma cried, and the heads of the other customers on the terrace turned in their direction.

"You won't do that," Emma repeated in a quieter voice.

"And why not? You don't want to do what I ask. You don't want to help a person in trouble. Why should I stay silent? You remember our motto: we helped you, help another."

Emma did not say anything. She sat with her face turned towards the city street, with its usual daily bustle, pedestrians and car drivers going about their business and absolutely indifferent to the problems of others.

"I hope she won't start crying now," Martha commented in a whisper.

"Here's what we do," the stranger spoke again, "I give you time until tonight to think."

Then, he got up and left. Emma stayed. She took a sip of her cold coffee, reached for a napkin, and Martha and Lisa saw her shoulders shake. And then Lisa darted off her seat. Her name was not mentioned, but she still knew – it was about her and about the incomprehensible events of the last days. Without permission, she sat down opposite Emma.

"And now, tell me everything from the very beginning."

Terrified, shocked by her sudden appearance, Emma stopped

crying and tried to run, but Lisa used the same trick the stranger did.

"Or I'll tell everyone about you."

"You... did you know?"

Lisa didn't answer.

"Then, why are you asking?" Emma started sobbing again, smudging her mascara with a napkin even further.

"I know that you've done something wrong, and now you're being blackmailed, while you're blackmailing me. That alone is enough to derail both your career and your life if I tell Danny. Believe me, he'll know what to do with you. He's an experienced journalist and editor."

Emma looked at Lisa again with eyes swimming in tears.

"No, it's not what you think. It's not blackmail. Yes, I did a terrible thing and they helped me... yes, believe me, I couldn't share it with anyone. I was afraid to tell someone and just started looking for help on the side among strangers..." Emma sobbed jerkily, "One day, I came across a club of lonely people who had no one to share their pain with. Pour out your soul if you hurt someone, but there is no way to fix it... Just talking, you know?"

Lisa nodded, encouraging Emma to continue her story.

"You could say nothing at all, just come to meetings and communicate with the same people who were ready to talk about their wrongs or the pain they caused other people. No one forced anyone to speak. No one said their last names, only first names, any even then, not real ones. The hall was always half-dark and it was impossible to see faces. You can't even imagine what a relief it is to talk about what has been tormenting you for so long, about the sick feeling you've been having and can't break free from. Some of the members of the group, those who could not speak out in such an environment, asked for a personal meeting with the guru. I heard by chance that in private, members of the club talked about real crimes that they, ordinary people, committed through negligence or stupidity... not criminals or repeat offenders. Just.... people..."

"So, basically, a club of anonymous murderers, thieves, and child molesters! Have I forgotten anyone?"

"No, no, most of them are just ordinary citizens who have made a big mistake..."

At this point, Emma looked into Lisa's eyes for the first time during their conversation, as if trying to convince her with that look that this was exactly what happened.

"Are there really that many..." Lisa hesitated, choosing her words, "unusual citizens in our city?"

"I don't think so. When they confessed, some sometimes mentioned details that made it clear that they were not from around here."

"Well, at least that's good news. Go on, I'm all ears."

Emma looked her straight in the eyes again, this time without defiance, rather searching for understanding in Lisa's eyes.

"I also couldn't speak in front of everyone and asked the guru to listen to me in private. After meeting him, it really became easier for me. I just treaded on air," Emma even laughed, remembering that week of happiness, freedom from her secret... "There was also a mandatory ritual of sorts. I had to go through the forgiveness ceremony, and I was told that my obedience would be to help someone go through forgiveness, who could not come to our meeting, and I..."

"And you thought to offer me up, that it?"

"Yes, I really wanted to help you..."

"What makes you think I've done something terrible?"

Emma quickly lowered her head, but then she raised it and looked Lisa in the eyes.

"The police suspected you of Alexander's murder."

"And? I was cleared of all suspicion. There was no evidence against me."

"Yes, they didn't find any evidence," Emma agreed.

"Go on," Lisa urged on.

"But you told me yourself at the Christmas party..."

"What exactly did I say to you?"

"Well..."

"Just say it. What did I tell you then?"

Emma rubbed her already dry eyes with the same dirty napkin again, but Lisa grabbed it from her.

"I'm waiting!"

"You told me how you followed Laura to some old house and saw what Alexander was doing to her. You couldn't let him do that, so you picked up a bottle from the floor..."

"And?"

"And you didn't remember whether you hit Alexander with it, and you didn't remember how you got home, and that all this wouldn't let you live your life."

Lisa leaned back in her chair. So, Emma just blabbed her secret to the blackmailer, a secret Lisa told her when drunk.

"Did I tell you any specifics?"

Emma shook her head.

"That's all you said, and it's very short, I barely made out the words. You got really wasted that night and just mumbled something to yourself."

"Who else heard?"

"No one. I'm telling you. You were just mumbling to yourself."

"Did you come up with all the bullshit, too? The forest and meeting with Alexander?"

Emma nodded quietly.

"It's just ridiculous and makes no sense. Then again, you have always had problems with logic and plot building."

Emma pursed her lips, and even now, caught and discovered, she could not bear listening to criticism.

"Was that man the guru? The one that sat with you?"

"No, no! No one has seen his face, even at a personal meeting. He wears a mask and sits in a dark corner of the room."

"Figures. Why would he show his face? And who was here just now?"

"One of our own."

"Another criminal?"

"No... why would you think that? Just a man..." Emma seemed offended.

"... just a man who did a bad thing," Lisa finished for her. "I've heard that before."

"I don't even know what happened to him. He was always quiet at our meetings. It was the first time he came to one. In fact, recently I've been receiving instructions via phone."

The waiter, who, for the hundredth time, approached them for an additional order, again left with nothing.

"And what does Alexander have to do with all this? Is this his idea? He's going to report me?"

Emma looked away again, towards the crowd of people on the

street. It would be nice to go about her business now, smile at her reflection in the shop windows, buy a fruit ice from an ice cream vendor on the corner, and never meet Lisa again, who kept asking for more answers. But most of all, Emma wanted to be in the dimly lit basement now, where no one reproached you for what you once did, where everyone was understanding and did not vilify one another.

"That's what we wanted you to think. To make it easier for you to make the decision to go through forgiveness."

Lisa exploded. "Emma, what the hell is wrong with you? Are you in your right mind? Or did your guru just hypnotize you or some shit? I do not know what you have done, and what you are so afraid of, but ... but this is not normal. Don't you understand what is happening? Some kind stranger suddenly, absolutely unselfishly... Do I understand correctly? Yes, he absolutely selflessly helps all the suffering people. Is he a saint?"

Emma shook her head. "He's just like us. He was like us, and at one time, someone helped him with some, I think, very heavy stuff. Now, he's helping others."

Lisa waved her hands at her. "This again! Your entire group belongs in prison! And here you are playing at forgiveness!"

"And you don't?" Emma shot back.

"You know what? You will have to look for someone else. I am not playing your game. If Alexander reports me, he will have to explain what he really did. The only thing I'm interested in right now is Laura. Where is she?"

"Laura? I..."

"You what?"

"I don't know."

"But you have a theory, and I think you do know something. Who were her friends? You were in touch, weren't you? She called you. I know you'd become close lately, and it's strange because you're my friend."

"No, no! I really don't know anything else. Why did she call me? Maybe she wanted to be closer to you, but you were like a mother to her, and you can't tell your mother everything... and I'm sorry..." Emma sighed.

"Then tell me about all the chatter, rumors, everything they say in the office."

Emma thought for a while, then began talking, carefully choosing her words. "I only know that there was one guy who was hopelessly in love with her. He used to work in our office, but Danny fired him."

"Who was it?"

"It was Arthur. You must remember, we called him Arty. He was your typical loser, not exactly a looker... At one time, we even suspected him, but he was too much of a sissy and couldn't possibly harm Laura."

"Who else?" Lisa pressed on.

Emma's phone had already rung several times, but she rejected the calls every time.

"Just answer already," Lisa could not stand it anymore. "Maybe it's work-related, they'll let you go faster."

Emma held the phone to her ear, listened, and then handed it to Lisa.

"It's for you."

"Me?"

Lisa picked up the phone and heard the same metallic voice that had become too familiar.

"Now, you will get up and go where I say. Go alone, get rid of the old woman."

Lisa couldn't breathe.

"Do you know where I am? Oh, yeah, of course... And if I don't go?"

"You have to go through forgiveness," the metallic voice insisted.

"Yes, well, you can go to hell with your forgiveness! I am so sick of you!"

"Then, you'll never know where your sister is."

Lisa was taken aback.

"Do you know where she is?"

The blood surged to her head, and the booming sounds wouldn't let her focus properly.

No! Not this! She needs to keep a clear head!

"Who are you? Why are you doing all this?"

"It doesn't matter who we are. We just help people get rid of their guilty conscience."

"By forcing them to blackmail others?"

"They have to pass through such obedience."

"Will they be shooting at me again?"

"No, that was not us."

"Then who was it?"

"It doesn't matter. He won't be there."

Silence fell. No one was on the line anymore.

Emma moved in and out of Lisa's vision. Everything was blurry. So, these people knew where Laura was. She turned her head towards the table where Martha was supposed to be but did not see her either.

Trying not to make eye contact with Emma, Lisa looked for Martha again but still couldn't find her. Then, she moved quickly to the exit. Emma left the cafe soon after. The boy who had been playing with the puppy ran up to her table and, tearing the phone attached with tape from under the countertop, took it to Martha in exchange for some money.

Chapter 11

The evening breeze played with the bamboo curtain on the door, which responded with a gentle chime of small bells. The soft, dim light from the wall lamps in the room with full-length windows beckoned with homely comfort. The young woman was setting the table for dinner, arranging the plates, laying out cutlery, napkins, and from time to time, glancing at the clock over the fireplace. Soft music came from the sound system. The violin sang about happiness, love, a dream come true. The scent of deliciously cooked meat spread from the room.

It's good that she and Martha had lunch. Otherwise, Lisa might have choked on her saliva from such a mouth-watering smell. Through the foliage of an old spreading willow, behind which she hid, Lisa saw how the woman, once again, looked at the clock, took a bottle of perfume from the mantelpiece and sprayed her wrists.

A romantic dinner? Lisa asked herself since there was no one else. She was simply ordered to go to this address and watch the house. So, she did.

There was something familiar about the woman's look: curly blonde hair, chiseled shoulders, a dress that couldn't hide the thin arms. All of her – lithe, slender, long-legged, very young.

Only for a moment Lisa thought that this was her younger sister, grown up, but still remaining a graceful girl. Everything was very much like Laura – body, height, hair, even some of her gestures resembled Laura's, but it wasn't her. Lisa's heart missed a beat from an unexpected feeling, and then, it began to beat again as usual, only slightly more quickly.

Lisa narrowed her eyes and then opened them, desperately hoping the woman was Laura, alive, healthy, just older. All Lisa needed to do was enter the room, call out to her, hold her and never let go again. But the miracle did not happen.

While Lisa was rummaging in her pockets, hoping to find a handkerchief or at least a napkin to wipe the tears that had the worst possible timing, she missed the moment when Alexander entered the room.

It was, without a doubt, him – his gait, his mannerisms. The woman darted to him. Lisa thought she caught the smell of her perfume as the tenderest breath of a spring breeze that flew after the impetuous hostess. She hugged Alexander, ran her hands through his hair, stroked his face and pressed her lips to his mouth. All in him, all about him. Probably, another man would have already dissolved into this flow of love, but not Alexander, always personable, always mockingly ironic, able to put a person in their place with not even a word, only a careless gesture if, as he believed, that person deserved it. The same happened now: Alexander allowed the woman to kiss him but did not kiss her back. He raised his face and with a familiar gesture pulled a strand back from his face and put it behind his ear. She didn't even seem to notice his neglect. Stepping lightly, she flew into the kitchen and brought first a salad in a crystal bowl, then a hot meal, the sight of which made Lisa swallow again.

The woman poured Alexander a glass of wine, put food on his plate, pushed the salad and some other snacks closer and sat down opposite him, looking at Alexander with shiny loving eyes.

Just like Laura, Lisa thought. And not only Laura. All the women he met fell in love with Alexander. His irresistible charm, coupled with a certain degree of neglect in his manner of treating others, for some reason won women over. He also had a very pleasant velvety voice and the habit of talking with everyone from the first minute of introduction as if they had known each other for a hundred years. His confidence that no one would ever say no to him worked wonders with women, and not only them. Often men, even those who were infuriated by his constant success with the fairer sex, in some inexplicable, miraculous way, fulfilled his requests or even orders.

Alexander lazily picked at the food on his plate with a fork, sat for a while, leaning back and relaxing the knot on his tie, and then threw his napkin on the table and went to the half-open door to another room.

The woman whose efforts he had so mercilessly rejected was sitting with her eyes lowered into her empty plate. Before the door, Alexander took off his jacket and threw it on a chair, and then looked back at her, said something and, without waiting for an answer, disappeared inside.

The woman sat with her hands down for a few more minutes, but then got up, went to the mirror on the mantelpiece, fixed her hair and once again sprayed perfume on her neck, front and back, lifting the curls. Then, she also went to the other room.

Lisa heard the quiet vibration of her phone and held it to her ear.

"Well, why are you standing there and saying nothing? I told you. You have to tell me what you see. What's going on, that's the order."

"Nothing is happening," Lisa wanted to shout, "It's just that Alexander, in his usual boorish manner, humiliated a woman who had been cooking dinner for him all evening and was waiting for him, not taking her eyes off the clock, and this narcissist, this bastard..."

But Lisa didn't say any of that.

The metallic voice on the phone demanded, "Tell me!"

"There's nothing to tell. He didn't want to have dinner, apparently wasn't hungry, and went to sleep in another room."

"And why are you standing there? Why didn't you move to another window?"

Lisa decided not to argue, realizing that all the trumps were in the hands of an unknown person, and if this crazy guru wanted her to go through the ritual of forgiveness invented by him, then to hell with the man, she'd do it, and then... she didn't know what was yet to come...

Stepping over the glowing white decorative stones surrounding the flower bed, pushing through the thickets of climbing plants, Lisa moved around the house to where the window of the room where Alexander was should have been.

The curtains were not closed, and the room was lit as if a movie was being filmed there. At the request of the metallic voice, Lisa repeated what she saw, but it wasn't enough for him. He demanded that she tell him what she felt.

Damn you with your forgiveness! I'm so sick of this! she thought to herself while commenting aloud, "I don't like how Alexander treats this woman. First, he practically insulted her, and now..."

"Yes," the voice said, "What now?"

And Lisa suddenly heard it.

"This is the end, the end! Don't you get it? It's over. It's all in the past! I don't need you. I'm sorry for being harsh, but you don't understand. I've tried to tell you many times that I don't love you anymore... I'm sorry it happened. It happens when people... yes, when people were happy together, and then something happened, something broke... No, don't say anything, just, just... Life is such a complicated thing... I think you don't need to listen to tired tropes. Now we'll break up. We'll just go our separate ways, and that's it... don't ask why. I don't know the answer, and no one does... This is how life works. It's stupid, cruel... No, I asked you – don't come near me and don't ask! And, oh God, don't you dare cry... I didn't deserve this... I'm sorry. Forgive me if you can. Don't come near me, and don't try to kneel. I'm starting to feel like the worst possible bastard, but what did I do? I've simply fallen out of love with you... Please don't tear my heart out. Don't cry... I decided to be honest with you and tell you everything as is."

But the woman, like Laura, a beautiful little princess, still got down on her knees and crawled to him, begging him not to leave her, begging him to stay with her at least one more day.

Alexander did not answer, only looked down on her.

The woman hid her face in her palms, but Alexander threw her hands away.

"No, don't hide your eyes. Face the truth. I don't want you, just let me go!"

Lisa was very confused . This woman, Laura... her heart was racing, mind foggy...

Wasn't Alexander just repeating the same words that Lisa heard in the abandoned house? What's going on here?

The woman adjusted the shirt strap with a careless gesture. Stretched out her hands to Alexander, and he hit her again and again and again.

"Do you want me to be gentle with you?" Alexander grabbed the woman who looked just like Laura by the hands and dragged her to the bed, then took the rope, pulled her hands together and tied them behind her back. Again heavy and strong blows, again and again, striking her face, her head.

Tearing her lace shirt, he climbed on her, pushing her legs open with his knees... She didn't cry or scream, only her baby feet twisted terribly. She was in pain, she was in unbearable pain. Her barely adult body was not ready to accept the lust of an aggressive grown man...

Lisa's eyes let her down, and she literally went blind for a few minutes. When she could see again, she saw only Alexander's naked body thrusting in a crazed, hungry rhythm. And Laura's helplessly spread childish legs and small hands resting against the bed for support.

"I can't hear... I can't hear you," the rapist yelled, and Laura's thin voice followed with a plea, "Don't. Stop. Don't do it anymore, please, don't."

Alexander straightened up.

"No, that's not what you should be saying. You have to beg me to fuck you harder and harder. I don't want to hear your slobbering pleas."

"Tell me. Tell me what you see. Tell me what you feel," the metallic voice demanded from Lisa.

"I see how this bastard is abusing my sister! She's not fighting... she's still trying to please him..."

"What are you feeling. What are you going to do now? You have to go through forgiveness," the metallic voice insisted.

Lisa saw herself standing in the doorway of that room in the abandoned house where Alexander was doing the same to her little sister, and all her bitterness, all her pain burst through.

"What forgiveness? There will be none!"

Lisa felt something roll under her feet. Looking down, she saw that it was a heavy bottle. Without thinking about what she's doing, she reached for it.

"Tell me what you're doing," the voice in her ear insisted, "Repeat exactly what you did then..."

"Then... I... I bent down..."

"And... what happened next?"

And suddenly Lisa, as if through a heavy fog, heard a cry from behind.

"Don't say anything! Shut up! He needs your confession!"

She stopped, not understanding who was screaming. Colored circles appeared before her eyes, and someone pressed against her from behind and covered her mouth. Lisa tried to push the attacker away and reach for the murder weapon again, but the old hands held her tightly. Lisa turned around and recognized Martha, who was whispering fervently to her.

"He needs your confession. He has nothing on you. Your confession now means prison. Shut up and don't say anything."

The measured, metallic voice was still whispering in her ear, "You have to see this through. You need forgiveness. Send the old woman away. Tell me what you did then."

But Martha was strong, unlike most old people, and dragged her away through the bushes, fighting off the willow branches.

Lisa struggled and screamed. "I want to kill him!"

But Martha grabbed the phone and threw it against the white stones.

Chapter 12

"He has nothing on you! He needs your confession, your sincere admission of guilt!" Martha repeated over and over again, wrapping a warm blanket around Lisa, who was shaking.

She couldn't even hold a cup of tea. Martha held the cup for her, making Lisa drink, while the latter was sobbing, then trying to get up and run to the house where Alexander was doing horrible things to a woman who looked just like her sister.

Martha had no arguments left in her attempts to reach Lisa. She said the words in every possible way, but Lisa did not want to understand anything. Finally, Martha slapped her in the face. It worked – the sharp pain instantly sobered her up. Lisa even stopped shaking and screamed. "Why are you hitting me?"

"Let's think. If this Alexander of yours is involved in all this, and he is ready to go to the police, then why isn't he going and why has he been keeping quiet for so many years? And what is this nonsense about forgiveness? Perhaps, this guru simply gathers unhappy people into his cult. As usually happens, desperate people are promised all kinds of help, and then their property is taken from them."

"I don't have anything to take! My grandfather's house, yes, but it's so old it's about to fall apart."

"What about your reporter's salary? Perhaps they wanted to lure you to this club so that you could help recruit other members. You're a great journalist. I found your articles online and especially liked your interviews with different people. You inspire confidence. You know how to get them to talk. I think they would not have told other journalists what they tell you."

Lisa smiled bitterly: that was actually true. Both Danny and her former editor-in-chief forgave her a lot – Lisa's frequent absence from the office for no good reason, her unwillingness to do routine work, and slowness where other journalists raced one another for a scoop. They turned a blind eye to a many things because of Lisa's special talent of communicating with people without provoking them, without pushing or striking an accusatory pose. Lisa just listened, but for some reason, the people she spoke to were frank and sincere.

"Let's say he wants to make me work for him. But no! No and no and a thousand times no! If I don't want to, I won't work for him."

"Even to find Laura? You'll do anything for her, won't you? I repeat – he has nothing on you. You don't remember whether you hit Alexander or it's just your sick mind, so he puts a similar scenario in front of you and makes you confess, writes it all down. That's the dirt."

Lisa thought about it and then asked, "I still don't know. Is Alexander aware of this 'crime re-enactment' or are they just using that situation?"

"We can ask him," Martha smiled and a predatory spark flashed in her pale blue eyes.

Lisa laughed. "How? Just ask? Alexander, did I try to kill you?"

"Well, why so directly? Let's follow the fresh tracks to that house. Maybe in the light of day, we'll find something that will push us to more productive thinking."

However, the trip was fruitless. The doors were locked, the shutters were down, and during the whole evening they spent in ambush, no one appeared. After asking the neighbors, they discovered that the house was being rented out on a monthly, weekly, and even daily basis. Such a real, tangible thread that connected them to Alexander was no more.

Disappointed, they left in different directions: Martha returned home, and Lisa went to a press conference organized by the lawyer of the terrorist who held the bus hostage. The message about the press conference's time and place was sent to her by Danny.

The man who until recently had held the hostages, their families and even the whole city in fear, sat with his eyes lowered to the floor. Life seemed to have completely left him, but for some reason, the event holders brought the corpse and sat it down here. Instead, his lawyer spoke and answered all the questions – red as a freshly baked cherry pie, with thin coppery hair carefully slicked over a bald spot, a man in an expensive suit and glasses, which he put on, then took off and set on the papers in front of him. He explained how an ordinary employee of an ordinary company was robbed blind by the bank, leaving him without savings and without money for his son's college, which he had been putting aside all his life. The lawyer claimed that his client did not want to harm people, the only requirement was that the head of state or the bank read aloud on the air the fine print from his contract, which not all people read. That was where such contracts hid the most important information, which allowed banks to rob ordinary hard workers with impunity. He'd decided to do this out of complete despair – everything was taken away from him, both his house and his savings, and in addition, the son called his father a sucker.

Listening, Lisa looked at the man, who never raised his eyes. Now, they would send him to prison – a terrorist attack was a serious crime, but she also knew those present at the press conference were on his side. The lawyer promised that they would definitely win the lawsuit against the bank, since public opinion was on his client's side, and this was not a single case, and the terrorist's son would absolutely go to college... but did anyone believe his words? Lisa left with a heavy heart. Even if it went their way, why did justice prevail only after such terrible shocks?

She saw the faces of other journalists, heard the voices of loud and unceremonious TV people, who believed that they were the main carriers of information, although the Internet with its social media had long ousted them from the media Olympus, and knew that for most it was just work. Her good friend, young Sophie from the City

Bulletin, was making notes on her tablet. Evan, as always, the first, had already sent information to his website "Only Honest News" and was now stroking his stomach with satisfaction, apparently anticipating a delicious lunch. She also saw how two inseparable friends, the charming dark-skinned Marcia and the unusually tall Chinese woman June, after sending the necessary number of words about the event, each to their own editor, had already moved on to discussing something more pleasant, perhaps the evening presentation of a new French-Japanese perfume.

Lisa worked on her text, sitting on a bench in the city square, not far from the building where the press conference was held. She still didn't want to go to the office with already yellowed, but still visible bruises. Fortunately, her non-existent illness and the editor's kindness allowed her to avoid the office.

After making the last edits in her text, she sent it to the office and leaned back on the comfortable bench, and for a moment, it felt like she had never been to a terrorist's press conference today and that she was not being terrorized by a crazy guru. Lisa wished all this just did not happen! Today, the sun was particularly kind, warming and calming, as if saying, "no matter what happens, I am here. I shine all the same for victims and criminals, and life goes on anyway." Oh, she would like to lie somewhere on the shore of a warm sea, drinking coffee and be where there were no terrorists or crazy gurus who wanted god who knows what.

Martha's phone call distracted Lisa from her thoughts.

"What if you just passed out from anger, but then why don't you remember how you ended up at home? And what if you didn't just faint? You could have been knocked out. Did you have a bump on your head the next day or a bad headache?"

"Yes, Martha, it all happened, because I fell and hurt myself."

"Was the bump in the back or the front?"

"What does it matter?"

"If you were hit from behind, then the bump should have been there. But you could have fallen headfirst and then there could also be a bump somewhere in the front. And if you just fainted, then the bump could be both in the back and front, depending on how you fell. So where was the bump?"

"I don't remember. I didn't care about some stupid bump then."

"You said there was someone else in the room. And I know who it was."

"Well, who was it?"

"I figured it out. Emma said that some boy named Arty was in love with your sister and he's a sissy. We've both heard it. And the man who shot at you and then cried... doesn't that give him away as a ninny?"

"So what?"

"He was there. I know it. Why else would he be shooting at

you?" Martha insisted.

"That's right. Why would he be shooting at me?"

"Perhaps he was afraid that you would remember something at the scene of the crime. Well, admit it. It could be so."

Lisa was still saying something, arguing with Martha, who, apparently, was tired of sitting idly all day and was now looking for adventures and fun to run from boredom. Yes, salvation from boredom – that's what she was for Martha – a lonely, well-off elderly woman. But Lisa didn't want to entertain anyone at all. Still, Martha's arguments were tipping the scales more and more in her direction.

"Fine, have it your way. Let's go visit Arty. Although I'm not sure that he was the shooter. We just need to find out where he lives."

"I already know!" Martha shouted with joy.

"You do?" Lisa was surprised. "And, by the way, what does the father of the boy who played with the puppy think about his classes? Didn't he stick your phone under the table where Emma was sitting? Does the father know?"

"You mean, the owner of the place? He's not the father. The boy tries to be at home as little as possible because his mother is always drunk, and some random men come and go. The owner of the cafe feeds him out of pity, and in gratitude, he entertains the audience with all sorts of tricks with a puppy. Someday, we'll go there again. It's impossible to look at them without laughing."

"What about the phone?"

"Sometimes he does such tricks with the phone, and runs other errands for customers, because he has to make a living somehow."

Chapter 13

Contrary to assumptions, the sad loser Arthur lived in a prestigious part of their town, with beautiful new houses and well-groomed front gardens.

"I've always wanted to live in a house like this," Martha whispered when they arrived, "The building has only four floors. There are few neighbors, and there are trees and flowers, and the park is very close."

Lisa was surprised once again. Martha had her own big, beautiful house, and the neighborhood was no worse, but she did not comment.

The doorman believed their story that they were Arthur's colleagues, and the company had sent them to check on their sick friend. She did, however, escort them all the way to the elevator, pressed the button for the right floor and, apparently, wanted to go up with them to check whether they were who they claimed to be, but someone rang the front door again, and she returned to her post. Martha and Lisa breathed a sigh of relief when the elevator door closed.

"Will you tell me where you got Arthur's address?"

Martha snorted dismissively, demonstrating her attitude to how she did it. "I called your work, said that I was from the post office, and a package had arrived in his name, but he seemed to have changed his address, and I needed the new one to deliver it."

Lisa looked at her incredulously. "That simple? Did they just give you the address?"

Martha chuckled again. "Well, not that simple. They said they didn't know his new address. I told them said the address I presumably had as if to clarify. They said they had another address, the old one, from when he worked for them, and gave me that one."

Lisa once again didn't comment on Martha's behavior.

One of the three doors on the bright, clean landing, lined with potted plants, seemed to be no different from the others, and yet the women immediately went straight to that door and were right to do so; the number on the door matched the one Martha got from Lisa's office. They stood listening to the sounds from the apartment, then Martha just up and pressed the button. No one answered. There was still silence behind the door. After pressing the button a few more times, Martha fished out a bunch of keys from her pocket and, choosing one, inserted it into the keyhole. The lock clicked softly and the door opened. Lisa's eyes widened, about to finally ask Martha about her espionage skills, but her neighbor pushed her into the semi-dark hallway and slammed the door behind them. When their eyes got used to the darkness, they could see part of the room from the open doorway. An uncertain light shone through the curtained windows and fell on the couch by the window, revealing something resembling a pile of rags. As they approached, they saw in this pile a man covered with a warm blanket. He was shaking so terribly that they could see him tremble even in the dim light, sweat rolling down his face.

"Of course, I knew it. He's a damn junkie! Well, nevermind. Now, he will tell us everything for a fix," Martha declared in a victorious whisper.

The man on the couch, sensing the presence of strangers, opened his eyes and whispered, "Who are you?"

"We are your doom!" Martha said solemnly.

At that moment, he recognized them and hid under the blanket, pressing himself against the wall.

"No, don't you dare crawl away. Tell us everything," Martha was on the offensive.

"I didn't want to! I didn't mean to kill you," Arthur wailed and coughed. Then he continued, "I was just scared."

"Scared, huh?" Martha was enjoying playing bad cop and was ready for some brutal questioning, but he did not know where to hide and stared at Lisa.

"Why did she go to that house? Why did she go there? It's all her fault!"

"Wait, just start from the beginning. You were there when

Alexander was abusing Laura, weren't you?"

"Yes," he squealed, "He was doing such terrible things to her!"

"But you didn't stop him!" Martha attacked him with words.

"I was just filming it all. I was the man behind the camera!" Arthur cried out and started coughing.

"Filming? For what?"

Arthur had another coughing fit. When it stopped and he was able to catch his breath, he told them about filming specific movies, for those who liked it rough with beatings and violence.

"And there is a demand for it?" Martha was astounded.

"Of course! Henpecked husbands who only consider how to take revenge on their wives, sons of heavy-handed mothers and just perverts in general. Alexander needed money for a big movie. He wrote some super script and wanted to make a movie out of it."

"And there were no people willing to invest in his great script?" Lisa, who had been silent until now, joined the conversation.

"I don't know. He didn't tell me."

Arthur's face was a terrible sight – red eyes, sunken cheeks, crusty lips, sweat trickling down his thin, sinewy neck and horribly protruding collarbones.

"You were in love with Laura, and you just calmly filmed these scenes?" Martha had gone on the offensive again.

"No, I wasn't doing it calmly. That day, I decided to kill him, kill him, destroy him... although I was very afraid... I'm frail and knew what they would do to me in prison, but I decided to kill him anyway."

"And why didn't you kill him?"

"She ruined it. Got there at the worst possible time. I was ready, determined, but out of nowhere, she appeared," Arthur looked up at Lisa for the first time, and she saw how much hatred was in his eyes.

"What is on that tape, and where is it?" Lisa asked.

"You know better than me what's in that video," he looked at Lisa again, "But I don't know where it is now. When you passed out, Laura took the flash drive and ran away."

"Where is Laura now?"

"I don't know," he shook his head violently and started coughing again, spitting right into the wet, torn pillowcase.

"Have you shot many such videos with Laura?"

"I don't know. I wasn't the only cameraman. At first, there were other girls, but Alexander only wanted Laura. He said that only with her he could earn money for his film."

Another coughing attack followed, and Arthur fell face first into the dirty pillow.

"He's not a drug addict. Just very sick," Lisa suddenly realized.

"Yes, I see. At first, I thought he was in withdrawal, but it looks like it's either pneumonia or tuberculosis," and both women instinctively stepped back from the couch.

"We'll call you a doctor now."

"No," he shook his head, "I don't have insurance."

"You have the money for this apartment, but no insurance?"

"My grandmother left me this apartment when she was still alive..."

"Do you have any other relatives?"

"They don't speak with me."

"There are still hospitals for the poor."

"It's bad there."

"Do you need it to be good too? Do you want to die here?" Lisa snapped and began calling.

Arthur coughed again and again. The dirty pillowcase was completely darkened by his saliva, and Lisa feared more and more that red spots would begin to appear on it.

Chapter 14

Lisa spent the whole evening locked in her house after sending her neighbor out. She went over what Arthur had told her and always returned to the same phrase, "When you passed out, Laura took the flash drive and ran away."

Laura ran away, leaving her next to the corpse.

"How could you? How could you?" She kept saying over and over, "How could you?"

That night, she did not turn on the lights or answer phone calls or messages. She just walked from one wall to another and stupidly repeated the question that had no answer. Later, she found her grandfather's old icon of the Holy Mother in the closet and tried to pray, but there was no relief. There were no tears that could heal the soul.

Little Laura, for whom she would do anything, whom she loved and protected so much, for whom she was like a mother... At least that's what she thought... Little Laura left her and ran away... And she never showed up or called again. If she was no longer alive, the hopeless thought returned, it would at least be understandable, but why did she do that? Why? Why? Why?

That night, Lisa could not calm down, and only around dawn, fatigue finally overcame her, and she fell into an anxious sleep.

The doorbell woke her up. Trying to ignore it did not work. It just rang again and again. Reluctantly lifting her head from the pillow and first sliding off the couch to the floor, she got up and shuffled to the door. A delivery boy in a bicycle helmet and a bright shirt stood on the threshold, holding the bike with one hand and handing her a white envelope with the other.

This again, was her only thought.

She had a terrible headache, the bright morning sun was too blinding, and Lisa had no desire to take the damn envelope. Yet she took it, signing the courier's tablet with a doodle instead of a normal signature. It didn't make sense to ask him who the sender was. She knew already – her tormentors simply organized the delivery through the service, as did thousands of respectable citizens.

Lisa went back inside, threw the envelope into the trash and trudged to the couch.

But they wouldn't let her sleep. Martha called. Of course, she probably sat at the window all night watching her house and saw the delivery man.

"I'm not calling about the package," Martha immediately stopped Lisa before she could say anything. "I've got something. Remember, I told you about a girl who went to school with my daughter and committed suicide.?"

"I remember something. But..."

"You didn't finish listening to me... Lily was indeed blackmailed. She paid the blackmailer several times, but he demanded more and more money. No one wanted to discuss this lead, because the story about the millionaire husband who allegedly killed his wife was much more interesting. Nobody likes millionaires. But I called my daughter, asked her to find out about her friend's case. My daughter is a very good lawyer and she found something. Yes, indeed, Lily was blackmailed. She complained to her friend but did not say anything to her mother and husband, didn't want them to worry. The husband was suspicious... but didn't want anyone to know. Reputation was very important to him."

"Yes, you already talked about the husband," Lisa said indifferently, waiting for Martha to finish so she could finally go back to bed.

"But something else is interesting. Another young wife of an elderly judge also committed suicide, and you know what unites them? He is also a very famous person, and his reputation should be impeccable. At first, they hushed it up because he is a very influential person, but now it seems to be gaining momentum."

"And what do you want from me? Please, Martha, this is police work, and I'm not going to get involved. I'm not a crime journalist, as you know, and have enough worries of my own."

"Do you not believe that this has something to do with your case?"

"Oh! No! I don't see any connection, and I have a headache. I didn't get enough sleep. Please leave me alone."

Without even glancing in the direction of the white envelope in the trash can, Lisa went back to the couch with only one thought – to fall fast asleep and, better yet, not wake up at all.

However, she still had to go out – after a few hours, her stomach demanded food. After getting some rest, Lisa seemed to have come to life. She didn't want to remember yesterday. The sun was shining brightly again, and a fresh wind burst through the open window, bringing the smells of rain-washed asphalt and greenery.

She decided to have a snack and, without delay, since all possible deadlines for her alleged cold had been exhausted, go to the office. The fleeting thought that Danny, with all his patience, should have already been angry and just fired her (but nothing like that happened, on the contrary, he seemed to keep giving her more time), she dismissed as unnecessary and stupid.

She couldn't begin to suspect Danny too.

The meat pie in a small cozy family cafe on the next street was fresh and very delicious, and the coffee with a white foam cap smelled mind-blowingly amazing. Both the owner of the establishment and his rosy-cheeked wife smiled affably, and if she didn't think about yesterday, then life would be a very good thing.

Suddenly, a simple idea occurred to her. What if she quit her job and just went somewhere near the warm sea, sit on the shore, watch the waves, drink coffee or wine and just enjoy her life. Quit her job? But work had always been more than just a job for her. It was both the meaning of life and the drive, and prestige. She simply could not imagine herself not working. It had always been that way, but not today. To be honest, similar thoughts had visited her before, but they seemed blasphemous. Besides, she'd had Laura to care for, and no one but Lisa could do that. Even the fact that her sister was missing did not stop her. After all, someday, Laura would resurface, and she would need her even more than before.

So Lisa thought until yesterday, but yesterday, something broke in her, and she no longer wanted to see Laura or analyze her cause. She did not want more of yesterday's pain. Something had snap in her.

When the phone rang, she answered automatically, without even looking at the caller ID.

"You can still fix everything. We will arrange a meeting with Alexander, and you will ask him for forgiveness," she heard the same voice, but the usual metal somewhat changed. It had became softer, heartier.

"Go to hell!" were the first words she wanted to throw at this mad guru, who was still trying to lure her into his traps. She would have screamed and used stronger words, but she remembered that there was also a video recording and decided to be more careful.

"You know, I don't care anymore. Alexander is alive, after all, and if he hasn't sued me yet, then I don't think he will."

"You made an attempt on his life!"

"But he's alive!"

"Are you sure?"

"Damn it! I'm so fed up with your mind games! Then who was it with that girl who looked like Laura?"

"A man who looks like Alexander. By the way, a great actor. And here he is, turn your head to the right, he's at the counter buying cigarettes."

Slowly, unwilling to believe, Lisa turned her head and saw Alexander. He paid the clerk, took a pack of cigarettes from the counter and turned to Lisa, and then she saw his face for the first time. Yes, everything was just like him: the clothes, and the hairstyle, and the characteristic gesture with which he brushed a strand of hair from his face, which Lisa believed most of all, but it wasn't Alexander.

She was shocked. The man smiled at her, showing snow-white teeth, and quickly left the cafe and got into a car.

Looks like she killed Alexander after all.

"You have to go through forgiveness and help others," the insinuating, enveloping voice drilled into her brain, "Help yourself."

Chapter 15

The huge dark blue dome of the sky indifferently and coldly covered the earth. Myriads of stars scattered across looked lazily at the earth, reflected in the silted and partially reed-covered river. On the rapids, where the water flow broke out of the dam, the reflection seemed to be shrinking. The stars huddled together, trembling slightly, and disappeared, as if being sucked into a black hole. And not somewhere out there in the universe, but very close, in a river she knew from childhood.

Lisa was sitting on the hilly bank of the river. The earth, which had not cooled down after a sunny day, shared its warmth, holding her in place, lulling her to sleep. A warm breeze whispered – tomorrow the sun will rise, a new day will come, just calm down... But

Lisa's soul was striving upward, to where we will all go in the end, and this was the first time in her life. Thoughts about what would happen next never bothered Lisa. She considered them "old-people's things" and always teased those who started a conversation on this topic. She did not like the darkness and the endless abyss opening above her. She always preferred a roof over her head and the cozy yellow light of a floor lamp by the couch to romantic walks under the stars. But now, for the first time, the abyss seemed to have opened its arms to her – come to me, dissolve into me, only in my arms you will receive the desired calm, only here are the answers to all your questions; free yourself from everything that torments you on earth, which makes life unbearable; none of this makes any difference.

For the first time, she did not want to hide from the endless expanse calling out to her. She just needed to open her arms to meet this call and fly up to where there was no betrayal from the closest people...

Emma's words came back to her, "I treaded on air..."

A simple thought came to Lisa: maybe she should repent, repent out loud in front of everyone, ask for forgiveness from Laura, from Alexander. To apologize for not saving her sister, for being too busy earning money to feed them. Too soon, such a burden fell on her shoulders. She was simply not ready for this. Now she had both the experience and education, and could sometimes argue, and back then she snatched any opportunity to earn money, went with the police to any call, filmed crime scenes that children were not supposed to see. When something like that was on TV, mothers took their kids away.

She also was still a child at that time, torn from a warm home and thrown into adulthood.

So maybe Lisa should repent for taking Alexander's life. After all, she missed those moments when she needed to pay more attention to her sister and her friends. At the very beginning of his relationship with Laura, she could have prevented its development had she not been so busy and withdrawn into herself by then. Her little sister came to her when she was crying quietly from fatigue, grief, from resentment at her parents. Laura snuggled up to her, stroked her hair with her warm palms, but Lisa never responded to her call, never hugged and cried with her sister. And the little girl would go to her room, sit alone for hours on a bed covered with a warm blanket.

Alexander, of course, was a bastard, but something made him like that. Why didn't Lisa try to understand this man, find out everything about him? Why, when she realized that something was wrong with Laura, did she give free rein to only one thought – to kill him? However, until the moment she snuck into the old house and saw everything with her own eyes, this thought was not framed in a clear desire. Until the last minute, Lisa did not believe that this could happen to her sister. The decision to kill had come instantly.

She killed him and what? Did she feel better? No. Laura was gone. Alexander was dead. And her heart was aching...

Perhaps if she repented, it would make her feel better. She just needed to go where she was being called and repent.

Chapter 16

In a room with windows covered with old newspapers sat a simple wooden table with a computer on it. Lisa arrived at the specified address, climbed the stairs, entered through the unlocked door and stopped at the threshold, looking around. There was an old office chair, with a sunken seat and worn upholstery, by the table. There was no other furniture in the room.

Walking carefully across floorboards as old as the table, listening to them creak under her steps, Lisa approached the table and touched the chair's back. Despite the first impression, it easily turned, as if offering her to take a seat. She sank into the chair, pushed off lightly with her foot and faced the computer. Lisa placed her fingers on the keys and a familiar room appeared on the screen. A room with stripped wallpaper in the abandoned building, a table with dirty dishes and a metal bed with a nickel-plated headboard. And then... then came what she had already seen. She was being shown a recording of Alexander beating Laura. Lisa looked at what was happening on the screen with detachment, as if all this was not happening to her, as if someone had turned off her emotions. Did she burn out? Did she really not care what that scumbag was doing to Laura? Could such terrible pain really crumble into dust? And why? From the fact that it hurt too much, and she could no longer endure it? Or did her resentment for her sister, her new pain overwhelm the previous pain, like two huge oncoming ocean waves canceled each other?

The video stopped at the moment when she picked up the

bottle.

Leaning back in the chair, Lisa reached for a cigarette, but remembering that she had quit smoking a few years ago, cursed instead. That's the great force of habit, it's like the effect of a severed hand – it had been gone for a long time, but sometimes it still hurt.

"How did you get this tape?" all this time, she had been on the call with the blackmailer.

"It doesn't matter. Tell me, what do you feel? You care for him. You were just jealous of Laura and wanted to be in her place."

Lisa grinned. This guru had decided to play therapist.

"You're the one mentally crawling to him. You always liked him. All women liked him. And you were no exception. You need to free yourself. Just tell me how you felt then."

"I'll disappoint you. I never liked him. I don't like narcissistic pompous dandies. Not my type."

"Well, at least now, when you already know that you are to blame for his death, ask for his forgiveness. Just say what you've been wanting to say to him all these years, what you've been living with," the voice on the phone said softly, as if listening to her thoughts.

And Lisa was again overwhelmed by yesterday's melancholy, the black dome of the starry sky once again opened above her. Yes, she felt guilty; all these years, she had been living with the thought that if a miracle suddenly happened and she could meet Alexander, she would ask him to forgive her and thereby free herself from a terrible burden. Maybe this guru was not really that crazy, maybe he just saw it as his mission to save people by holding such sessions.

Lisa became more and more lost in the soft voice coming from the phone, and finally, the question arose in her head – why not? It's so wonderful to repent. It's not for nothing that in all religions at all times, people who wanted to throw off an exorbitant burden from their shoulders either went to the temple to the priest, or in the old days, simply went to the square, knelt down and repented of grave sins in front of all the people. Her soul had been asking for repentance for a long time. So why was she avoiding it so? Lisa even thought that she was in a temple and through the colored tiles the light fell on the faces of the saints, the organ sounded high and solemn, and smelled of something special, as it always did in temples. Lisa breathed in this smell that filled her lungs and turned her head. She felt so good, so light as a person who finally made a difficult choice. Through this splendor, she did not immediately hear the annoying call on her second number, ruining the goodness that enveloped her.

She didn't want any calls or conversations and pressed the button just to get rid of the caller, but suddenly heard an unpleasant snotty voice.

"She's at St. Paul's cathedral."

Lisa did not immediately understand what had happened. Still in a daze, instead of hanging up, she switched to the other call, and now someone she knew, someone terribly unpleasant, was talking to her.

"It's Arthur. Laura is at St. Paul's. And I think she's in danger."

Now Lisa recognized the voice. The man who was in love with Laura.

"How do you know?"

"I had a dream."

"Junkies have dreams?"

"I'm not a junkie and you know that."

"I know, it's just...

"How are you? Your voice is strange, like you're stoned..."

Keep mocking me, Lisa thought, and then rushed to the window, almost falling from her sudden movement. She tried to open the window but failed – it was sealed. Choking, coughing, on the verge of passing out, she ran to the door, to the stairs, pushed the door with her entire body, again and again. The old plank barrier could not withstand such pressure. Flying out onto the staircase and hugging the cold, painted wall, she began to exhale, coughing up whatever shit was in her lungs.

Meanwhile, Arthur kept yelling into the phone, "Are you okay? Where are you?"

After catching her breath, Lisa returned for the phone and again jumped out onto the stairs, cleared her throat, croaking, "Why didn't you tell me before?"

"In front of the old woman?" he sounded surprised.

"So what?"

"You still don't understand about her? She probably appeared in your life quite recently when strange things began to happen, right?" Arthur started coughing. When the attack stopped, he continued, "And of course she helped you, but didn't her sudden appearance raise questions?"

"Yes," Lisa hesitated, "But she always had an explanation for everything."

"If you're with her, run," and he coughed again.

"I'm not with her, but I'm... I'm somewhere else."

"Oh," Arthur said, "If so, then run still! Looks like they broke you after all. And don't tell anyone that I called you... just... Thank you for sending me to the hospital."

Lisa rolled down the stairs to the street, into the fresh air, exhaling from her lungs that strange... whatever it was. Out!

At least she finally knew where to look for her sister.

Chapter 17

Climbing the mountain across winding turns, the bus finally brought Lisa to a picturesque area with a magnificent view of the valley, surrounded by greenery and still swirling morning fog. A handful of tourists with cameras and backpacks on their shoulders, barely after stepping off the bus, gasped and clucked their tongues, expressing their admiration for the panorama that opened before to their eyes.

They were talking among themselves in a language that Lisa did not understand. There was so much to admire! From here, a high mountain, the land with perennial olives barely illuminated by the morning sun, seemed like paradise. A flock of birds took off from the mirror surface of the lake in the distance and, after circling once, twice, sank back onto the water. The blue-green spurs of the mountains afar had not yet been freed from the descending fog, which was creeping over the lake, over the gardens, over the roofs of tiny houses and over the winding road, gradually melting in the sunlight.

Lisa also froze with admiration for this beauty, this magnificent expanse. For thousands of years, people had been cultivating this fertile valley, growing olives and fruits for themselves, grazing sheep and goats, raising children and defending their land with weapons in their hands from invaders who repeatedly tried to bring these people to their knees. When it became absolutely unbearable, and the enemy won, the inhabitants fled to the protection of the mighty walls of the ancient monastery on such steep cliffs that not anyone who wanted to enslave them dared to climb there. And now, in peaceful times, the stone walls of the temple, cut into the rock, were still impregnable and very dangerous.

After admiring this fertile valley for quite some time, taking several deep breaths and filling her lungs with mountain air, Lisa followed the diverse flock of tourists that was also headed for the temple. Now, a stone-paved road led there, still open to the eyes of those who watched them from the stronghold, as in ancient times.

Tourists were allowed only to the part of the territory reserved for visits at a small gatehouse church. Here, they could kneel before the faces of the saints, asking for the fulfillment of their most cherished desires. And the saints always helped – at least, numerous pilgrims said so.

With the others, Lisa sat down on a stone bench but did not listen to the guide. Questions kept running through her head: Was it really true that Martha was playing her? Was Arthur right? Had it occurred to Lisa before that Martha acted almost like a professional detective? Lisa refused to believe that Martha had started this whole game with her. Why would she do all this? From boredom? A wealthy old woman just got so bored that she came up with detective stories where she played a central role? Why were there no pictures in her house, and why did the house look nothing like a place where an old lady would live? And what else did Martha really know about her situation? Almost everything, actually, because Lisa told her everything herself. But was Martha actually dangerous?

Arthur was very ominous with his warning: "Don't tell her about Laura. If you find her, then you'll be useless to the old woman."

And then what? Would she make Lisa's story public? Or would she blackmail her? But why? And why did she need Laura? What if she was Alexander's relative and wanted to avenge him? Why hadn't she thought about Martha before, about her suspicious behavior? Why did she turn a blind eye to so many weird things that raised so many questions? She had just wanted to believe her. Lisa had just wanted to have a friend.

Yet, suspecting Martha was like a lazy plot twist from a bad movie, and movies rarely were like real life. In life, everything was much tougher, and no screenwriter or writer would come up with something that life would throw your way. Lisa was taught this by her very first editor-in-chief, with whom she worked straight out of university as a young girl. He taught her everything she knew. Remembering this amazing man, her teacher, Lisa smiled. Julius paid a high price for his passion, even obsession, with the profession, but that's a completely different story.

The woman guide, having delivered her lecture, lowered her voice and said that they were all in for a very pleasant surprise. At her request, the abbot himself would bless their group. The tourists hummed softly to show their approval. How lucky they were to have such a story to tell upon returning home.

"We'll just have to wait a bit," the guide warned. "The abbot kept vigil at night and is now resting."

After a while, a thin, elderly smiling man with a slightly swollen face entered the church from the closed part of the monastery. Must have just woken up. Along the way, he moved the boxes left in the aisle by an acolyte to the wall, as if he was not an important person, but a simple monk, and approached the group. The tourists quickly lined up, one by one coming up to be blessed. Lisa, too, rose from the bench and watched them. She had expected to see a full-bodied, well-fed man – after all, he was the abbot of a famous monastery, even outside the country, but this old man looked so much like her grandfather. Lisa had never been very religious, and it seemed inappropriate for her to approach him for a blessing. So, she stood there until the last tourist stepped aside. The abbot looked up at her. There was no call or question in these eyes, just a soft glimmer of understanding in a very old man who had seen a lot and, apparently, had lived through just as much. Lisa's feet carried her to him, as if enchanted. She knelt, a soft hand touched her head, and then she decided to ask.

"I'm looking for a girl named Laura. At least that was her name before. I was told that she was in this monastery, but I'm not sure that the man was telling me the truth – yours is a friary, after all – and I'm in despair. I have so much to say to her. I'm so sorry... I thought I had replaced her mother and had the right to know everything about her life... When I began to notice bruises on her body and face, I tried to just talk to her, but she screamed at me, demanding I stay out of her affairs. But I did as I saw fit, and she disappeared and I, I have to see her..."

Lisa knew she was just raving like a lunatic and this old and apparently very busy man might not know where Laura was, who she was. What did he care about Lisa's problems? But still, she talked and talked, and he listened without interrupting.

When she finally finished, when the words ran out, the abbot beckoned Lisa to follow him and went to the far door from which he came.

Behind the door, Lisa saw the closed part of the monastery with a well-kept garden and a small sparkling fountain with tiny goldfish swimming in it. A little further down the mountainside, already behind the monastery wall, there was a low building. The abbot pointed to this building and explained that this was a school for children from nearby villages and kids from the orphanage at the monastery.

"There are three teachers working at the school," he explained, "Among them, your sister. But first, I have to ask her if she wants to see you."

"No, she won't. No, she won't... and can I at least look at her from afar? That's it. I'll leave and never come back... I promise you," Lisa stared at the abbot pleadingly.

"I think she loves you," he said and went towards the school, leaving Lisa waiting on a bench under a flowering rose bush.

Sitting on that bench, Lisa constructed her dialogue with Laura. In no case should she give in to emotions and show how much she missed her, how guilty she felt about everything that had happened. After all, it was Laura who betrayed her, and betrayal could not be forgiven by a single act... These correct and clever words were spinning in her head. She was a journalist, and now, she just needed to build her conversation, discover why Laura had run away, why she hadn't contacted her for so long, because everyone thought she was dead... Lisa even forced herself to remember some lectures for journalists about the rules of conducting interviews. She was very thirsty. As a city person, Lisa drank only bottled water from the store. Now, she just forgot all usual caution and caught a trickle from the fountain with her mouth. She rinsed her hands and face, took a deep breath and exhaled, trying to calm her desperately pounding heart.

A woman in a long-sleeved dress, a floor-length skirt and a scarf on her head was walking along the path to her. She stopped just a few paces from Lisa.

Lisa peered into her face, trying to catch something familiar about her features: the stubbornly turned up chin, the victorious smile of a spoiled child whom everyone loved and who was forgiven for all pranks, but she saw nothing. It wasn't Laura and a wave of disappointment overwhelmed Lisa. Yes, in the world, indeed, not only her sister was named Laura, and she was not the only one who ran away from home.

The woman noticed Lisa getting up from the bench and went straight to her.

After greeting her, she began to apologize for the abbot who had given Lisa hope. A girl named Laura really worked for them, but she recently left and did not say where she was going. Whether this was the girl Lisa was looking for, she didn't not know. The Laura who worked for them said almost nothing about herself.

Lisa listened with her head down and felt that she was a sandcastle and the oncoming wave was washing away her walls, towers... A little more and nothing would remain of Lisa. Perhaps the Laura who lived here was really her sister. Otherwise, why would Arthur send her here? And Laura left – this time, no one knew where she went. Or maybe Arthur lied. But why? Why would he say that

Laura was in danger? Perhaps he told Lisa about the monastery and then regretted what he said and somehow warned Laura, so she ran. She left because she didn't want to see Lisa and didn't need her apologies.

Muttering, Lisa wandered to the gated church entrance, behind which ordinary life was going on. Again, she felt an emptiness inside. Perhaps Laura was right to leave, and she would not need to have a serious conversation with her. She would not have to blame her for anything. She was not ready to demand any explanations anyway. She's not ready to meet her sister at all.

After grabbing the heavy door handle, Lisa remembered that she had not said goodbye to the woman. Looking back, she saw another woman walking along the same path. When she saw Lisa, she stopped and then ran, and Lisa ran towards her. Both of them, like wounded birds, stumbled, fell and soared again, rushing to each other, to join bleeding hearts, cry out, scream, kiss each other's faces, hands, inhale the smell of their hair, which had not changed at all since happy times. Holding each other, they wouldn't let go and stood close. Inseparable.

Chapter 18

Martha had already tried Lisa's number many times. Failing once again to reach her, she cursed and put her phone on the table covered with a perfectly ironed linen tablecloth. The stubborn girl didn't want to talk to her! The story was coming to an end, and without Lisa, none of this mattered.

After walking aimlessly around the living room and dialing Lisa's number a few more times to be sure, Martha left the house. She pushed away the cats that hurried to her, got into her Volkswagen and drove to the city center. Near the city hospital, she started to slow down but then kept driving past the hospital parking lot and stopped the car around the corner.

At the hospital, she asked the nurse on duty for a particular patient's room number, but the nurse refused to give it to her – they did not give out information about this particular patient and no one was allowed to see him. Martha did not argue. She would solve this problem some other way.

Passing by a door labeled "Staff only," she considering waiting for the right moment when one of the cleaners would come here for their brooms and buckets, but changed her mind. Instead, Martha went outside, called the police and said that there was a suspicious bag left unattended in the hospital building and it could have explosives in it. When the police and rescuers arrived, and the entire hospital staff hurriedly ran out into the street while the specialists were deciding whether to evacuate the patients, Martha quickly went up to the second floor where the intensive care unit was. Here, she immediately saw the one door in the long row with an officer on duty, looking out the window to see what was happening below. It seemed he had not yet received his orders, and not knowing what to do, he was pacing between the staircase and the window. Martha waited for him to return to the window and slipped into the room.

She left the room before much time had passed and quietly sneaked onto the back stairs behind the police officer, who was now hovering by the stairs.

Martha made it back to her car and once again called Lisa only to hear the same ringing. She left a voice message, turned off the phone and leaned back in the seat, her heart pounding intermittently. She took a bottle of pills from the glove compartment and put one in her mouth. Scanning the car for a bottle of water that always lay near the seat, she noticed a man running quickly to her car. Martha thought that she had seen the man before, but there was no time to remember. In a panic, she tried to block the door and raise the window, but before she could, someone else's hands grabbed her by the throat.

Chapter 19

The sisters could not stop talking. Words and tears mixed together as they cried, then laughed, then began talking again. Each told the other about what she had experienced during this terrible time, how they missed each other.

Laura had run away from Alexander. First, she hid in the basement of an old building and did not go outside at all for three days, drinking mostly rainwater because she was afraid that he would look for her and find her. Laura didn't have a phone nor did she have any change to call from a pay phone. Because she was wearing only a nightgown, she couldn't show herself to people in this state. She was afraid to go home, too. On the fourth day, hunger overcame fear and late at night, when all sounds had died down, barefoot and almost naked, Laura went out on the road. She did not dare to hitch a ride like that, and to say that she had been robbed meant going to the police station – no, Laura did not want that. So, she stood at the night stop, hiding from random cars behind a billboard, not knowing what to do next, waiting for who knows what, when only one passenger got off the night bus: Arthur. He had been looking for her all this time, realizing that she would not get far, scared and undressed, and that day, he had decided to search for her at night, in case Laura had decided to come out of her hiding place. He helped her then, sent her to the village near St. Paul's, where his very distant and very old relative lived. She brought Laura to the abbot and asked him to give her shelter.

Laura was temporarily given shelter at the monastery, where no one asked what happened to her or why she was running. Here, in the monastery's silence, she gradually calmed down, trying to forget the past. She eventually began going to church, even though God had never interested her before, and learned to pray. To somehow thank them for their help, she asked for a job at the school – cleaning, washing, mopping floors, anything, really, but was offered a teaching position for young orphans. Laura herself was a child not so long ago, and they would probably find a common language, so the abbot thought.

Time passed. The terrible events gradually retreated. Simple healthy food and fresh air did their work to heal her. There was nothing here that reminded Laura of her past life. There were no drugs and alcohol, and Laura thanked God every day that Alexander failed to get her hooked on the serious stuff, because of her mother's very strict, absolutely intolerant attitude towards drug addicts, which, if the girls did not obey, she frightened them with. "If you behave badly, you will become junkies," she said. It seemed that there was no scarier punishment than this.

Laura learned to thank God that her mother had scared them so much as children. Here, in the shelter, she heard a lot of stories about the lives of children who had been through bullying, abuse, and drugs.

A year later, Laura began to take time off. She came to town, rented a car, and parked in the shade of old trees near their house to watch Lisa. She wanted so much to meet her sister again and tell her everything...

"I couldn't survive this shame. I didn't want you to know what I was doing for Alexander, but you saw everything anyway... I was afraid you wouldn't forgive me.... You look so much like our mom, and Mom wouldn't approve."

Lisa wanted to but could not ask why her sister left her in that terrible house, in a situation where she could have been accused of murder. She wanted to but couldn't bring herself to ask. Laura herself started talking about it, telling her how she ran away from Alexander in a panic, how she feared that he would kill her after she said, "That's enough, I won't do it for you anymore!"

"At first, he pleaded, 'You will ruin my future. You know why I need the money and why we're doing this.'

'Are we doing this? No, you're doing this, and it looks like you're enjoying it, and it excites you, and only that. I don't remember us making love like normal people. You can only do it after you beat me up.' And then he snapped... I ran and only then saw you with a bottle in your hand. It was so scary."

"So, I killed Alexander after all?"

"No! No! There was someone else, someone hiding behind the door. Arthur was late, but Alexander didn't want to wait, he placed the camera on the tripod. You appeared in the doorway with this bottle in your hands, someone pushed the door very hard from the other side, and you fell. And then I just ran. I'm sorry that I left you there alone. I ran and ran, not knowing where I was going, just away from that place, until I was completely exhausted and fell through the wooden, rotten roof of the basement."

Gradually, the disparate events of that day formed into a much clearer picture. Lisa remembered how, after repeated attempts to talk to her sister about the marks on her body, she simply tracked her down and witnessed that horror. Anger blinded and stunned her then. She was ready to smash the head of her sister's tormentor.

"But who killed Alexander? Arthur?"

"I don't know, I don't think so... it's unlikely. Arthur is too weak. He will run from a street dog. He is afraid of well... everything. There was supposed to be another man on the camera that day. Alexander ordered many close-ups, and Arthur was afraid to even get close to us."

"Perhaps it's this guru person?" Lisa suggested.

Her sister's confused look was her answer.

"At least, there is one good thing about this," Lisa tried to joke. "Everything is fine with my head. And I don't pass out just because I'm very angry."

Lisa thought about it, because indeed, she heard some muffled sounds outside the door. Someone was hiding behind it. But who and why?

"Why did Arthur tell me that you took the flash drive with the recording?"

"I don't know," Laura gave her sister an apologetic and pleading look. "Maybe he just lied to protect himself?"

"I would really like to have it because it is proof of my and your innocence. That's our alibi. This recording would be very useful."

"Could it be one of the neighbors? Saw the light, snuck in?"

"No one lived there. The houses were completely abandoned. Alexander wouldn't take any chances and would have found another place to shoot his films. I heard there are refugees living there now, but there weren't any then."

Several times during their long conversation, Lisa's phone started ringing frantically, but she ignored it. Whoever was calling now could wait. She and Laura had so much to say to each other.

They sat holding hands, near the same bubbling and sparkling fountain, and it felt like such terrible things could not happen in this beautiful world. Everything that had happened to them was just a very bad dream.

When the words and tears dried up, and they were finally able to let go of each other, Lisa said, "Well, let's go."

Laura looked up at her blankly.

"Where to?"

"Home, dear sister. We're going home."

Laura smiled lovingly and shook her head. "My home is here now."

Lisa didn't understand at first what she meant.

"But I've been looking for you for so long. We will be living as before, and I won't let anyone hurt you anymore." Seeing that Laura was going to refuse again, she added, "I need you."

Laura shook her head again and looked down, saying softly but unflinchingly, "You're strong. You're extraordinarily strong. You're my sister, and you can do anything, but these kids need me."

Lisa grabbed Laura by the shoulders and shook her. "No, no! You don't know what you're saying!" At that moment, Lisa completely forgot about her promise not to choose for her sister anymore, not to play mother hen and give her freedom of choice. "You're not a nun!"

"I'll be soon."

The bright sunny day was no more.

"No!"

Lisa could not imagine that her sister, full of life and strength, would imprison herself in the walls of some monastery among submissive and faceless nuns.

"I can't go back to the world. In the gaze of every person I meet, I will be reading the same question, 'Is this that little whore?'"

"Do you think Alexander was selling the video?"

Laura lowered her eyes.

"So what?" Lisa persisted. "You were underage. He was humiliating you. You don't have to hide. On the contrary, we need to hold a press conference and tell people everything. We don't have the video yet, but we will find it and the person who really killed Alexander."

Laura was silent, staring into the distance at the garden, at the peaceful clouds floating over the valley, over the monastery and the road, the lake.

"You've been through so much, we've been through so much together – Dad's death and then Mom and all that happened after. We have the right to be together and be happy."

Laura was quiet still, and Lisa's heart sank again. She had just found her sister and was losing her once more. The happiness, which nothing could destroy seconds ago, was collapsing like a sandcastle on the beach beaten by the wind and waves.

Laura looked up, and for the first time, Lisa noticed something different in these eyes – not a spoiled girl in pink clothes and bows, whom everyone loved, but a grown woman, who had made an important, the only important, decision.

"If you could listen to these children's stories, listen to what they went through before they got here, how they were treated in shelters, in foster families, how they were beaten, kept in basements, raped by their families... There is so much grief in their little hearts, but they did not deserve this grief. They are not to blame for anything... They need me, you know?"

"But they didn't lock you in the basement," Lisa was confused.

Laura pulled away. "You have no idea what he did to me..."

And she started crying again. Lisa held her tight, stroking her hair, her shoulders, not knowing what other words to say.

After a while, Laura finally calmed down and continued, "I want to help these children. It is very difficult to earn their trust, but gradually they've warmed up to me, they... began to smile. You have no idea what it really is. I've never seen children so drawn to knowledge before. They all have different levels of training. Not everyone was allowed to go to school, and now they are catching up in a way that other children never dreamed of. Language, literature, mathematics, chemistry, physics – they love all the subjects. At least they're trying."

Laura's face seemed to be lit up by the morning sun.

"And PE! Volleyball, football, gymnastics, dancing. The abbot insisted that they must have all that too. We even teach them self-defense and shooting. And recently we've held an all-around competition."

"Shooting? Does the abbot mind?"

"Of course not. He was even a judge at these competitions. He understands that these skills give them confidence that they can stand up for themselves."

Lisa really wanted to ask, "Aren't you afraid that having acquired such skills, they will begin to take revenge on their abusers?" but restrained herself.

"You will come here to see me," Laura hugged her. "I'm not dead. I'm just different. I'm still your little sister..."

Chapter 20

Lisa returned to the city absolutely depressed: she found her sister only to lose her again.

"It's fine, everything will work out, everything will be well over time. I'll figure something out," she kept telling herself, but she knew that nothing would be the same as before.

Out of habit, she checked her phone and saw more than ten messages from Martha but decided against calling back yet. She needed to think. Why did Arthur forbid her from telling Martha that Laura was in the monastery? Did he really suspect her of something? She needed to meet with Arthur soon. He obviously didn't tell Laura everything.

Lisa was distracted from her somber thoughts by a dialogue between two passengers on the bus as she was returning home. Two women were discussing another terrorist attack, another hostage-taking... Wasn't it enough?

Were they remembering that last time, or was there another crisis in the city? Busy with her own affairs and her own worries, Lisa had not watched the news for a long time. She took out her phone and – oh shit! While she was in the monastery, some stranger took a woman hostage. He was armed. The car with the terrorist and the hostage was now on Freedom Square.

Freedom Square again! It looked like the first terrorist had himself a copycat! How many more would there be until dust settled, until some other drama gripped the attention of the townspeople?

Lisa decided to go straight to the square. She called Danny to say that she was taking this job if he hadn't fired her yet, but her boss wasn't answering.

Their bus stood at a stop for a long time before entering the city. The driver took coffee at a roadside stand, but an elderly lady in a hat with a creamy satin ribbon snidely remarked that they shouldn't drink coffee at work since they already made too many stops. It would serve them right if someone wrote a complaint to the Minister of Transport – let them cancel these stops near small villages. Their residents may very well walk to the next one.

She also expressed the same idea to him in a shriek, and the driver, quite purposefully, was in no hurry to get back on the bus and, in response to her heap of reproaches, sipped his coffee, enjoying his position. The woman threatened him with complaints, fines and all sorts of punishments from above if they did not move immediately. Of course, he could have finished his coffee in three sips, but her screeching voice seemed to only provoke him more.

Some passengers joined the old lady, but there were also those who thought it would be better if the evil old hag shut up.

When Lisa changed buses and arrived at Freedom Square, she was expecting to have deja vu – the same roadblocks, and the wind driving a used paper cup across the empty square. And cameras aimed at where the action was.

And when did they even manage? For some reason, Lisa thought with dislike.

The only difference was that in the center of the square there was no bus with hostages, but Martha's car. For the first few minutes, Lisa didn't believe was she was seeing. No, couldn't be. Martha was supposed to be at home, looking out the window and waiting for Lisa to come back. Maybe someone stole her car, Lisa thought, calling Martha. That was self-deception, of course. No one answered the phone. She pressed the redial button again and again, but it kept ringing. Lisa stared in confusion, looking for someone she knew to ask what she had missed this time. She saw Evan first. Another familiar thought – he was the first, as always, the best and fastest. However, Evan was not where he should have been, not with journalists.

Had he managed to get so close to the terrorist already? That's a reporter! But then Lisa realized that Evan was the terrorist, and it was he who was holding a gun to Martha's head and using her as a shield.

Emotions did not allow Lisa to think clearly. She was on edge, so she grabbed the phone and dialed Martha, Danny, Evan... Useless. No one answered. And then, finally, she remembered the voice message from Martha.

Chapter 21

When Martha passed out from suffocation, the man who attacked her dragged her into the passenger seat, looking around to see if anyone saw him, got behind the wheel and sped away, dangerously overtaking others, trying to get further away from the hospital. He had not yet decided what he would do with her, with this clingy old woman. He noticed her slipping out of the hospital by the emergency stairs and immediately realized that, somehow, she had managed to discover that Sergio was here and had gotten to him. If Sergio regained consciousness, he could have explained how, for the first time in many years of their behind-the scenes competition, he beat Evan and was the first to arrive at the apartment of the stupid wench, who, it turned out, had left a suicide note. He, Evan, failed. He was too late this time. Whoever asked Sergio to come first would, as always, be second, and this was not bad for a photojournalist, but he asked for trouble. If he had been late, as always, he would be alive and well now. Evan could still see him dazed, confused with the note that had fallen out of that woman's hand. Then his astonished look at the sight of Evan appearing in the doorway.

This time, the officer, whom Evan paid to report all emergency incidents in the city, had screwed up. Thanks to this, he was always the first to arrive at the scene and took the best pictures. Had Sergio outbid his informant?

Evan had no choice but to hit his competitor, slightly, under the left nipple, where the large pectoral muscle ends. Usually, the knuckle of the middle or index finger there resulted in an uneven heart rhythm and a fatal outcome. Evan learned this jiu-jitsu technique from a man who fought for many years in various hot spots around the world. There were no external injuries, and it would be unclear why a person's heart suddenly stopped.

Sergio then fell and Evan began to call the police, who were waiting for the forensic team on the street. He shouted that a photoreporter had lost consciousness; it looked like he had seen a corpse for the first time and should be sent to the hospital immediately. So, it happened, and Evan took the note.

But when the same informant from the police called Evan and reported in a joyful voice that his colleague had not died, but simply passed out, he realized that he had screwed up again, only temporarily taking his opponent out of the game. Thus, he had returned to the hospital, hoping to finish the job.

For unknown reasons, Sergio was assigned protection, and Evan had to wait at the hospital all night, puzzling over how to get into the room. Had his competitor regained consciousness and managed to tell them everything? No. That was unlikely. Did the detective on the case suspect something? This was becoming more complicated, and he had to finish off his restless competition before the man spoke. When all this commotion began with the arrival of the rapid response team and sappers, Evan was confused at first, and when he saw Martha, he understood everything. How did she get wind of it, that old crow?

He had to act immediately; first, he must discover from the old woman whether Sergio had woken up, and then deal with her. He just needed to go to a quiet place and then quickly return to the hospital. Perhaps all this fuss with miners and special forces was in his favor. He just had to hurry.

Evan was looking for a quiet, deserted place, and drove into the city park, but as luck would have it, it was full of people. He drove through the city center towards the quarter with abandoned houses occupied by migrants. Here, he could definitely complete his tasks quietly. Stay under the radar. But then his engine died. In the middle of the stupid square. And Martha began to move. Wheezing and struggling, she tried to jump out of the car – a surprisingly tenacious old woman she turned out to be. Evan began to strangle her again, but a guard was already coming to them, and it would not be possible to hide her.

And then Evan started screaming about a bomb he had in his car and the hostage.

Chapter 22

"Just in case, I'm giving you my daughter's phone number if something happens to me... But you know, nothing will happen to me..." that's how Martha finished her voice message, and Lisa, who listened to it again and again, dialed this number. The call was immediately answered, and a dry business-like voice said, "I know, and my plane is taking off now. I'll be there in a couple of hours." Short beeps followed.

Lisa sat on the steps of the TV crew bus, loitering in anticipation of something changing – long negotiations were being held with the hostage taker. She gulped the hot coffee offered by crew and went over the events of the last days. She first saw in her head how Martha bravely climbed the tree, trying to help the screaming cat down from a branch, and this memory made her smile, and then her neighbor, her partner fearlessly jumped Arthur, who tried to kill them in the old house.

How could she ever doubt her? After all, Martha helped her so many times and took care of her like her own. Lisa remembered and punished herself, because if she answered Martha's calls, her neighbor's car wouldn't be sitting in the middle of the square right now.

Then, Lisa mentally returned to Martha's voice message about a new suicide and the wife of a rich famous man who left a suicide note, "I don't want to pay him anymore." Sergio, who happened to be close to the scene of the accident, told her this. A small bribe to a friendly police officer opened the door for him to the scene even before the forensic team arrived.

And there was more: Sergio quickly scrolled through the list of calls on that woman's phone and suddenly found a number he knew —another mistake on Evan's part, when he was just starting out, communicating with this woman from his phone – with this rich bitch, whom he milked like a cash cow for a long time and very successfully. Sergio, who found Evan's phone number, became suspicious, but that was just that - suspicion.

Evan, of course, had now deleted his number from her phone – he should have done it a long time ago. He did not repeat the same mistake with his new wards, but everything was going so well. He could not imagine such an outcome. And why shouldn't she share it? Her husband was rolling in money, she would give him a little, as before and that's it. But no, this stupid cow decided to repent! It looked like he went overboard with repentance. It was, of course, good that his method worked, but he did not immediately believe that such a large number of people needed forgiveness. All he needed was to find out their weak spot. The business he organized worked so well. However, for the future, he would have to consider such negative side effects. Cash cows should live and bring him money.

He would rather take the device, but the detectives might notice – where have you seen a person without a phone today? Just in case, he first dunked the phone in a vase of flowers and then left it next to the overturned vase.

Martha's words sounded in Lisa's head, "You won't believe who it is. You know this person very well."

But now, Lisa was not at all sure that she knew Evan well.

A couple of hours later, as promised, Martha's daughter arrived. Lisa first watched her from a distance while she was talking to some people. Martha's daughter did not look like her at all – tall, thin, resembling a thoroughbred greyhound, dressed in an excellent business suit and thin heels. These probably cost at least five thousand, Lisa thought. Nice haircut, straight, beautifully styled hair. In her hands was a leather briefcase, like Lisa imagined for an expensive lawyer with whom fate brought her together. But then, Martha had said that her daughter was a lawyer, a very successful lawyer.

The woman did not cry, did not demand her mother be released immediately. She just carried on a businesslike discussion with two inconspicuous men in ordinary city clothes, who, having met them in another place, Lisa would never have thought that they could lead an operation to free hostages.

Lisa didn't like Martha's daughter. She was completely cold in such a difficult situation, like a stranger. The face of the boy, the son of the former terrorist, sobbing, burying his face in his hands, flashed before her eyes. But here there was complete calm.

After waiting for them to finish their conversation, Lisa approached her, introduced herself, and wanted to express her condolences, but realizing that it was unnecessary, only said that she was Martha's neighbor, and they had been talking a lot lately.

"I guess your mom was talking about me."

Helene nodded dryly.

"So what?" Lisa shamed herself. "Everyone experiences grief in their own way. Need to leave her alone."

The woman seemed to be waiting just for this. She immediately turned away and began to call someone.

Suddenly, Lisa saw how the special forces were regrouping. Were they really going in for the assault? *Damn it! But what about the negotiations, what happened with that?* After all, it usually didn't go this way – they talked to the perpetrator for a long time, discovered their demands, bought time, and... why was it different now? If they attacked, Evan could just kill Martha. Lisa rushed to the car, to the two men, who were in charge of the operation, but they did not let her through.

No, Martha must not die! Lisa ran to her daughter. She must tell them no. Judging by how respectfully they treated her, she was, indeed, an important person, but Helene had disappeared. She was here just a second ago and was gone the next. Lisa looked around, turning her head in all directions, intending to break through to these two, if she was not allowed to pass again, she would scream, yell – everything to prevent the assault, when suddenly she noticed Helene behind one of the cars, where there were no people at all. Martha's daughter was talking to someone on the phone, covering it with her hand.

What a great time to talk! Didn't she understand her mother could die? Lisa ran up to her, about to angrily tear at the sleeve of the suit but stopped when she heard the end of the phrase, "You will release her immediately. There will be no 'otherwise.' Do it now."

Lisa was blindsided. What was it? Who was she talking to? Was that Evan? This was Martha's daughter, right? No mistake? And Evan was the terrorist who captured her mother. Bewildered, Lisa quickly retreated behind the car.

Meanwhile, something strange was happening in the square. Evan, fat bald Evan, the most successful reporter in their city, was getting out of the car with raised hands. He lowered the phone he was holding near Martha's head and imitating a pistol, knelt down and was immediately pinned down by the police.

Lisa's mind was racing. "Is he giving up? Why did he do it?

Why? Why did he decide to surrender? If Martha's daughter really called him, did she tell him to surrender?"

While Evan was being lifted from the ground and quickly led to the car, Lisa desperately broke through. She didn't care at all whether she would be shot. She just wanted answers, and she screamed, "Why, why did you do all this? Why, Evan? Just don't lie that you wanted to help me and help all these people!"

In those seconds when they were face to face, he shouted with hatred, spitting out the words along with saliva. "Why? Do you want to know why? Because I have seven children and all girls, and they all need to be fed, and I always have to be on top, the best, the very first, so that she doesn't humiliate me that I can't give her a boy..."

Lisa was taken aback, but he continued, "And why do you need this money? You're lonely. You don't have a family..."

"What money?" she asked in confusion, but he had already been taken away.

Chapter 23

Lisa kept pestering the paramedics until she was allowed into the ambulance that was taking Martha to the hospital. She was outright lying, claiming to be Martha's daughter, and again, she didn't care what people thought of her.

In the hospital corridor, she had to spend two hours waiting for the old woman to be examined and a doctor finally come out. The smile on his round, rosy-cheeked face spoke volumes: Martha would be fine.

"Your mother turned out to be an extremely strong person, although, of course, she got hurt."

He spoke some more, but Lisa hardly understood him. She only knew that Martha was alive and would stay so. After receiving permission from the doctor, she ran towards Martha's room.

"Just a few minutes," the doctor called after her. "Your mother needs rest."

Inside, Lisa rushed to hug and squeeze Martha, as if she really were her family. For a moment, she let go of her, looking into her face, and again hugged the old woman and cried shamelessly.

"Well, that's enough, stop! You'll drown me in your tears!" Martha protested.

Having freed herself from the embrace of her unexpected daughter, Martha, hardly pronouncing the words, first proposed to open a detective agency together.

"We worked well together!" she wheezed, her eyes shining.

"What agency at your age. You'd better nurse your beloved cats," Lisa laughed.

"I hate cats!"

"You do?" Lisa was confused.

"It's Helene, my daughter. She brings me her foundlings,"

Martha mused. "And she only comes when she has to give me the next one. My husband and I raised our daughter with love, helped her to become a lawyer. She is successful enough she can provide me with a house but has no time to come see me. Yes, she bought my current house after ours burned down, furnished it to her taste, and just put me there. And my husband died even earlier. We always dreamed that she would come to us and bring children. Instead, she brings cats..."

Lisa was silent, not knowing what to say.

"There used to be pictures hanging in the house, her pictures and I talked to them, but then I got mad and cleaned everything up."

"But she came right away yesterday!"

"Yes, she was there, in the square, I know... She checked something at my request. Turns out that both her friend and that other woman were being blackmailed. Each had a secret. These secrets tormented the women for many years, and they could not tell anyone about them. Somehow, Evan figured them out – he was a good reporter. He offered the help of some unknown guru, and he became something like a confessor for them."

"I understand that, but what does it have to do with me? Why did he blackmail me? I am not rich, I live paycheck to paycheck, and believe me, they are not so big in our office. Serious cases, such as a terrorist attack, when you can earn money, don't happen often."

"You really don't know anything?"

"What should I know?"

"Have you been in contact with your father's lawyer recently?"

"Well, it's been a long time... he didn't promise anything. He said it was unlikely we'd win the case, and I gave up on everything long ago."

Martha lifted her head from the pillow and sat up in bed. Lisa tried to make her lie back down, but Martha stopped her with an impatient gesture.

"Several more people have joined your lawsuit. Including some people from a neighboring urban settlement, who also suffered in a similar situation. The owner of the plant resisted for a long time but realized that it would be even worse if similar cases were unearthed all over the country and abroad, because he had more than one plant with a terrible security system, and then he would be in trouble. Well, when my Helene took up the case, he agreed to pay both material and moral damage to the victims, and it's quite a large sum."

"A large sum? How large is it?"

"Helene said that you would get five million each."

"How much?"

Martha just nodded to confirm her words and added, "That's why Evan needed your confession. He was going to cause you to have a nervous breakdown. You would have confessed to a murder that you did not commit, but since doubts had not allowed you to live normally for several years, confession and forgiveness would have seemed to you a release from torment... As well as those girls who chose to die."

Lisa fell silent, shocked by what she heard. Could she get that much money? And what about the lawyer, why didn't he tell her anything? Somehow Evan had found out about the money... that's why he forced her so persistently to confess to the murder. To blackmail her?

"Helene will take care of your lawyer, so don't worry about that," and the same reckless sparkle appeared in Martha's eyes.

"Yes, by the by," she continued, "I want to ask you to do something for me. If I suddenly die, well, I'd die of boredom," she foresaw Lisa's reaction, "please check on my cats, feed them, and ... go see them later, well, not immediately, and then..."

Lisa looked at her, not understanding a word.

"It's just that if something happens to me, well, you never know – the work of a private detective can sometimes be dangerous. This time, of course, I set myself up. In the future, I will be very careful... I promise you! And I'm fine, I'm totally fine! I just wanted to ask you – don't forget my cats. There's food in the pantry for them and there's more... there are instructions on how to feed them and when..."

"Yes, I'll figure out how to feed your cats," Lisa laughed.

Martha tried to get out of bed again to begin some kind of investigation right now. And again, her eyes shone, her face lit up with a dazzling smile, and even the hospital gown couldn't spoil the impression – a warrior, an Amazon, the ancient Roman goddess avenger Fury, Marianne on the Parisian barricades, the American

Statue of Liberty ready to fight any injustice. She got out of bed anyway. Lisa hugged her, lifted her off the hospital floor and spun her around. Martha was laughing and trying to get herself free. Fragile in appearance, she turned out to be not so light and weak and, in the end, they both fell on the bed.

"Well, fine, you convinced me," Lisa wiped the tears from laughing too much, "Tomorrow we'll talk about our detective agency, but don't rejoice ahead of time, we haven't decided anything yet. What matters is that you're fine now, and tomorrow we'll discuss everything, deal?"

The door to Martha's room swung open and first Helene appeared, followed by the doctor with rosy cheeks. He wasn't smiling anymore. His face was flushed with anger, and apparently, he was preparing to kick out the impostor.

Helene stopped him.

"It's all right, Doctor. This is also her daughter, just not by blood. You don't have to worry anymore." And in a more authoritative manner, with a polite, venomous smile, she added, seeing his hesitation, "Leave us, please."

When the door closed behind him, Helene approached her mother from the other side, kissed her and patted her cheek.

Lisa followed the doctor out, realizing that she was the third wheel. But she couldn't just leave. She grabbed a coffee from the vending machine, sat down on the couch in the hallway opposite Martha's room, and decided to wait as long as it took.

She did not have to wait long. Before she had finished her coffee, Helene emerged of the room. When she saw Lisa, she stopped for a moment, and then approached and sat down on the other end of the couch, speaking in the same even, dry voice, "I will answer all your questions. Yes, I told Evan to surrender. Yes, my mother asked me to find out about your insurance. She thought it strange that your lawyer had been biding his time to contact you lately, and his frequent calls to Evan looked suspicious. In recent months, we have been monitoring their actions. I won't tell you the details. It was a special operation. I'm only saying this so that you will stop all investigations."

"Who planned all this?" Lisa interrupted her.

"What exactly? Hunting you? Oh, it's not that simple. Alexander wrote a script for a film about blackmail and forgiveness, and when he was gone, Evan got the script, and he tried to bring this idea to life. And not only with you, as you probably already realized."

"How many of them were there, or rather, us?" Lisa corrected herself. "How many people has he almost driven mad, driven to suicide?"

But she wouldn't answer. "This is a special operation. Mere mortals are not supposed to know the details. I've been working on Evan and his group as part of the investigation, and lately, I've been doing the same thing to him as he does to other people."

"That is, he also wanted forgiveness?"

"Many people want forgiveness. But that's not the point."

"Ha! They want forgiveness! Some people deserve to be

punched in the face, and more than once, but they don't deserve pity for sure!" angry thoughts were racing in Lisa's head.

"You already know that the unexpected appearance of the second photojournalist forced Evan to take serious action," Helene continued, ignoring Lisa. "Now, the answer to the following question: no, I didn't know that my mother would play detective, and when I found out, I was ready to kill you for dragging an old woman into this mess."

Lisa tried to object – who dragged whom remained to be seen, she had tried to talk Martha out of it. Helene stopped her with an imperious movement of her hand.

"It's over for you. After my mother is discharged, I will sell this house, and she will move to another place, perhaps even to another city. And you won't look for her."

The blood rushed to Lisa's face. She barely restrained herself from cursing Helene to hell. She forced herself to look at her beautifully manicured hands, calmly lying on a stylish bag, at her hands that didn't shake or twitch restlessly, the hands of an absolutely indifferent person.

"And you're going to bring her cats again?"

Helene did not even turn her head in Lisa's direction, only closed her eyes for a second and pressed her narrow lips together until they were a very thin line. Having coped with the desire either to tell Lisa where to go, or to say, "It is none of your business, we are a family and we will figure it out ourselves," Helene inhaled and exhaled, leveling her suddenly uneven breath. Lisa looked at her thin, sharp, bird-like face and wanted to make her snap, yell at her, but no, the mask slipped only for a moment and quickly the face turned into alabaster again.

"Thanks for the insurance. Although I do not know what to do with such money..."

Helene again did not react, and judging by her bored face, she had heard such words repeatedly from people who suddenly had come into money.

They were silent for a while. Lisa wanted to say so much to this cold woman, and she also wanted to express her gratitude somehow, but only standard phrases came to mind, like, "I will never forget it" or "I will be grateful to you all my life."

She only blurted out, "You have such a wonderful mother... You are such a heartless bitch!"

Helene didn't look hurt and, again, not a single muscle twitched on her face.

"I know. I've been told that before. For various reasons."

Chapter 24

The next morning Lisa woke up with a feeling of unspeakable happiness. The sun looked kindly into her windows, bathing all the flecks of dust that had settled on the panes of dirty windows with golden light. However, this did not bother Lisa; if someone didn't like it, they should not look into her windows. She remembered yesterday, and peace filled her heart. Everything was fine – she'd found Laura – she was alive, and what happened next – they would see. Martha was safe, Evan was caught, and she would receive more insurance money than she knew what to do with.

The entire time Lisa was washing, dressing, drinking coffee with dried cookies, she was making plans for the future. It didn't matter that Helene forbade her to see Martha and even wanted to move her to another city. After all, Martha was a grown woman and could decide for herself. She could live with Lisa. The house was big and empty, and Helene could sell that other house. Lisa's face blossomed into a satisfied smile when she imagined how her old house would be filled with the smells of fresh pies and patties. They would decide about the agency with Martha, and not with her terrible daughter. First, they would find those who worked with Evan, no matter what Helene said, and bring the whole gang to light.

Lisa remembered how shameless Helene was and muttered, "A covert operation? Mere mortals are not supposed to know the details? We'll see about that. You can't forbid a journalistic investigation. And finally, we will find out who killed Alexander."

On the way to the hospital, Lisa stepped into a deli where they sold homemade food and bought some patties. Most likely, they were not as good as Martha's, but she could eat these until she got better. Lisa also took some hot soup, a salad and a homemade blackberry pie.

In the vegetable shop, she looked at the fruit display for a long time, trying to remember what Martha liked, but couldn't, and then she bought at random, oranges, apples and grapes. She also wanted to grab a cup of coffee for Martha, but changed her mind – probably coffee wasn't a good idea in her state.

Walking down the corridor to Martha's room, she saw the same rosy-cheeked doctor come out and stop at the door.

Well, now he didn't want to let her in – just let him try to stop her! But the doctor just stood there and stared at Lisa in some confusion. She came closer, stopped and looked inside. Helene was kneeling by the bed, sobbing, "Mom, Mommy! No! No! I love you so much, Mommy! No!"

Lisa looked at Helene – her skirt rode up poorly, one shoe had flown off her foot, and the second rested with its shiny toecap on the leg of the bedside table, her leg bent in an unnatural, uncomfortable position, a leather briefcase thrown aside... Lisa looked at her shaking shoulders... Watched as she hugged and pressed Martha's motionless body to her, hugging her the way a sick child was hugged, hoping to share warmth. Then Lisa looked down at the orange and red balls falling from the shopping bag she was holding in her hands, and suddenly everything went dark before her eyes. She tried to focus on the doctor, but everything was blurry.

"She died in the night. Her heart gave out..."

Chapter 25

Lisa did not leave the house, did not answer any phone calls or the doorbell. She didn't go to Martha's funeral. She just couldn't see the funeral ceremony and huddled in a corner under the old staircase, whined softly, "She won't come anymore, she's gone... you're such a tease, Martha. We had plans for the agency, and where am I going to put your stupid cats now? You left me, you, and Laura, and Mom, you all left me..."

Lisa knew in her heart that what she was saying was useless. Those who leave us forever do not return, and nothing can be changed by pleading or reproaches, but she had to cry her fill to live again and write an excellent article about everything that had happened. Danny even hinted at a possible book deal. Two days ago, it would have been simply great, but now Lisa knew that she would not write an article or a book... And why wouldn't they all finally leave her alone...

She repeated all this incoherently all day and all night, and the wind outside the window muttered something along, sometimes breaking into a long moan.

At some point, her strength finally ran out, and she fell into a heavy sleep and dreamed of Martha again, trying to climb the tree after a screaming cat. The cat jumped higher and higher, and Martha, barely pulling up her already not-so-young body, went after it and Lisa was worried – after all, she could easily fall, and then what would happen...

... Lisa felt a warm palm on her forehead and started awake.

Her neighbor was floating away into the misty distance with her Lord. At first, Lisa didn't understand why she was curled up under the stairs, but then she remembered everything. Next to her, kneeling down, stood Laura, gently stroking her hair, and then pressed Lisa to herself and sang a lullaby to her in a thin voice, as their mother used to do when they were little.

Chapter 26

Laura lived with Lisa for a few days. Together, they cooked real homemade food, went for walks, holding hands – just like little girls. They wandered along the riverbank and sat for a long time on the trunks of trees felled by the storm, fed pieces of bread to birds that flew everywhere, but never came too close. Laura talked all the time, told Lisa about their childhood, how she saw their relationship then. These were good memories, until she met Alexander. The sisters avoided this subject.

In a burst of remorse, Lisa sent Danny a message.

"I'm sorry! It wasn't me who sent those first reports about the hostages, and I don't know who did it. I was trying to figure out what was going on around me. I think you fired me a long time ago. I don't blame you. I've tried your patience for too long and abused our friendship. Anyway, I'm sorry."

Danny didn't answer, but she didn't expect him to.

They didn't notice the cats silently opening their mouths in

Martha's windows right away, only a few days later. It was too painful to look at her empty house, and the sisters instinctively turned away as they passed by it.

"Oh, my God. They're hungry! They must have eaten everything Martha left them a long time ago!"

The sisters rushed to the house. The key was under the flower pot, near the porch. When Lisa opened the door, they smelled such a stench, as if military-grade nerve gas had been released. Then, the cats all flew out into the street at once, pushing one another aside, rushed to the puddle that had not dried up after the rain.

After opening all the windows to air out the house, the sisters also ran outside to catch their breath, and only after a while returned inside – the trapped animals had already ruined Martha's stylish carpet, her couch, and all corners of the house.

Lisa did not do the cleaning – after all, this was someone else's house and Helene could come at any minute. If she wanted to...

Lisa wondered who she was going to sell the house to now. Who would be her new neighbor?

It didn't matter though. Now she needed to feed the animals, who, having quenched their thirst, returned to the sisters and surrounded them, staring at them with expressive hungry eyes.

"Let's look for some food," Laura suggested. "Otherwise, I'm afraid they'll eat us too. Look, that red one with the torn ear... he's licking his lips!"

The red cat, indeed, licked his lips and prowled towards the sisters. Laura backed away, screamed, and ran across the street to their house.

Lisa barely refrained from following her sister, but then had a clever thought. Surely Martha had a supply of food. She couldn't feed such a horde without a stash. Holding her nose, she went to the back of the house, looked around, found the pantry and opened it. Indeed, large packages of cat food were stored here. And Martha had said something about it to her in the hospital room. She even left instructions.

"Yes!" she let out a triumphant cry in her head, "We are saved!" Lisa looked around and saw cats approaching her in a pack.

"Wait, it's coming."

Despite the open windows and doors, the cat smell became increasingly unbearable, Lisa pulled some rags from the shelf to cover her mouth and nose, dislodging a thick notebook, which fell to the floor.

Hastily wrapping her face, Lisa ran for a kitchen knife and opened the package. The cats, having lost interest in her, kindly switched to the spilled food, crunching and swallowing it. All sounds except chewing and slurping disappeared.

Lisa couldn't believe her ears – cats slurping like piglets? How hungry they were!

She picked up the notebook without thinking, flipping

through it; some columns of figures caught her eye, and Lisa realized it appeared to be an accounting book. Martha had written down her shopping expenses and other costs.

Why hide an accounting book behind bags of food? Then again, what did it matter? Now it was Helene's concern.

Lisa was about to throw the notebook on the shelf and let the animals eat, and then she would put the bag away, but some belated cat flew in from the street, slid across the tiled floor, as if on ice, and crashed into her. Barely able to stay on her feet, Lisa dropped the notebook on the floor, and a picture fell out from behind the cover.

Why hide a photo in an accounting book?

She picked up the photo, walked out of the dim closet into the room, closer to the light. Two people were looking at her from the picture. Rather, they did not look at her but at each other with loving, happy eyes. A man in a light summer shirt and a woman, her hair fluttering in the wind, on a yacht. In the distance was the blue-blue sea. The woman's face seemed vaguely familiar to Lisa. *Wow! Why, it's Martha, only young and so dazzlingly beautiful! Wow indeed!* She was a real beauty, and next to a man. As young Martha looked at him, she glowed with happiness. Lisa turned her gaze to this lucky man and froze. It was her father, also young and very happy.

Martha and her father? Did they know each other? She refused to believe her eyes. Or was it a mistake and he just looked very much like her father? No, the crisp image left no doubt that it was her father and Martha next to him in the photo. When was it taken?

Perhaps even before meeting her mother, but her parents got married quite early, very young – Lisa remembered their wedding pictures, and in this one, her father was a middle-aged man. He already had a family.

In search of an answer, she turned over the photo but found neither the date nor any other notes.

Memories immediately came flooding back – her father's frequent business trips when he would always return refreshed, happy. How her mother was upset about these trips. Some fragments of memories resurfaced. The quiet but irritated voice of their mother arguing with their father about something.

"Lisa, where are you? Get out of there already or you'll suffocate," she heard her sister's voice.

Lisa started. Her sister should not see this picture, should not see their father happy next to another woman. She needed to put the photo back behind the cover and place it on the shelf, but Helene could come here any day and she didn't need to see it either, so Lisa shoved the photo into the waistband of her jeans, covering it with her shirt.

Chapter 27

Yesterday, at the thought that it was time for Laura to return to the monastery, to school, to her duties, Lisa felt utterly discouraged, but today, she was glad when her sister started talking about it. Not being able to meet her sister's eyes was unbearable. All she wanted was to share her discovery because they agreed that they would not hide anything from each other. But she couldn't tell her this.

"I will tell her," Lisa promised herself. "But not today."

After walking her sister to the bus and quite sincerely promising her that she would never be sad alone, would definitely do something interesting, Lisa returned straight from the bus station to Martha's house. Once again, she carefully examined the deserted, orphaned house, rummaged through the shelves and drawers, but didn't find any more photos. After sorting through a thin bundle of letters and greeting cards in a box from the bedside table drawer, Lisa stopped at the postcards from Martha's sister. Martha had never mentioned having a sister. The stingy, even routine, words in the greeting cards only confirmed Lisa's suspicions – the sisters were barely on speaking terms, just cordial congratulations without any of the warm words usually written to relatives and loved ones.

The next morning, Lisa fed the cats, leaving some food out for later and filling several bowls of water for them. Then, she locked both houses and went to the bus station.

A few hours later, she was standing near a modest pink terracotta house shaded from the street by large trees. Hesitating for a moment, she made herself ring the doorbell.

An elderly woman in a robe and old slippers opened the door. She was all kinds of lardy and unkempt.

Nothing like Martha, neither the face nor the figure. Even in her old age, Martha looked much better than her sister, Lisa noted.

After listening to the unwelcome guest, the woman slammed the door in her face. And never opened it again no matter how many times Lisa rang the bell.

Lisa didn't dare kick the door, despite really wanting to. The owner could simply call the police and then she would have to explain the purpose of her visit. No, Lisa didn't want that. She really hoped to learn at least something about that period of her neighbor's life, one of the moments that remained captured in the picture. The frugal words in the greeting cards prompted her to consider some serious disagreements between the sisters. Perhaps, the relationship with someone else's husband was the cause.

Crossing to the other side of the street, Lisa found a small shop with two coffee tables for visitors in a row of houses and bought herself a coffee. She thought to ask the shopkeeper about Martha's sister but then immediately discarded the idea. Of course, in a small town, everyone knew everything about everyone else, but most likely, they would not confide in strangers. And, again, Lisa didn't want too much attention.

The bus stop was located almost opposite Martha's sister's house, just a couple dozen steps further down the street. She could see the door of her house from where she stood perfectly, and Lisa decided to settle down with her coffee. She knew that she was also being watched, so she showed in every way that she was not going to leave and would wait until the bitter end.

After her fourth cup of coffee and two sandwiches, Lisa placed the empty cups in a row on the bench. She didn't know how much coffee she would have to drink and how many hours she would have to wait, but she would prevail.

"Martha, you wanted to become detectives and do private investigations. Consider this our first case."

Lisa spoke to her deceased neighbor for the first time after she found the photo, and now her inner anger and resentment burst out. Rare passengers getting off the bus at this stop stared her and quickly moved away.

In the afternoon, the sky suddenly clouded over, a strong wind blew. Lisa tried to wrap herself in the thin windbreaker, but it did not save her much from the cold. And then suddenly it started pouring.

"Such a cold rain at this time of year?" Lisa was amazed. "I guess I'm just that lucky. Of course, I should have checked the weather forecast before coming here, but still – it's too cold."

The weather was worsening by the second. At first, the rain was coming in straight streams, but under strong gusts of wind turned into sharp, angled spikes, chilling her to the bones. Deep puddles immediately formed on the road and sidewalk. Lisa blew on her fingers, rubbing her hands together, but it didn't help much. It was getting darker.

The headlights of the next bus blinded Lisa at first, and then the door of the warm, softly lit interior opened. The driver stayed at the bus stop longer than usual, without closing the door, silently inviting her to plunge into its warmth. She had already decided to accept his offer – it was so cold and lonely – but with an effort, she suppressed this desire. No, she would wait, as she had promised herself and Martha.

The doors closed. The bus left. Lisa was once again alone. She didn't want coffee anymore, and perhaps, the owner had already closed shop.

Meanwhile, it was getting colder. The gusty wind, suddenly changing direction, hurled quite unseasonably cold jets at her lonely crouching body. Lisa already deeply regretted that she had not taken the bus. She could spend the night in a hotel, and tomorrow, she would come up with something. However, the next bus, as she already saw on the real time display, would only arrive tomorrow, and Lisa, barely moving her frozen feet, wandered across the road, climbed the slippery steps and pressed herself against the door.

And the door gave way.

Not believing her eyes, Lisa pushed it further open, seeing the hallway and then the living room, illuminated by the light of a large floor lamp with an orange shade.

Lisa stepped into the hallway and heard a woman's voice.

"And I thought you decided to freeze at the bus stop."

"But... but you wouldn't let me in the house."

"Well, yes, at first I wouldn't, but then I unlocked the door. And why would I want you to freeze and die, so they put me in prison for not helping?"

Lisa listened to her and absorbed the blissful warmth as her whole body shuddered. She wanted so much to ask for a cup of tea.

"I'll bring you tea. You can sit here," the woman pointed to a chair covered with a throw knitted from orange yarn.

"But don't assume anything. This is still just me helping those in distress."

The hot sweet tea was a heavenly delight now, and Lisa sipped, burned herself, and tried to drink again. Her hands were still shaking so much the hot drink spilled over the top of the cup.

Martha's sister threw her a dish towel.

"Don't spill it on my carpet. Here, put that on your lap. And here's what, let's get real. Martha sent me a letter a long time ago, asking me to give it to a certain Lisa, but only in case of her death. Martha was always a romantic, believed in fairy tales and other nonsense. Back then, I didn't attach any importance to it, just threw the letter into the drawer. I didn't read it. Could be something very bad in it, some kind of confession, and I don't want to know anything bad about my sister. And I won't give it to you."

"But," Lisa objected, "It was her wish, her last wish... You can't do this to us. To her."

"If it was just about you, I wouldn't care, but I do care about her. She was foolish and unhinged, but I loved her," the woman suddenly finished, and her voice trembled. But then she coped with her emotions, crossed her arms over her stomach, under her big, saggy breasts, as if defending herself. "That's all. Finish your tea and leave."

"Where am I gonna go in this rain?"

"That's not my problem, girl. Call a taxi and get out of here!"

"I'll take you to a hotel," Lisa suddenly heard another voice and a boy of seventeen or so came out.

"No," Martha's sister shouted at him. "You're not going anywhere! And I told you to stay where you were."

"Then let her stay until morning, until it stops pouring. And give her the damn letter. Aunty Martha wanted it very much."

The kid went to the dresser, pulled out a drawer and took out a white envelope.

The woman grabbed the envelope from him, hesitated, then said, "I'll do it."

She pushed the envelope into Lisa's hands and threatened, "God forbid! God forbid... you, filthy little journalist, publish this... I'll ruin you. I'm only giving it to you because Martha is screaming at me from heaven. That's why the weather has gone crazy."

Someone knocked loudly and rudely on the door, and then a big and noisy man in a raincoat barged in.

"You called me. Who needs a ride in this weather?"

"This one. Take her to the hotel."

"Can't she wait here until morning?"

"Take her. I'll pay."

Chapter 28

Lisa would begin reading Martha's letter, then pause. The rain outside the window had already stopped and the deep puddles that flooded the road, flower beds and pedestrian paths silvered in the light of the moon peeking out from behind the clouds. In the clean post-rain air, the shadows of trees and houses looked clearer, and the objects themselves seemed larger. She didn't notice any of this.

"I started writing you this letter many times… I started writing it every day and then tore it into small pieces, burned it. I don't know if I can finish this time. Yes, your father and I were close. We met on a business trip, at an eco-symposium. After it was over, the event organizers arranged a boat trip along the amazingly beautiful lagoon for all participants. It was a beautiful day – the sun was shining, the spray behind the stern sparkled with all the colors of the rainbow, light wine turned heads, and people who escaped from their offices were just happy. And after the banquet, you know how it goes – two people who were free for an evening spent the night in the same bed. A pleasant memory, nothing more.

However, after we returned home, your father called me and offered to meet. I refused – a fleeting relationship it was and passed.

If it wasn't for the shiny happy day, nothing would have happened. Well, if it happened, I should have just turned the page. That night meant nothing to me or him. That's what I thought.

He didn't call again, but two years later, we bumped into each other on the street. I understand that it doesn't matter to you, and you may not read all this at all, but I'll tell you anyway – I didn't want to keep the affair going. We both had families, quite good lives, but he wanted, really wanted, to. Then your father had a midlife crisis and had to assert himself. He had to feel like a man, desirable and desiring. But, according to him, his wife did not understand this. She was annoying him with her constant petty care, her hair-splitting, and he wanted to feel young, strong, healthy. He wanted to feel like a hunter, the way young men see themselves...

Every time we met, I told him that today was the last time. I asked him not to call and not to seek dates with me, but he begged me not to break it off, to leave everything as it was, at least for a while. And every time I gave in. I punished myself, hated myself for my weakness, but I gave in all the same. It could have gone on forever, but one day, I found the strength. I called your father, said that we would no longer meet, there would be no hotels, motels and "unexpected work lates." He insisted on one last meeting and even came to our garden. I asked him to leave, but he kept trying to kiss me, undid the buttons on my dress, then suddenly fell to his knees, begging for one last time.

I was in despair. My husband or daughter could wake up any moment, and everything would come out... But a teenager, a neighbor's boy, suddenly appeared from behind the gazebo. At first, we were dumbfounded, and then your father ran away. And I remained standing in my unbuttoned dress. I thought the boy would run away too, scared, but he made a sign for me to be silent, whispering, "Turn and bend over." I was angry, but he threatened me, "Or I will tell your husband everything. I know everything."

I should have slapped him in the face, of course, so that he knew his place, but I chickened out and just did what he wanted, hoping that this was the last time I would hear his snotty snuffling. How wrong I was! The boy announced that now he would take your father's place.

And then the nightmare began. I hid from him when, under some pretext, he appeared at our porch. But every night, he came to our garden and whistled like a midnight bird, and I... I went out to see him. He took me behind the barn to an old iron bed. And even though the barn was quite far from the house, I was still afraid that one of my family members would hear us.

Then it got even worse. I got used to it and even began to like it. I really liked it. Every time I told him, "Don't come again," but I couldn't wait for the night to fall. He was quite rough, caresses and beautiful words – that's not him. He either sat down on the bed where the old mattress had been for ages and, lifting my robe, sat me on his knees, or rather, of course, not on his knees... Well, you know what I'm talking about... Or crucified me, not caring at all whether such a pose was comfortable for me. It's just that he wanted it that way now, and then something different. God, why am I even writing this?

The boy was handsome, he was maturing every day, and, of course, I saw how girls and older women looked at him. He would come to our intersection and do funny tricks – dress up as a clown, with that stupid hat and the big nose and juggle balls of every color; he would drag an old, broken hurdy-gurdy (where did he even find it?) and sing Santa Lucia horribly out of tune.

The house where he lived with his mother and sister stood at the end of our street, but he always arranged his performances next to our house, in a small square at the junction of two streets. The kids from the entire neighborhood gathered to watch his antics, as well as adult boys and girls. And each of these girls wanted him to entertain her, but I knew he was doing all that for me.

I've aged now. I have wrinkles, but back then I was, as they say, in my prime, with bright eyes, smooth skin and firm breasts. "A mother you'd like to fuck," a young caretaker who tended to a neighbor's garden once said. Apparently, he hoped to win my favor with such a "nice compliment."

My boyfriend's name was Alexander. He already had grand plans then – to conquer the world. At that time, he had not yet figured out how, but there was an unshakable determination in his eyes, and I did not doubt for a minute that it would be so.

I fell in love, imagine an adult woman falling in love with a boy, a blackmailer! But how good he was! And how incredible, dangerous and exciting it all was!

One day my worst fears came true. Alexander came to our garden and began to call me loudly. I hurried out of the house and ran to him. He was drunk and demanded we have sex then and there, and no amount of my persuasion or pleading could stop him. He screamed that he had a fight with his mother and sister, that these bitches had kicked him out of the house. I didn't know how to calm him down. I was desperate, and he was coming at me, when suddenly Helene appeared with a gun in her hands. She pointed it at Alexander and cocked the hammer, but this did not stop him, and he went at her, tearing his shirt and exposing his chest – drunk and crazed. And then Helene fired. First into the air, and then she shot him. At that second, I felt like the sky fell on my head – Helene killed Alexander, and this was the end, the end of everything – my family, my love, my life... I did not hear the sound of a gunshot. Perhaps it was my personal Guardian Angel who turned off my hearing at that moment, because no avalanches in the mountains, no rockfalls could compare to this sound, which meant a disaster...

The bullet only grazed Alexander's shoulder, but the pain sobered him up, and he retreated to the gate and then ran. Helene shot again and again. I was sure she would finish him off. She would definitely finish him off.

My husband came running to the gunshots. I said it was a robber who'd run away, and I persuaded him not to call the police.

I never saw Alexander again. Soon Helene left for her college, and we never talked about this with her. She never asked anything either, but I think she knew what was going on.

A few years passed. My husband died and then our house burned down. At first, I lived with my sister, and then Helene, who had already become a successful lawyer, bought me this house. As fate would have it, right opposite your grandfather's house. This is where I've been living for the last few years, hoping that I put all that mess behind me. I didn't know it was your grandfather's house.

And one day I saw Alexander, who was escorting a girl, one of the sisters, who had recently settled in this old house – Lisa and Laura, and whom I was in no hurry to meet. I didn't want any new acquaintances or relationships, even just neighbors. Loneliness, when you get used to it, is quite a good thing.

That was until I saw Alexander and your younger sister. These two kissed for a long time by the gate, they just couldn't keep their hands off each other. I was shocked because I thought that everything was over, and I would never see him again. But I was wrong.

Alexander was very attractive as a boy, and now he had become a dazzlingly handsome man, like a prince from a fairy tale. And the girl he was kissing was also very pretty – young, trembling, radiant somehow. Jealousy blinded me. I turned into an old wreck. The death of my husband, my estranged daughter, the fire ... it all took a toll on me... Was I overwhelmed by late love? And for whom? A narcissistic boy? Of course, it will seem funny to you, but old people can also love and burn with passion. After all, what is old age? Only wrinkles on the face and creaking joints. But the heart beats as strong as it did when we were young. My daughter turned away from me, but what could I explain to her? She wouldn't have understood me and couldn't forgive me, and neither can you, but I'm writing you this letter anyway.

I ran away then – went to my sister again and decided to sell the house, but how would I explain my desire to Helene, because she'd bought this house for me?

I lived with my sister for two months, tormenting myself with doubts, but I still could not decide. I wanted to kill him and be with him, at least one last time. And then I found out that Alexander was killed, and Laura was missing.

This shouldn't have happened! It was impossible! I wanted to know how it happened. I had to find out. I'm sorry, but I wasn't helping you when I was looking for Laura.

I did write you a letter, but I couldn't send it – it's too insulting to you. I just left our picture in the pantry in case my old heart failed at some point and you found it, and then this letter. Stupid, of course...

I'm not asking for your forgiveness, I know that there is no such thing as forgiveness. All this was invented by the churchmen, and modern Internet and other gurus picked up the mantle and made a very profitable business out of it. Still, no forgiveness will help either you or me. I just had to tell you that.

You know, I don't regret at all that Alexander was in my life. I loved and was loved passionately, even if that love was mad and forbidden. And as I die, I will remember every kiss, every meeting with him. I was happy. It's hard for you or my very good daughter to understand. You both aspired to success – work, career always came first. You have become a good, an excellent, journalist, my daughter is a wonderful lawyer, but where are your families, where are your beloved men? Why are you both lonely and unhappy? A woman should be happy and loved! I'm afraid neither of you can understand that. Just look at yourself – always disheveled, skinny, unkempt, in worn jeans... remember when a man gazed at you for the last time with such a look in his eyes that your whole life before that seemed empty and meaningless."

Lisa looked up from the letter: ordinary city life was beginning outside the window – a garbage truck drove by, then the first intercity bus. She came here on a similar bus yesterday. Came to find answers about that damn picture. And she did. The edge of the letter was torn, but the first part was enough for her.

Some fragments of memories leapt into her mind. Mom was always unhappy with her father's frequent work nights, his unexpected and urgent business trips. In recent years, it was as if he lived in the family and didn't. Lisa remembered her mother's angry face and her father's guiltily happy look when he returned from another trip. How gradually he seemed to fade away, lost interest in life, how he became indifferent to everything. She also remembered the boy who was playing a clown on their street, but all this did not interest her much then – she had already started her own life, college and new friends, and with them, entertainment and travel.

There was a soft knock on the door. At first, Lisa did not

understand what the sound was and then she shouted, "Who is there?"

It was the owner of the small hotel where Martha's sister's neighbor brought her yesterday. In one of the hotel's rooms, she'd sat all night, wrapped in two blankets -- one an extra the owner had brought her. Now, he was asking if she wanted some hot coffee.

Lisa took the tray with the coffee pot and fresh rolls from the hands of the caring owner. Closing the door behind him, she took a sip and set the cup aside. All she could hear in her head was, "What a bitch you are, Martha! You took my family! You took the most important thing in life – the belief that your parents are the best, the rightest, the holiest! I wish you'd never written that letter. And you know what? Why won't you go to hell with your happiness and your instructions! People like you don't like skinny, fat, tall, or short. You see, we don't know how to break up other people's families, fuck with boys and then revel in these memories on our deathbed. Are you still going to teach me how to dress and comb my hair? Fuck you! If hell exists, then you belong there and may the devil kiss you all over!"

She didn't hear the phone at first, but then she felt its vibration and pressed the button. Danny again.

"I have three things to tell you, and all three are bad: First, Evan may be released soon. He's cooperating. The information he has collected about many, including influential, people can be used for further investigations. Well, you know how it is – who is Evan compared to the big shots?"

"But he's killed people."

"There is no hard evidence of his guilt, and lawyers will easily prove that if the case goes to court."

"And Martha's abduction? Martha's death?"

"Martha's daughter is not pressing charges against him."

"But why?"

"I don't know... The second thing: Press-Accord Publishing house has signed a contract with him to publish a book, and in it, he is going to explain how he, in fact, exposed dirty officials."

"But if he's cooperating with the police, he can't have anything made public, or am I missing something?"

"Unless it is dished up as 'a brilliant operation of the special forces,' and it turns out that Evan has been working as part of this special operation for some time. Well, as you know, the book will be a bestseller, and if you give it a name like, 'How I chose my victims,' then it's a win-win."

"And what will be in this book? Will Laura be there too? Laura's not connected to these people!"

"Your sister is too memorable a character – an underage prostitute who became a nun. That will add zest to the book. You know how respectable citizens really like those details."

"How does Evan know about the monastery?"

"I don't know..."

Lisa felt dizzy. The window and the wall swam before her eyes. No! No! She wouldn't pass out! Not now!

"And the last one: they found the murder weapon used to kill Alexander. So, if you have anything to do with it, don't show up until I know more and call you back."

The murder weapon... But she never saw a bottle of sparkling wine in that old house!

"I realized almost immediately that those were not your reports – not your style. I was just waiting for you to explain everything. We really were friends. Why didn't you just tell me?"

"I'm sorry, Danny. I wanted to figure it out by myself first. Please forgive me!"

Danny hung up.

Alexander had been killed by someone else, and Laura saw Lisa fall after being hit by the door. But would they believe Laura? Lisa's fingerprints were definitely on the bottle. Who pushed that door? Arthur? The second cameraman who was late for the shoot?

Lisa remembered the letter. Why was the last page torn off?

Throwing aside the blanket, Lisa jumped up, put on her clothes, quickly laced up her sneakers and ran to Martha's sister. On the way, she fell on the slippery steps, scraping her leg that had not yet healed, but another pain pushed her forward. She pounded on the door, kicked it with her feet, but no one answered. The house seemed to have died, only the swinging curtain in the window betrayed the presence of people.

"Don't come," Danny told her, but she wasn't going to hide! She didn't kill Alexander. Yes, she was holding the bottle in her hands, but she didn't do it. No, she'd go home right now. And then what? She'd be arrested. After all, her fingerprints were on the murder weapon. Well, so what? Let it all come out! She should have killed the bastard who did that to her sister! Let all the papers write about it, all the mass media tell about it. She no longer had the strength to hide the truth.

Chapter 29

The bus was taking her home. Despite the sleepless night and the soft rocking of the comfortable chair, Lisa could not sleep. She would go to the police and confess everything.

"You wanted repentance from me. There will be repentance for you," she muttered to herself.

The passenger next to her moved to another row.

"That's right. Get away from me. Soon, you'll all be running from me. As people say, there's no smoke without a fire... Even if a person's guilt is not proven, they will forever be branded as complicit," she muttered softly after him.

Busy with her thoughts, Lisa did not immediately pay attention to the scooter that had caught up with the bus and was now driving parallel with it. The driver was waving at her, apparently urging her to stop. Lisa recognized Martha's sister's son, the same boy who helped her get the letter.

She shouted to the driver, "Stop! Stop right now!"

And rushed to the door.

The driver refused at first because there was no stop close by, but eventually, he slowed down, and Lisa, rushing off the bus, literally fell into the hands of the zonked scooter rider.

"What? What did you want? Martha killed Alexander, didn't she? And the second part of the letter is about that?" Lisa shook him.

He looked at her blankly and then his eyes changed. Now, they were filled with contempt. He pushed her away violently and went back to his scooter.

"What? What? What happened? What else happened?" Lisa screamed, "Say something! Anything!"

The boy got back on his scooter, turned it in the opposite direction, then spat, "Aunty Martha did everything she could to keep you safe" and took off from the spot, showering her with a stinking cloud of exhaust...

Lisa waved to the bus driver to go without her and, picking up her backpack he'd kindly brought out for her, started walking along the road.

Once Lisa reached a gas station, she had coffee, sitting on a small garden bench behind the building with a view of the field and blue forest in the distance, birds flying about their business, then soaring up into the sky only to strive for something on earth moments later.

The message from Danny was brief, "Tomorrow at noon, Evan is holding a press conference."

So fast? She hadn't come up with anything.

Arthur's phone number, from which he called her and which she dialed now, rang without answer. Lisa tried another number – Helene. Martha's daughter already knew about the upcoming press conference. She only added that Evan would be taken to court first and then would give the conference.

"Make sure he doesn't mention Laura's name."

"I can't."

"But you spoke to him directly in the square..."

"I did then, yes, but now I can't get involved," Helene snapped.

"Then, I'll spill all about Martha."

"So what? It's just my mother's private life. She didn't kill anyone."

"No, no, you do care," Lisa didn't believe her, "I saw you crying in the hospital room. You care about her memory."

"I can't do anything."

"Try to... Please... I'm begging you..."

"You're asking me? You're afraid that people will talk about your sister? How do you think I felt knowing that the entire street and all my classmates were talking about some brat fucking my mother behind the shed as she screamed with delight?"

Helene was breathing heavily, finally she stopped. Just ended the conversation. And with it, all the threads, all the possibilities to somehow influence the further development of events were gone.

Lisa discarded the stupid idea of somehow contacting Evan. Well, yes... it was her fault that he lost such profit... If it hadn't occurred to him before to put Laura's story on public display, then after talking to her, he would do it with much greater pleasure.

Having learned from the station attendant that the next bus would not be coming soon, Lisa went out onto the road, raised her hand and got into the first car that stopped.

Chapter 30

Lisa got lucky. The doorman at the beautiful new house where Arthur lived was not there. Perhaps she was only gone for a few minutes, but it was enough for Lisa to sneak up the stairs. She did not dare to use the elevator, avoiding unnecessary noise.

At first, no one answered the doorbell. Then, she heard a hoarse voice, "Who's there?"

Lisa gave her name. Recognizing her voice, Arthur opened the door and stared at her with eyes wide with horror. She pushed him back, stepped into his hallway and slammed the door behind her.

"Why, why are you here?" Arthur was being fidgety as always. "I've already told you everything. You found Laura, didn't you? You did find her?"

Lisa went into the kitchen, poured herself a full glass of water from the tap and drank it all. Arthur was about to follow her, but stopped, keeping his distance.

Wiping her lips and chin, Lisa sat on a kitchen chair and showed Arthur to another one. He shuffled around a bit more and then move closer but did not take the offered seat. Instead, he chose to sit next to her and grabbed the back of the chair.

"Did you kill Alexander?" Lisa finally asked.

"No! No! I wanted to... But you stopped me! You had such bad timing... And I left..."

"Who hit me?"

"I didn't see it!"

"How did I end up back home? Who drove me?"

"I don't know! I told you – I left, ran away..."

"Chickened out, you mean. You had a chance to kill the bastard who raped the girl you loved... Raped her right before your eyes... Repeatedly... You had a chance to commit, maybe, the only courageous act in your life, but you ran away..."

Lisa's face was burning with anger. She barely managed to restrain herself so as not to punch this slobbering, sweating fool.

"Next question. Why did you tell me that Martha was a danger to Laura? What do you know about Martha?"

Arthur threw up his hands, jumping up like a goalkeeper who was trying to block a ball but knew he would not be able to reach it.

"Nothing, I swear, nothing! She just hung around you all the time. You've been inseparable for the last few days, so it seemed suspicious to me that you were suddenly so close. I assumed that she was somehow interested."

"Did you know from the very beginning that Evan was behind all this? Was he the second cameraman?"

Arthur lowered his eyes.

"I can't hear you. Was he the second?"

"Yes," Arthur mumbled, absolutely broken.

"And after Alexander's death, he took matters into his own hands. Was that so?"

"Yes," Arthur managed to say.

"What happened next?"

"He offered me a share, knowing that I was already on board, but I didn't want to be a part of it anymore. I immediately refused."

"But he didn't leave you alone. Yes?"

Arthur didn't answer right away. He never raised his eyes to look at Lisa.

"I was afraid that he would kill me. I lied to him. Told him I'd written a statement for the police, and it was in a safe place. He let me be for a while, but then it started again. He came and came to me, intimidated me, said that either I was with him or my days were numbered... That's when I went off the rails, went to that house. I don't know... I wasn't going to kill you. I wanted to end... end it all, but there you were again..."

"And you started shooting."

"I didn't shoot at you, I shot at the walls, all over that disgusting apartment... And Evan really needed you. He wanted to get your confession... oh! No! I didn't know back then that it was about money. But he was in a big hurry and tried to break you. He said that you were being watched around the clock. He had sent his people to follow you. That's when I thought about Martha... And called you..."

Arthur stopped talking. The wall clock ticked softly, a muffled noise came from the street. Someone had their TV on behind the wall.

"Give me the weapon you fired. Don't lie and say you got rid of it."

"Why would you need it?" Arthur clearly didn't expect this.

"Just give it to me!"

Arthur stared at her, still not understanding, until gradually the meaning of her words became clear. It dawned on him why Lisa had actually come to him.

"Do you even know how to shoot?"

"My father took us to the shooting range when we were kids. I was pretty good."

"How long ago was it? You're probably out of practice."

"It's fine. I'll practice today."

"I'll have to disappoint you. I really did throw it into the lake..."

Chapter 31

Lisa stopped for the night in a roadside motel. As she went up to the old, shabby room, she threw her backpack on the floor and fell on the bed but couldn't sleep.

What? What could she do? How could she stop Evan? Ask Helene again? Try to get a weapon somewhere else and kill the bastard? Get one where? She didn't have much time left. Or maybe she should just go and smack him in the head, like the other asshole, his mastermind? With what? If she even managed to get close to him, it was unlikely that she would be allowed to do anything. It was also possible that she would be detained as soon as the police saw her, because the murder weapon that ended Alexander was found.

Lisa tossed and turned all night, running through with different scenarios, making plans each crazier than the last. She didn't care what happened to her if she killed Evan. If she had more time, she would have found a way out, but there was less and less time left...

As she approached the courthouse, she saw Helene in the crowd at the entrance. She tried to catch her eye, but Martha's daughter turned away. So, Lisa just needed to watch the last act of this terrible performance, at least until she was arrested, most likely the fingerprints had already been run through the system, and they'd found a match. Lisa.

The waiting period for the hero of the day to appear dragged on for an incredibly long time. How many times, how many times she, a journalist, waited like this for some famous person to emerge, for whom so many people had gathered here. Chatting with colleagues, drinking coffee, perching on the steps of the building, running for a smoke break to a nearby square when she was still smoking. Back then, Lisa was on the same side as other journalists, on the same team, ready to expose the criminal to the public. To be honest, modern journalism was all about going after some wrongdoer, and journalists easily forgot that their professional duty was simply to inform readers, viewers, listeners, Internet users, but certainly not take sides, let alone impose their opinion, even indirectly through intonation, prioritizing certain facts or keeping silent about others.

What would these journalists carry to their public today? Sympathy for the victims of a blackmailer, sympathy for a seduced girl? Information that another of their colleagues attempted to kill a man whose corpse was recently discovered? Or just an ad for a scandalous book?

Lisa wanted to get ahead so that she could see Evan's eyes, but every space was already occupied by the TV people, and she didn't want to be recognized yet. With all her heart, she was praying for a miracle, for something to happen and Evan simply to not exist. It didn't matter how. She prayed to God, in whom she didn't really believe, prayed to the Holy Mother and the universe...

When Evan, accompanied by several people, left the courthouse and approached the microphones installed outside, everyone seemed to freeze at first – this was their colleague, one of them, a good guy, though not very young anymore, balding, with a belly. Everyone knew him as a family man, a father to a whole bunch of kids. They knew that he was a very hard worker, one of a kind...

Evan did not hide his smug smile. Finally, he was the real hero of the day, neither a terrorist nor an extortionist, but a hero fighting against the powerful of this world, the hero of our time. He was ready to greet his audience, probably with a prepared speech, perhaps written and well-rehearsed over the years, or considering the changed circumstances, hand-scribbled minutes ago.

Suddenly, the smile disappeared from his face. He seemed petrified, staring at something. Then shots were fired – one, two... Evan crouched down and scrambled on all fours to the door. More shots followed, one after another... another shot... another moment... and he disappeared through the door.

The panic began. People fled in different directions, screams were heard everywhere. Lisa stood upright, trying to see the shooter, who had already been knocked to the floor...

"Damn it!" She swore. How can one be so clumsy?

When they came to their senses and realized that they were no longer shooting, some journalists returned and filmed Arthur's pale, angry, desperate face.

Lisa caught Helene's gaze in the crowd, and it seemed to her that she was also disappointed with Arthur.

Meanwhile, the panic grew stronger. People could still hear gunshots, even if these were most likely in their heads, and were running away. Someone dragged Lisa along, someone else's hands grabbed her, pushed her, someone's hard fists beat her in the back, urging her away from the terrible place. But Lisa didn't want to go. Because someone had disappeared behind that door. Someone who would destroy both her sister's barely improved life and her life and, at the same time, get away with it, appearing before people as a hero, a fighter.

With effort, she extracted herself from the crowd of runners, turned onto the side alley and plopped down on a bench. Lisa used the last of mineral water from the bottle to wash her face, but only smeared the tears that wouldn't stop falling down her cheeks.

It was all over. Arthur found the courage to kill the bastard, but missed... And if not today, then tomorrow Evan would continue what he had started.

No one would help anymore. After today's incident, Evan would be assigned security as if he were the fucking president.

Lisa reached into her backpack in the vain hope of finding more water. Only now she noticed her backpack was open. The rope that usually held it was loosened. Damn it! Did thieves never sleep? She checked her phone, wallet with her bank cards, documents – everything was there.

But there was something she had never expected to see inside – a small white envelope.

Chapter 32

Carefully, with two fingers, Lisa took the envelope out of her backpack as if it were a dead rat.

Again? Evan's business was alive and thriving?

What did they want from her this time? To give them the money? She would have if it helped. If it shut Evan's mouth permanently.

The phone rang, but this time, Lisa didn't hear the hateful, mechanical voice that had been harassing her lately. The voice belonged to Helene.

"Have you read it yet? No? Then read it!"

Helene? Was Helene behind all this? She knew about the money before anyone else, she ordered Evan around in Freedom Square and he obeyed and let Martha go. She did not want to help Lisa... So, Helene?

A thousand little moments, words, glances that pointed to Martha's daughter, that Lisa failed to notice, now became absolutely clear.

Helene. It was her.

Lisa, as if blind, ran over the text. The letters danced, not wanting to form words. She closed her eyes and told herself to let go of emotion and focus. Perhaps if she gave them all the money, she and Laura would be safe. Hope, which had already left her, seemed to have returned even stronger.

Lisa rubbed her eyes, temples, face, and stood. Walking by the bench, she inhaled and exhaled several times, trying to calm down. She wanted to do a few squats, but her nerves couldn't take it, and she grabbed the piece of paper with the top edge torn off.

"Perhaps I have earned your forgiveness after all – I saved your sister's life. I was there too, in that old house where Alexander shot his movie, and I saw everything.

A lot of things had already become clear to me as I watched them. You know, an old woman attracts the least attention – an old hat covering her face, glasses and a shapeless gray raincoat are an excellent disguise. After I saw what he was doing to her, it felt like everything turned upside down in me. I had to stop him. Lately, Alexander had become too crazy, obsessed or something... Laura drove him mad with her innocence, her submissiveness. And that last scene in the abandoned house... It was unbearable. Alexander didn't see or hear anything or anyone but her. My presence behind the door went unnoticed, although I was very afraid of being discovered when I snuck and hid first in the opposite apartment and then behind the door, merging with the darkness, forbidding myself so much as to breathe loudly. Alexander did not wait for the cameraman. He installed the camera and ordered Laura to start.

"We'll rehearse first," he commanded in a hoarse, unhealthy voice.

I don't know why, but I had a very bad feeling – he humiliated her on purpose, provoking her to protest, and then... then something irreparable could happen. But why the camera? Only a mentally ill person could film himself in the part he was going to play that evening.

I had to do something. I had to stop him, but what could I do? Scream, burst into the room? So what? A madly jealous woman – that's how I would look in the eyes of both Alexander and your sister. And he would have done something terrible to her anyway, just another time.

He did not seem to notice Arthur, but Arthur climbed the stairs, stopped on the threshold and froze, as if some force wouldn't let him go further. I barely had time to hide behind the door. The cameraman's stooped back seemed out of place and superfluous at the border of the light from the room and the darkness of the corridor, and this silent presence was so out of place with what was happening.

Through the crack in the door, I could see how Arthur's hand pulled down the zipper of his large loose jacket. Then, I realized that he had something hidden under it, and he didn't just freeze. He was on the verge of making a very important decision. Time froze, and the waiting became unbearable – on the one hand, Alexander's screams and Laura's crying, and on the other – a man ready to do something desperate. I had repeatedly seen his face before as he left another shoot. It was impossible not to see – Arthur was in love with Laura and hated Alexander, and I was sure that, at some point, he would snap. I wanted it to happen. Someone had to stop Alexander... But I waited in vain. He choked, just turned and left and did not do what he really had come for. Arthur lied to us when he said that it was you who stopped him. He ran away before you appeared. And Laura probably told him about you.

There was no end to my disappointment then... I wanted to run after him, bring him back... I could imagine what it would look like, because he didn't know that I was watching them.

Then suddenly, you appeared, as if from nowhere, burst in like an angry fury, first frozen on the threshold and then bent down for the bottle. But no! You shouldn't have done that! You shouldn't have gone to jail, then Laura would have been all alone. At that moment, I saw in her my daughter, who rejected me, but still desperately needed love and support. There was no time to think. It was me who hit you with the heavy door I was hiding behind all that time. I pushed it as hard as I could, it was just supposed to sober you up, but you fell. There was silence for a few moments. Laura was stunned for several seconds and then rushed to the exit, jumping over you. Alexander ran after her. He didn't care about you. He needed to finish what he had planned. I'm afraid he would have ripped her to pieces if he had caught up with her.

I followed them. Alexander was running among the houses, calling her, shouting threats. He seemed to be distraught, and I was very afraid for Laura, fearing that he would find her. This went on for a while. I don't remember how long. I didn't know what to do — you were upstairs, and I didn't know whether you were alive or dead.

Nevertheless, I returned to the apartment and began to shake you, slapping you on the cheeks, but it was all useless, and it was a damn mess! In a panic, I feverishly wiped my prints with an old rag wherever they could presumably remain. I didn't want to have anything to do with your death. And suddenly you moaned, and that sound was like the voice of an angel from heaven. You were alive, which meant you had to be taken away urgently. But if you were not here, then your fingerprints shouldn't be here either, so I wiped both the bottle and the door. Cursing myself for being reckless, for getting in such a scrape, I stopped to rest, then dragged you out. Why your lean body turned out to be so heavy, I don't know. Still, I managed to carry you to my car, which was safely parked under the trees. But having already dragged you inside, I remembered the camera in the room and ran back.

But I was too late. A car drove up, and a man got out, went to the apartment and a few minutes later, came down with the camera and tripod. Soon, Alexander returned and demanded the man give him the camera.

I hid in the shade of the trees and did not see the stranger's face. I only heard their voices. The stranger yelled that he was tired of Alexander's antics, his hysteria, uncontrollability, drugs and that it was time to stop all this. Alexander objected, said he had *everything under control. They screamed at each other very loudly and for quite a long time, until Alexander, in response to the accusations, said that he refused to work with the other man.*

He went back to the apartment. The stranger followed him.

For a while, I didn't hear their voices. It became suspiciously quiet, so I thought that Alexander had killed the stranger in a fit of rage, and I could be next. I didn't try my luck anymore, just left. I drove you home, carried you inside and called 911. But I couldn't calm down. I looked at the windows of your house, then forced myself to undress and go to bed. But I couldn't sleep. After a few hours of suffering, I drove to Alexander's house.

There was a scooter outside his place. Thousands of people use them, and Arthur also did. So, you'd better ask him your questions. Or the one who took the camera."

Lisa slowly lowered the white sheet to her lap. Tears continued to stream down her cheeks.

Chapter 33

Lisa did not remember how long she sat on that bench.

It was Danny's call that snapped her out of her musing.

"Have you seen the latest news yet?"

"I've been to the press conference... I saw everything with my own eyes... I can do the report," the crazy phrase suddenly burst out, although she knew that Danny would never forgive her and would not allow her to return to the office.

"Were you there until the very end?"

"Until the moment the crowd dragged me away from the square."

"So, you didn't see who killed Evan?"

"Killed him? No! Arthur fired several times but missed."

"I know, but that's not what I'm talking about. Evan was shot later, in the building."

"Shot? Is he dead? Or just wounded?" Lisa still couldn't believe it. So, she did hear new shots when she was running away from the square. She didn't imagine it.

"Try to survive when three different people fire at you."

Lisa froze, shocked, thousands of questions running through her head, but she asked just one, "But who?"

"They don't know yet, and actually, that's insider information for now. Three different people shot at him: first, a female guard. Perhaps she mistook him for an attacker – yes, that's a version, but it is doubtful. There is also a rumor that she is a member of some radical feminist organization, but this is also preliminary information, and it needs to be checked. The guard wounded Evan. He ran to the side door but saw his wife at the end of the corridor and rushed to her, but she opened fire and also wounded him. Maybe the distance was too great, or she wasn't a very good shot. Evan managed to open the side exit, jump out onto the street and that's where he was finished off by someone from a car that fled the scene. They already found the car – it was just left on the street. A rental, paid in cash, fake ID. The car rental service employee could not remember what the customer had looked like – just an old man. They are still looking for the third shooter."

Lisa could not utter a word. Her throat was dry, and there was no water left. Yet, she managed to get out a few words, "What now?"

"Now? Now you write me a report. Fast. For the coming issue. And also," he hesitated, paused, choosing his words. "You have to make a decision – tomorrow you either return to the office and get to work, or I won't cover for you anymore or pass off Emma's reports as yours."

"Did Emma write the reports for me?" Lisa was rattled.

"Yes. Yesterday she came to me, crying... said she was completely confused... that she was forced... I already told you – I immediately suspected that these were not your reports and was waiting for an explanation."

"Danny... Danny, I'm sorry," emotions overwhelmed Lisa, "Thank you, thank you for everything!"

Chapter 34

Lisa was still on the bench. She started crying again, then laughing with joy. She needed water and, as if by magic, the desired bottle appeared in front of her. And this bottle was held by her sister.

"How... How did you find me?"

"As soon as I heard about the upcoming press conference, I came. The abbot had urgent business in the city, so he gave me a lift. I saw you among the journalists, but then the shooting and panic started. I was looking for you everywhere and remembered this favorite shop of yours."

"Weren't you afraid to come here?"

"You said it yourself – stop hiding. I don't know what will happen next, but I'm no longer afraid. Even if Arthur decided to do this, and now we don't know what happened to him. What matters is that Evan is dead."

Helene called Lisa the same night.

Lisa interrupted her before she could say a word, "I do not know what you did, but you did everything just fine!"

"What are you talking about?"

"It's just..." Lisa hesitated, realizing that she had said too much on the phone.

"If you're talking about Evan's shooting, then I have nothing to do with it."

"Yes, of course," Lisa tried to backpedal.

"Did you really think that I could stoop to putting a hit out? It would be so ridiculous and rude," Helene was indignant. "We now have a lot of problems with this incident: all the materials and all the video footage have been seized, and they will be dealing with this case at another level. Besides, most of the video footage turned out to be damaged, not recoverable, and this will also be investigated."

"Damaged? What? What does it mean?" Lisa didn't know what to say, how to avoid another mistake.

But the short beeps in the phone saved her from making that decision.

And then the phone rang again, "And you know what? You're just as much a bitch as I am!"

Chapter 35

This time Lisa didn't try to dissuade Laura from staying longer. She looked at her little sister, whom she was ready to protect even at the cost of her own life and did not recognize her. The frightened, hunted look had disappeared; the lowered shoulders had straightened. There was even a healthy blush on Laura's usually pale cheeks. This little girl, who had suddenly turned into a grown woman was now strong and no longer needed constant care. She herself could protect anyone and stand up to the offender.

Such a change in a broken person could only happen if they made a very important decision for themselves.

Or they did a very important thing.

Now Lisa averted her eyes, afraid that she would not hold back and ask a question, the answer to which could again drastically change her life and her relationship with her sister. Yes, she thanked the Lord, the universe with all her heart, blessed the man who shot Evan, but... but she didn't want to know the answer to the question of who did it and who took part in it. Let it be anyone, but right now she didn't want to know the answer.

So, let everything remain as is. And whatever comes, let it just come.

I am a hacker! Save me!

A Novel

Chapter 1

With caution, she looked out the crack in the door and listened. All sounds disappeared. There was a deafening silence or maybe she just had gone deaf. She couldn't check or rub her ears because she was holding the door with her fingers, letting herself see what was happening in the room. If she were to take away her hand, the cabinet door where she was hiding would close, but then she wouldn't have any air to breathe. Her body had become numb in this uncomfortable, hunched pose. She really wanted to straighten up, to stretch her shoulders, arms and legs, but that wasn't possible.

Sitting like that in the cramped lower compartment of a bookcase on a pile of old magazines was becoming less and less bearable. Because of her knitted dress, she was in constant danger of slipping on the glossy covers of the magazines. She shoved them to one side when she decided to hide here and now she lay on an icy mound, every minute risking slipping at the feet of those from whom she was hiding. Her head was throbbing. There wasn't enough air. She was perspiring heavily, literally drenched in sweat, but most of all, she feared that this disgusting smell of the terrified person she had become would draw attention to her.

Eventually, she couldn't sit like that anymore and had to move. Besides, she could no longer hear any shots.

"Maybe they are done and just left?" she thought.

She opened the door just a little more and stuck her hand out, reaching out and touching the floor, or rather something sticky on the floor. What is this? She jerked her hand away and saw blood. Trying to fight nausea, she wiped her fingers on the inside of the cabinet and moved to the back wall, although it seemed there was no space left. She inhaled and exhaled several times, trying not to make any noise, and decided to try again. Somehow coping with disgust, she again slid her hand through the crack, moving it further to avoid the pool of blood. But her fingers sank into blood again. Gritting her teeth, with an incredible snake-like movement that she would never have been capable of in a normal situation, she stuck out her other hand and dropped it into the disgusting puddle, then stuck her head out and looked around...

Chapter 2

The magnificent, dazzling Mediterranean sun flooded the square in front of the cathedral with a flat facade topped with a spiraling tower. Against the background of this tall, flat facade, resembling a fortress wall, the front door of the cathedral seemed quite small. The priest usually stood on the top step of the entrance and greeted everyone who passed by, probably trying to draw attention to the church, to religion, but now the entrance was empty. The service must have already begun, and Lisa was late.

She liked coming to this cathedral on Sundays. It would be wrong to call Lisa a believer, but she really enjoyed the sunlight streaming through the high stained-glass windows and that special church smell. She liked the priest's serious voice, telling the few parishioners something very important.

The multi-colored joyful spots of light, the voice of the old priest, and the face of the Madonna with baby Jesus in her arms were all pacifying. It felt like she was dissolving in this magnificence, and when the sound of the organ suddenly rose, her heart was carried upward as well...

Today, however, Lisa was late. In anticipation of Sunday's service, she was about to run up the steps to the entrance when she heard a quiet voice, more like a groan.

"Help me..."

She caught sight of a figure huddled near the steps on the shady side. She could have gone by and not even noticed. God knows how many people felt bad in this world, but the voice stopped Lisa.

"Save me," he repeated.

She looked down at him. Dark eyes under the hood of a knitted jacket, pale skin like crumpled paper...

Lisa stopped. Usually, the beggars just asked for money and did so more often on the go, somewhere on the street. They just stopped for a moment and asked for it straight. It seemed the government of this country didn't encourage this kind of occupation, and the beggars tried not to draw attention to themselves. She never met any beggars under the church, perhaps they were there somewhere, but they'd certainly never been near this cathedral. The right thing to do would have been to tell the priest so that he would suggest a solution, but at that time, he was already giving a sermon, and the man, who was hiding behind the steps, was persistently asking for help. It's not that Lisa was very compassionate and couldn't just walk by someone in distress. No, it wasn't like that! But she understood that now she couldn't go and enjoy the Sunday service. She just needed to find someone else to take care of the beggar, and then she'd be happy once again.

"Wait, I will call someone," she promised him and touched the heavy door handle, but the beggar suddenly straightened up, looked around, put his finger to his lips, calling for silence, and sat down again, beckoning her with his hand.

Lisa sighed heavily, reluctantly trudging down the steps and carefully leaned toward the beggar.

"S-save me, I'm a hacker," he whispered.

This was bad. Lisa never had any business with hackers, but anyone who read the news online or watched TV knew that hackers were trouble. And this hacker also seemed to be badly beaten. Now she could see the bruise under his eye and the smeared blood near his mouth.

"P-please, get me out of here," he continued in a whisper. "I'll e-explain everything to you later."

Seeing the confusion in her eyes, he quietly pleaded with her. "J-just help me get out of here. Don't be afraid..."

A beaten up hacker asked her to save him and not be afraid! And not tell anyone! *That's something, all right.* Damn, why was she late for the service today? She could be bathing now in the mesmerizing sounds of the organ and squinting from the sun in the stained-glass windows. But no, now she had to think how to get rid of this unexpected problem.

"Let me give you money," the words just came out of her mouth.

He lowered his head, hiding his face under the hood, and in the meantime, she quickly pulled out the wallet from her bag.

"If you don't h-help me, they will kill me," he said, and tears glimmered in his eyes.

"God, why me!" she wanted to scream. Why today and why her? She used to come to this seaside town on vacation and recently decided to stay longer and got stuck here, although she had some serious work waiting for her at home... But she liked the measured lifestyle of this town, the smell of fresh coffee in the coffee house on the ground floor of the house she was renting, the rustle of plane trees over her head and the expressiveness of the locals. Here, she felt really well and surprisingly calm. And suddenly this hacker!

"Can you walk?"

"Yes," he said and rose slowly. "Go ahead, and I will f-follow you."

An alarm was ringing in her head, "take him to the police, and let them figure out what this hacker has done and who wants to kill him."

But, contrary to common sense, she went home, and, without even looking back, she knew that he was right behind her.

Chapter 3

A particularly bold ray of sunlight had broken into the room through the gap between the curtains that had been drawn since evening and was now tickling her forehead, cheek and was about to get between her eyelashes. Lisa opened her eyes, listening to the sounds. Silence. She remembered the hacker boy and thought what an unpleasant dream it was. Sometimes she had bad dreams from the past, unexpected dreams, but usually they disappeared in the morning. Smiling at this thought, she stretched, got out of bed, opened the curtains to let in the sunlight and then she caught quiet movement behind her. She turned abruptly, expecting anything — a shout, a blow, but she saw how that hacker boy from yesterday was watering the begonia on her windowsill. So, it was not a dream. He was still here. However, it was an absolutely peaceful sight, seeing a child simply watering flowers from a watering can. Her hostile mood changed at once, and Lisa thought, *no, he's not a hacker, no way. He's just a boy who had a fight with his parents and didn't want to spend the night with his friends, knowing that they would search for him there first, so he stuck with me.* She laughed softly, *what a little rascal!* Now she had to give him some tea and kick him out. His problems were his problems.

The teenager's head was perfectly visible in the sunlight against the window. Now he would turn around and she would see his shameless, guilty eyes. Maybe she should call his parents? Of course, they hadn't slept all night, looking for their poor little lost son. Their number was probably on his phone, but no, she was going to stay out of it.

She reached for her robe, and that's when she heard shots. Intuitively, Lisa threw herself on the floor, hid under the bed and plugged her ears but still could hear these sounds. They lasted a long, scary-long time. More and more, burst after burst...

All the time while shots were being fired, she lay, afraid to move, afraid to raise her head and see the worst possible thing: blood and the kid's motionless body on the floor. His head was such a great target against the window! And while she was trying to figure out how to get rid of him, the killer solved her problem. And now it was her turn, because no one would leave witnesses...

Now she would hear the sounds of steps on the stairs, the quiet creaking of the key turning in the lock, the breath of the person approaching her.

The wait had become unbearable, and she opened her eyes to anything. Whatever it was.

Near her bed, stood the hacker boy with a machine gun in his hands, looking at her with joy.

"D-did you b-believe?"

At first, Lisa couldn't say anything, not even a word, her temples were throbbing like crazy echoing wildly in her head, and he stood above her and smiled, baring his white teeth. Just stood and smiled... Finally, she was able to speak once again.

"Where did you get the gun?"

He nodded toward the pantry. Well, yes, of course, a toy weapon that was bought as a birthday present for the son of the woman from whom she was renting this apartment.

"You're a real asshole, you know that? Why'd you do that?"

"W-why did I imitate a shooting? Gosh, you're dumb! I'm being h-hunted. You didn't b-believe me... s-so I thought..."

Two conflicting feelings were now fighting in her: kick out the boy right now or first take away his phone and tell his parents what a moron their son was. However, most likely, this was not news to them...

"Y-you were so desperate with your pressing against the floor and whining, I felt genuinely s-sorry for you..." he continued.

Was he mocking her? That fucking stuttering asshole! Lisa was speechless.

"And what was I supposed to do, huh?" she finally said.

"Y-you are a journalist..."

"So what?"

"Ha! I read your articles... I thought you were c-cool... That's why I sought you out..."

"So us meeting was no accident? You know what? Get out! Get the fuck out!"

She jumped up and, grabbing his hand, dragged him to the door and threw it open, intending to throw the insolent boy out. But another surprise awaited her on the stairwell: a shadow appeared in the doorway and then transformed into three human figures at once. Lisa looked back at the kid, expecting to see the same impudent smile again, but seeing how his face changed, she realized that this was not some prank.

The old man, her neighbor, who always exercised in the mornings on his balcony and smiled hello, was the first to enter the lobby. Two thugs in black came behind him. They pushed the old man in front of them. While Lisa silently stared at the uninvited guests, the boy threw the machine gun at them, ran to the window, opened it and jumped out. They were on the second floor, so not that high, and if he fell on the loose earth of the flowerbed, there was a chance that he was alive and unhurt. The thugs rushed after him, also jumping out the window. There were screams and some intense cursing, looked like they didn't stick the landing.

Only she and the old neighbor remained in the apartment.

"You must run too," the old man said, "they can come back for you. Do you have a place to hide?"

"No."

"Remember this address..." He also said some other words, grabbed her clothes from the chair and pushed her toward the door, but Lisa looked at him blankly and didn't even try to resist...

Chapter 4

The old commuter train creaked plaintively and rattled around the bends, resisting with all its knots and joints. Outside the window were plowed fields, gardens and groves already bare, without leaves. Lisa would never have thought that the train could move so slowly. She rushed the driver in her mind, urging him on, trying to get as far as possible from her home and everything that had happened. She was headed to some distant village, to her neighbor's sister to wait until the situation blew over. The neighbor promised to contact her as soon as he knew that it was safe for her to return. Lisa had no clue how he would do that. First, she had to hide, calm down and then she would try to understand what the hell happened. Gradually, the slow movements of the train rocked her, and she closed her eyes, dozing off. She woke up to someone touching her. She instantly jumped up. The boy from yesterday was sitting next to her.

"What does all this mean?" she hissed angrily. "What happened? Who were those people?"

"Hey, I was one click away from death if you hadn't noticed."

"Oh, I noticed."

"I will t-try to answer your questions in order," he continued. "They w-want to k-kill me. And I already t-told you that. But I didn't expect them to find me so quickly. W-while you were sleeping, I m-met your neighbor. By the way, his name is Mario if you still don't know that."

Lisa lowered her eyes. Yes, she hadn't known what her closest neighbor's name was, nor did she want to know. She ran away from time to time, came to this seaside town not for the people or communication. And this boy had no right to blame her.

"He's a lonely old man," the hacker continued. "His k-kids rarely visit him. He has insomnia, so he wanders at night. By the way, he looks after you, knows everything about your habits..."

"Ah, so he's some kind of pervert, that old man..."

"J-jeez! You are dumb! Why do all women think that all men only dream of raping you?"

Lisa was confused and didn't know how to respond to that, but he continued. "Y-yes, some of you are so b-bad, you're not worthy of a hard-on or even to p-piss on, as a m-matter of fact."

"Enough, try to do without that teenage slang."

But he didn't listen to her. "He's j-just happy that you're there, in that house, maybe he sees you as his d-daughter..."

Lisa didn't know if she should believe the boy, but the way the neighbor came to her rescue spoke well for him.

"I uploaded a p-program on his phone so that when he couldn't sleep, he'd p-play chess with me, contact me at any moment, so he t-told me where he sent you. Did I answer this question?"

"Let's say, you did. Let's move on. Why do they want to kill you?"

He looked down, then turned away. It looked like he wasn't sure.

She elbowed him in the ribs. "Spill it! You got me into this mess, and I want to know what it is. Well? I'm waiting."

"I hacked s-someone..."

"Nice job. Well, sure, you're a hacker. Did you take a lot?"

"E-enough."

"Enough to kill you and everyone who happened to be around?"

The hacker was silent.

"So, how much? A thousand, five thousand, more?"

"More."

"How much more?"

He lowered his head again and then turned to the window.

"I'm waiting." She was so tired of all this. *What the hell? Some petty thief robbed someone...* "Fine. How many zeros are there? Couldn't be more than six, could it?" she was hoping that the stolen amount would turn out to be such that she could pronounce it without fear.

He waved his hands vaguely, still not looking at her, but she understood—more, much more!

So he's not a petty thief, he's a big one...

And then the same thugs appeared in the aisle. The boy cringed and slunk down in the seat. On instinct, she threw her jacket over him, as if he were just a sleeping passenger, maybe it would work...

The thugs were approaching. It was too late to run. The first leaned toward them, grabbed her by the shoulders and easily pulled her from the seat. Then, he just lifted her like it was nothing and carried her to the exit. At first, Lisa was speechless from such unceremonious arrogance and didn't even scream. Passing through the vestibule, he painfully knocked her against the door, her shoulder flashed with wild pain, then she cried out, and he easily shifted her to the other hand. He opened the next door with her feet, and her eyes shaded with pain, but realizing she was completely helpless was much worse than the physical pain. None of the rare passengers at this hour even thought to intervene, or even ask what was going on.

The goon carried her through the second, the third carriage. She tried to break free, to scream, but his stiff palm covered her mouth, and her body was only awkwardly floundering in his hands. She was scared to death, and it was getting worse and worse. No one would come to the rescue, no one would think to come look for her because now she was living as a hermit, trying to isolate herself from what had happened in the past. Nobody needed her, and no one would even know what these goblins did to her…

Chapter 5

Lisa woke up in complete darkness. Nobody and nothing around, not a single sound.

Where was she? She was lying on the floor in some unknown place. She listened but couldn't hear her abductors either. She moved her fingers, then she tried to straighten her arms. Her shoulder exploded with pain, her knees and feet too.

Well, of course, they used her body to open the door…

There was a rustling sound, and she stopped moving, frozen. The blood rushed to her face. The kidnappers!

Oh, Lord. Why did she ever pity that boy?

Seconds, minutes dragged on incredibly long, as if delaying the moment when she would be seized again…

Time passed, but there were no other sounds besides the booming beats of her own heart.

Did she imagine it?

She tried to kneel first, overcoming the pain, then moved to all fours, feeling the space around her with her hands. Her hand stumbled upon something soft and hairy, and Lisa drew it away in horror. So she was not alone and… was there someone else here or was this a corpse?

Having forgotten about the pain, she jumped to her feet and rushed away from the terrible find, stumbling upon something sharp and hard, some kind of corner, and immediately there was the ringing of broken glass. And then a smell...

A strange smell, something familiar... She knew that smell... She recognized this smell... It smelled like cold coffee. She probably hit a table or nightstand and the cup with cold coffee left by someone fell and broke... Hence the familiar smell. Lisa reached for the place where the table was, and she immediately found an object that felt like a table lamp. She pressed the button, the light came on, blinding her for a moment, and then she saw that she was kneeling on the floor in her rented apartment near the couch with the fur cover.

Was she at home? Was she at her home?

So, nothing happened, and... was it just another nightmare? But no, the room was a mess, there was a struggle, things were all scattered, and the pain in her legs and shoulder said everything that happened yesterday was not a dream. The boy and the two scary men, and the train... and she was kidnapped.

But why was she at home? Following logic, they should have left her in the basement of some abandoned building if, for some reason, they needed her. And thank God that they did because if the captors no longer wanted her, the end would be much more tragic... Lisa pushed this thought away.

Maybe they decided to hide her in the house and were just watching her from the outside. Another wave of panic swept over her.

Carefully, so as not to make too much noise, she crawled on all fours to the front door, opened the lock, flung the door to the side and rushed to her neighbor, knocking on his door and shouting, "Help! Help!"

First, she needed to call people, and then no one would dare to hurt her. The neighbor didn't respond, somewhere on the lower floors, doors slammed and she heard voices.

Wait a second! What was she doing? How would she explain to the peaceful inhabitants of this sleepy Mediterranean town what was happening? Best case, they'd take her for a crazy person.

Stop!

And she returned to her apartment, first in a half-bent position, afraid to straighten up. One by one, she turned on the light in all the rooms—the hall, kitchen, pantry, living room. But then she got angry and built up the courage to approach the window. Let them see that she was not afraid of them. She felt some strange intoxication... Now she would like to meet these bastards and tell them everything that she thought about them, to shout out... to cry...

It was gradually getting colder. Lisa went to the kitchen, took out a bottle of grappa from the cabinet and drank straight from the bottle, then more and more...

So... they just brought her back home, they only needed the boy. Perhaps, she could now return to her normal life and just forget about it. But what about the theory of unwanted witnesses? What about the boy? And where was the boy?

"Enough!" she cut herself off, "he's just a thief, and those who came for him came to take what's theirs." Which meant it didn't concern her.

Lisa took another big sip from the bottle and lifted it forward and upward, as if saluting in honor of her release.

She would just live on, as before. It was as if a weight had slipped from Lisa's shoulders, and a few more sips of grappa made her feel better and better. Having reached the couch, Lisa fell on the fur blanket...

Chapter 6

Several days passed after those events. Lisa lived her usual life. Every morning, she drank coffee in a new cafe. Having settled here, she came up with her own way of learning the customs of this town—to drink coffee each day in a new place, expanding her habitat more and more since there were countless cafes for every taste in this town. The holiday season was long over, but these establishments were still open, and she liked meeting new owners, waiters, and visitors every day. Such a mixture of entertainment and good practice was right for her.

Lisa firmly told herself that she was resting now and nothing else could distract her from having a good time.

The phone screen flashed briefly. Lisa opened the incoming message. To distract herself from all things negative, she had recently subscribed to the newsletter, "The funniest joke." This joke was selected after online voting and sent to the subscribers.

"Why does my connection speed drop drastically, when my washing machine's spin cycle turns on? It's hackers stealing your socks through the Internet."

"And what's so funny?" she muttered, displeased. The message again reminded her of the hacker boy. So she went online again.

The search for information about the abduction of a woman from the train in the news feeds yielded nothing. Honestly, she didn't even hope to find anything. And what would it change? Lisa's life returned to normal No one else tried to abduct her, and no one asked for help.

She spent hours on the beach, basking in the warm rays. The winter sun in these parts was gentle, not at all the same as in her home country. The seagulls were scurrying over the surf. There was no hungry despair in their cries, even they seemed quite content with their life here. Like her.

However, she still couldn't calm down. *And it's not even that in this blessed place, someone could ruthlessly break into someone's home, someone could drag a woman like a log through train cars, no.* She was concerned that she was thrown like a rag, like something unnecessary, used...

She took out her phone from her backpack and randomly typed the text, "Hacker steals money." No, that's too general. Better, "Hacker boy robs the wealthy." The search brought up many results with links from reports of hacker attacks during the US presidential elections to tips for beginner robbers on how to clean out a bank, apparently a very popular topic among Hollywood filmmakers and therefore the cherished dream of an ordinary man, tired of working his ass off his whole life and then expected to be content with a laughable retirement pension. Still, the banks were literally stuffed with money, and let's remember that it's not always earned honestly!

However, dreams were just dreams, and there was no information about the hacker boy or anything about her abduction.

Among other things, Lisa came across some information about Russian hackers, about a young hacker from Asia, who'd been hunted by Interpol agents for more than three years and was finally arrested and extradited to the United States. This guy hacked 217 banks and stole more than four billion dollars, and that's the budget of some poorer countries! For this, the hacker was facing the death penalty.

Although he was young, he was not as young as her hacker. Maybe Interpol was also hunting her guest? And these goons were some kind of agents?

But she had a feeling that these men were just hired guns paid by those who lost their money, and they quietly disposed of the boy. Of course, she could go to the police. She even considered calling the day after she returned, but a hunch made her not go through with it. If he really stole a lot of money, then why should she draw attention to herself as a witness to his death? She was in a foreign country and who knew how the local law enforcement officers would react to her being a part of this. First, Lisa wanted to speak with the editor-in-chief of her newspaper, discuss the situation, and decide the best course of action. She called her office, but the chief editor was not there, and Lisa didn't want to speak with her other colleagues. Yes, she was a journalist, and yes, this was a subject for investigative journalism, but as God was her witness, the last thing she wanted to do was investigate now when she decided to just relax and forget what she could not forget. She'd been so exhausted lately. She had a busy year, and she deserved this vacation. Still, it was a pity that the editor-in-chief wasn't getting in touch. He was also on vacation, somewhere in the mountains... Well, he also had the right to privacy... But she really needed his advice!

She tried typing different combinations of "hacker" and "stole a lot of money" in various search engines, but found nothing that could help her. And this was also haunting her. Even driving her mad!

She needed to remember what that boy was telling her about himself because he had said something, and she was missing it... However, she couldn't remember anything...

And where did her neighbor go, the one to whom she was "like a daughter?" Was he hiding at his sister's place? Or did the thugs take him too? Maybe he knew more. Maybe the hacker told him about his "special op" at night when they were talking?

The boy said that he read her articles and that's how he found her. But which ones? Lisa had been working for many years in journalism and wrote on various topics. What exactly caught his eye?

She threw the phone on the sand and wanted to kick it, but then she got a grip on herself and, grabbing it, opened the page of her newspaper and began to go through the articles.

No, not this and not this ... What then? What had interested him?

After reviewing her articles, she reluctantly opened the one that she didn't want to go back to at all. Too frank and too painful. She sincerely believed that she had gone too far when she published the true story of the girl who survived a terrorist attack. Everyone in the editorial office liked this interview very much, the editor-in-chief was over the moon, and the circulation of the newspaper went up so fast they even had to reprint. But it seemed unfair to her. To show the suffering of people in such detail felt like savoring the details of the killings. And nothing her colleagues said about a journalist's duty being to display everything impartially could reassure her. Too often, the community of journalists sinned by relishing in the details, and the more terrible they were, the higher the pay. Lisa still believed that the paparazzi, who filmed the dying princess Diana in the tunnel under Alma Square in Paris, were supposed to help her and not click the shutters of their cameras. Help with whatever they could! If you can save a person's life, just do it. Or at least, somehow ease the suffering of the dying. I think the princess would bless the one who just shielded her from the paparazzi at that moment.

Then again, how was she better than those paparazzi? Moreover, such an interview was not the first in her career as a journalist. Her natural gift of winning over people who shared the most terrible thing that happened to them helped her in her work. Sometimes she dreamed of the people in her articles, including that interview about children. Perhaps that is why she sometimes ran away to live in another country...

But she didn't help that hacker boy who came to her and was even happy that it was all over. It was purely human happiness... It's so natural to push the trouble away from you...

Someone came up from behind her. She hadn't heard the sound of footsteps and started.

"Maybe bring you something, coffee, wine?"

Lisa didn't immediately realize that this was the waiter from the hotel cafe near the beach. She drank coffee there last time, and then they had a little chat with this guy, and now he saw her on the beach and approached her.

"Thanks so much! Coffee wouldn't hurt."

He returned ten minutes later, and they again exchanged a few words about the weather, that probably after lunch the wind would begin with strong sudden gusts, so characteristic of this coast. The waiter was already leaving when suddenly she asked him, "Were there any terrorist attacks in schools in your city?"

"No, not here. Thank God, this is not America."

She did not remind him that the attacks in schools were not only in America, but more recently in Western Europe, Russia, and Belarus... And that this plague was spreading all over the world...

She was already leaving the beach when the waiter returned.

"Signora, I remembered something, maybe you'll find it useful..."

In his hands, he had a page from a notebook in which they usually wrote down customers' orders and seemed to hesitate whether he should be giving it to her, whether he should be talking about it at all.

Finally, he made up his mind and handed her the piece of paper.

"This address... This is my niece's friend... He is interested in computers. He calls himself a coder... in short, he creates various computer programs... I'm not good at it," he smiled awkwardly, as if apologizing... But seeing that she was listening very carefully, he continued. "You were asking about terrorists... Well, he created an application that allows you to find potential criminals when they are still in the planning stage of their crime. He told me, but frankly, I did not quite understand... I didn't understand how this can be done..."

The waiter smiled again awkwardly, as if he had said something stupid and knew how stupid it was and that she would laugh at him now. But she didn't laugh.

And then he continued, said that it would be better for he not to stick his nose into this business at all... when he offered his program to the police, at first, they laughed at him, and when he insisted and provided evidence that the local police officers had taken part in the recent robbery, he was badly hurt... And now he didn't like people and was afraid of them... He became a recluse, barely spoke to anyone and was peculiar...

He said something else, urged her to be careful, because those people were not fucking around and she should not get involved in it at all...

But she was already running to the station, holding the piece of paper in her hand.

There were no living people in the room... Only a crooked human figure by the window. It looked like he had tried to escape by jumping out the window, but the bullets stopped him.

Closer to the door was another body under the table, as if that person was trying to hide under it but was seen. They moved the table and gunned him down.

All the while listening to the sound of the footsteps of the returning murderers, she crawled out of her hiding place and, without straightening up, moved to the door. She froze, listening to the silence, then opened the door to the corridor. The entire space of the long corridor was literally covered with corpses. It looked like the victims were trying to escape from the shooters, scattering in every direction, but they were found and methodically shot, one by one...

There were still no sounds heard. None. She rubbed her ears, trying to regain their sensitivity and someone else's blood on her palms spread across her face. Despite the horror of what was happening, she still felt squeamish, so she wiped her fingers on the wall as best she could.

Now she needed to figure out which way the exit was. When the terrorists appeared in the building, she ran to the first door she could see and climbed into the cabinet, and, thank God, this saved her. And now she just needed to calm down and remember where the exit was.

At that moment, they were sitting in the math room, the angry math teacher left the three of them for an extra hour. She escaped, the two others were shot, and cowering in a frightened lump, she heard these sounds. The math classroom was on the second floor, almost above the entrance to the school. So, she had to go down the stairs as quietly as possible.

On the stairs, she saw another corpse that slid down the railing and fell backwards. "Don't look at the dead," she told herself and tried to pass by with her eyes squeezed shut. When she opened her eyes, she saw another kid who was also making his way to the door, but then someone laughed on the lower platform, the gun clicked. That second child realized that they saw him and ran like a frightened bunny, but the bullet was faster...

The shooter went down a few steps and shot at the writhing body two more times, then he turned it over with his foot and shot him in the open mouth, which was still trying to form words, probably asking for mercy...

Then the shooter turned to her, grunted in satisfaction, and threw the sawn-off shotgun in his other hand...

Chapter 7

Windbreak, roofs of houses, gardens, ponds, and meadows rushed outside the window, turning into a blurry picture, something similar to the work of the Impressionists. Oncoming trains flickered, sometimes appearing, then disappearing, leaving behind only a receding sound. The high-speed train slowed down only a little, passing smaller stations, and then, like a steed on a racetrack, rushed forward again and seemed ready to take off, driven by it, but even that seemed not enough. Lisa finally shook off that sleepy numbness and unwillingness to act like a chrysalis, shedding its skin, turning into a butterfly and spreading its wings. In her mind, she flung these wings behind her, helping the train, although it was already moving at a speed of more than 250 km per hour, which had not so long ago been considered unthinkable for rail transport. Nothing like the ancient commuter train, which she had to take recently.

The soft back of the chair should have relaxed and calmed her, but not now. Lisa would prefer a hard bench, if only the train moved faster. Scraps of what the waiter told her lingered in her mind. A friend of his niece created an application that allowed finding potential robbers when they were just beginning to search for information about banks and banking operations. But there were also the safe-breakers, experienced robbers, who didn't need to gather information, they already knew everything, she thought. Not everything. Then again, most of the robberies were committed by beginners, and because of their inexperience, many people died in these operations, and few even knew about the professional robberies. Most often, banks didn't even disclose the information about such robberies. They were afraid of losing customer confidence.

Finally, the web of electrical wires on the poles along the railroad track began to take on the configuration of complex rectangles and other geometric shapes. This meant they were approaching a big station. From behind the tops of the trees, the roofs and upper floors of tall buildings emerged, then the gray-pink cover of the railway platform appeared, drawn by a restrictive strip, behind which stood people with luggage.

Leaving the car, Lisa handed the piece of paper with the address to the station attendant, and he showed her where to go...

... A white house, the walls were covered with sweet lilac wisteria. The door was painted blue, a little ragged, as if tired of the touch of human hands for dozens, maybe hundreds of years. Drips on the walls, it seemed, the house had not been refurnished for a long time.

She pressed the bell button, but there was no sound. So, the bell was probably somewhere in the rooms. Pressed, waited longer, listened. Silence again. Then Lisa carefully turned the doorknob, hoping for nothing, and the door slid open.

So, that's how it's going to be?

"But what if they are already waiting for me here?" a panicky thought came over her, but she checked herself. Who'd even need her? They just left her alone. They didn't need her. She was of no use to them.

Lisa pushed the door harder, hesitated, stepped over the threshold, took a couple of steps forward and stopped, blinded by the darkness after the sunny street. Gradually, the furnishings appeared—an old kitchen sideboard, a table covered with a woven tablecloth, next to it, a bench and some chairs with high backs, a fireplace made of stones in the corner.

By the curtained window stood a chair with a straight back. In the chair there was someone. Through the half-closed curtains sunlight was coming through, illuminating the figure.

"Why are you here?" came the faint voice from the chair.

"Hello." She didn't immediately know what to say. And really, why did she come here? After all, everything ended fine for her. But still...

"I am glad that you are alive... I don't know how you did it because they found us, and I want to ask you, maybe you need help?" They will not leave you alone..." The man in the chair didn't answer, and she continued. "Is this about the money that you stole... or your application for a completely different reason, and you just lied to me about the money?

There was no answer again, and she took a couple steps toward him. She was not going to back down. She didn't come here to just stand and do nothing.

"So he told you about the money?"

The person turned to her on the wheels of the chair, and Lisa was shocked. It was a wheelchair, and a complete stranger was sitting in it. For several long minutes, she looked into his face, realizing that she jumped to a conclusion, indulged in wishful thinking. How stupid she must look now! She invaded someone's house and blabbed everything to some stranger...

"Sorry," she said, the first thing that came to mind, and turned to leave.

"Don't run away. I barely ever talk to people face to face, not on Skype or Viber... I understand who you are asking about. You're offering to help him, so he's in trouble?"

His voice seemed to be strangely changeable, the breaking voice of a teenager, then an adult, exhausted by some illness. For a minute, it even seemed to her that this was not an old man at all like she'd thought at first. Turning again to him, she took several uncertain steps forward, looking into his face.

Yes, it was a teenager, and a young pale hand was working the control lever of the chair. A child could have such skin too.

"I don't even know..." stumbling and gabbling, Lisa told the stranger why she was there, how she met the hacker boy near the church, and everything that happened after...

"Yes, I really know the person you are talking about. I really knew him. We used to hang out at one time, like boys, like distant relatives, very distant. When we were little, our big family gathered quite often, spent the holidays together. But then I heard something about him later. I heard that he was a big dreamer, liked to tell stories... But, what you are telling me is too much even for him... Then again, I lost contact with him a long time ago..."

"Even in spite of your kinship and family tradition?"

"Yes, the world is changing, and traditions are changing too. Unfortunately..." He remained silent for a while. Then he continued. "I'm sorry, but I can't help you... I have no way of contacting him, no information..."

"That waiter told me said you were a coder and also created some kind of program to fight corrupt law enforcement officers..."

"Not anymore... Now I just read books, listen to music, and look out the window..."

"He also said," Lisa insisted, "that you suffered because of your application... Maybe I can help..."

"Are you Mother Teresa? Helping everyone?" he grinned.

"That's none of your business," Lisa became angry.

"Then, please, when you leave, close the door properly. I do not want to let the cool air outside."

"Don't you want to know what happened to him? Whether he's alive or not?"

The man in the chair shook his head tiredly.

Lisa went to the door, but stopped on the threshold, half-lit by the sun, half- hidden in the shadow.

"Still... how much did he take?"

"How much? Billions..."

"Billions? From whom?"

"Don't let the cool air out. Please go away."

Chapter 8

Lisa came out of the shadow under the hot southern sun. She was shaking. She didn't know whether it was from disappointment or from the cold...

This was a completely different person, a crippled boy, and he didn't want to let her into his life. As if confirming this, a bird flapped its wings somewhere above. Lisa looked up—the whitish sky looked like it was burnt out by heat, not a cloud in it. Somewhere very high above, a plane was leaving a vapor path.

She got to the gate, left the courtyard, walked along the street, and then suddenly changed her mind. Adjusting her backpack, she clambered awkwardly onto the fence and jumped down. Landing in the flower garden, she was scratched painfully by the hydrangea branches. Well, good thing it wasn't the neighbor's agave otherwise she would have needed medical help.

Trying to step quietly, she crept to the door, carefully opened it and heard the boy's voice. Now he was speaking loudly, dryly, abruptly.

"Yes, yes... They are looking for you... I had to lie that we were related... No, of course... No, I don't want, no... Go screw yourself..."

He disconnected the call, threw the phone on the table next to him, and then noticing her out of the corner of his eye, he abruptly turned his chair.

"Now tell me everything," she said, hissing like a snake, ready to scold him with the worst words for fooling her. "So he is alive! And you know that!"

"I still don't know where to find him. I can give you his phone number, but I'm not sure that he will take a call from an unknown number."

"Then with your permission..."

She approached him and, taking his phone from the table, pressed the button to repeat the last call. Everything was actually pretty simple! There were long beeps, but no one answered. She pressed the button again and again, only long beeps...

"What does that mean?"

"I told you. This means that he's most likely thrown out the phone."

"Come on, what the hell is happening? Who is he? Ah, well, a thief... A thief, who stole a lot of money. Only I want to know how the hell am I part of this? What did he or they need from me? Come on, spill it! Who's after him?"

The boy's face was a storm warning. He could simply call the police, and they would detain her or even arrest her, but Lisa carried on. "I want to know everything! Both as a person and as a journalist, I have the right." Her thoughts were messy, she paced in front of the cripple, clenching the useless phone in her fist.

"Too many journalists are interested in him. That's weird."

"What do you mean? Are you kidding me?"

He shook his head, looked out the window, where through the translucent curtain one could see the silhouettes of trees and the path from the gate to the house.

"They came to me, offered money for his program."

"What's in it? Who came to you?"

"I don't really know."

"You're lying!" She stopped right in front of him, angry, prickly. She couldn't wait anymore. "Stop! Are you changing the subject, or is it somehow related to the application that the hacker created?"

"I don't know."

"Yes, you do!"

He hesitated and then decided to say, "Yes and no. I'll say no more. Go away, I'm tired, or I'll call the police."

She turned and went to the exit.

"I didn't tell them," he called after her.

"Who are they? Who came to you?"

"I don't know them. I thought one of them was a journalist."

"What's so strange? The journalist is gathering his material for an article."

"He offered me a lot of money, too much. Why would a journalist do that? He wants to get paid for his work. And he offered too much money..."

The phone rang softly and the screen flashed for a moment, Lisa automatically clicked on the message sign. The text appeared. "If you need to open a door in a building that has an intercom, whom do you turn to, to housebreakers or hackers?"

"To delivery men."

"Damn it!" swore Lisa. "Hackers and thieves! Again! Is my phone bugged or something?"

Chapter 9

Lisa was slowly wandering along the promenade illuminated by the midday sun. The sea was blue, motionless, like a huge aquamarine radiating all the shades of the Mediterranean summer, not a single breeze could be heard from the sides of the beach. She wanted to be in a cool, air-conditioned room and she also wanted to drink, drink a lot of cold water, sparkling water with bubbles tickling her nose. On the opposite side of the street, she noticed a café. At first, she wanted to run across the road, but the cars were flying one by one, leaving her no window for that. She looked around for a passage, and indeed, the railing of the staircase leading underground appeared ahead.

The faint coolness of the subway and the twilight enveloped her. Lisa was walking forward, striving to get to the place where there was water and didn't immediately notice that someone was following her. But just a minute ago there wasn't anyone. She must have been thinking about something and simply didn't pay attention. Meanwhile, that person was approaching...

Damn it! If she just turned around and it was just a passerby, she'd look like she was overreacting. So, she needed to speed up, which she did, but the pursuer also started walking faster. Lisa was ready to run but could she escape? There, on the surface, the street seemed to her the usual width, but now in the subway, the road to freedom was infinitely long. And, as luck would have it, no one was around, neither behind nor in front of her.

Maybe it's just a thief who wanted to snatch her purse and run away, but he could still hit her on the head so that she didn't call for help and didn't run after him... The stranger was now so close that she even felt his heavy breathing. Now. Now something bad was going to happen...

Lisa didn't understand at what point she simply jumped to the side. A stranger with a hoody pulled over his face passed in a business-like manner right in front of her eyes... He passed her and then disappeared, turning right, onto the stairs leading to the street. And Lisa just stood there, hearing only the booming beats of her heart and trying to restore her breathing.

Who was it? Just a thief, who didn't have the guts to do his job because maybe someone could see him stealing. Or was she still being followed? And she was too quick to think that they left her alone?

Lisa didn't know how long she stood in the subway afraid to

move. However, she managed to pull herself together, caught her breath and went back to the street. The cafe was closed for technical reasons, and she had no choice but to simply go on without thinking where she was going. Then she just turned into an alley and stopped at the hotel entrance.

There was no club soda in the hotel bar, but Lisa had plenty of plain mineral water. She drained the whole bottle in one gulp. Drowning in the soft, cool chair, she tried to put her thoughts in order and calm down. It wasn't going well. She could, of course, just have a drink. Whiskey, for example, was an excellent choice in this scenario, but then she decided not to drink alcohol in such heat.

Lisa knew from experience that everything would gradually fall into place, straighten itself out. And in order to give her brain time to calm down, she needed to do something, be distracted by something. But what? Wait a second! This was a hotel. That journalist interested in the hacker's program could very well be staying here. She had to try to make inquiries, come up with a believable story for why she was looking for the journalist. She could, of course, use the time-honored trick that repeatedly helped her out in the past. Maybe she had to give this journalist something he left or she borrowed from him and she just forgot the name of the hotel where he was staying, so now she was looking for him... What if that worked? But it didn't... After checking out a dozen hotels, where she gave a sweet smile and pretended to be embarrassed, telling her tale, Lisa was gradually losing hope. She knew that most likely she was mistaken for a woman with whom the journalist spent the night and then didn't tell her where he was staying. Just a one-night stand... But she didn't care...

She got lucky in a small hotel with a sweet name, "Spring Flower." The receptionist, who first eyed her with his greasy eyes, managed his rather unpleasant smile and told her that, yes, indeed, a quite well-known journalist from the capital had been recently staying with them. He kept his visit secret, but... but everyone watched TV, so... Lisa batted her eyelashes and blushed, almost naturally because the receptionist was smacking voluptuously and seemed to be undressing her right here by the desk. Lisa flatly refused the drink he offered and left the lobby, leaving him sighing about the missed opportunity...

Now she almost certainly knew where to look. True, she still thought about going to the local police station to ask about that scandal with the cripple's program and the accident that put the programmer in a wheelchair, but the law enforcement officers probably wouldn't be happy with her visit. Now she had more important business in the capital, and actually, Lisa wanted to get out of this city with its strange pedestrians in the subway as fast as possible.

At the door, she looked around, wishing to send a farewell encouraging look to the receptionist, whom she had used so easily, but contrary to expectations, he didn't look disappointed or baffled. He was quickly dialing some number on the phone, and Lisa realized that he was reporting about her to someone... And she suddenly felt very cold, just like in the subway. So she just hurried away...

Chapter 10

Again, the high-speed train was taking her into the unknown. Outside the window were the same fields, groves, vineyards, and smaller stations at which high-speed trains usually didn't stop. The landscape outside the window was changing so rapidly that it felt like a hurricane wind was blowing everything away, and the same wind burst into her head, refreshing, putting her thoughts in order, leaving the danger behind.

The conductor approached, glanced briefly at her ticket and proceeded on. Lisa decided to take a nap. At first she couldn't sleep, the receptionist calling someone and the stranger in the hoody kept popping up before her eyes, but still the smooth, lulling rocking did its job, her eyes closed, and Lisa fell into the darkness.

"God damn it! How many of you are there? I shoot and I shoot, but there's still more of you..."

"Maybe that's enough," she blurted out unexpectedly.

"What is enough? No! Today everyone will die! Because I fucking said so!"

She looked at him, too weak to move.

"Well, what is it? Why aren't you begging for mercy? Why aren't you saying your prayers. Come on, maybe God can help you."

With these words, he again moved the sawn-off shotgun into his other hand and aimed it directly at her face. Then he lowered the barrel.

"I can't hear you. Come on, do it!"

"What do you want to hear?"

"What do you mean, what do I want to hear? That you want to leave here alive. Or don't you?"

"I do."

"Then what is it? Tell me, little bitch, at least one reason why I should let you leave. Come on, I'm waiting!"

He stood so close, a little down the stairs that she could have jumped him and been at his throat... Just jump and go for the jugular... She was going to die anyway! Why was she hesitating? Just do it!

And he was playing with his weapon, throwing it from one hand to another and grinning. Then he pointed at the entrance, as if telling her to run! She knew that if she did, he would shoot her like an animal... And yet she took one step down the stairs to the exit, then the second...

He was no longer smiling, but looking at her with some kind of interest... Like in that old joke where the bus driver watches a passenger, who's late to board his bus every day at the same, and stops to think, "will he make it or not?" And then the driver just closes the door before that loser's face and grins again—ah, he didn't make it, maybe better luck next time...

No, she would not be that loser passenger! She would do it differently...

Bright light struck her face, and Lisa opened and then immediately closed her eyes. The train was slowing down, approaching the station. It was time to leave. It would be nice to catch the famous journalist in the editor's office, but there was no guarantee. He was, after all, a journalist, not, for example, an accountant, and he didn't have to actually be in the office all day.

On the train, before falling asleep, Lisa found some information online about that journalist, Mark Bukowski. Yes, he was a star, very famous, popular, in demand. He made a career reporting on events from the hottest spots on the planet, but the most striking stories, the ones that raised his rating sky-high, were the reports of terrorist attacks. Mark vividly described the suffering and fear of the people who found themselves in terrible situations. Just like her... True, Lisa never let herself give an assessment of what was happening, thereby instilling even more fear. She gave the floor to the victims, trying to show the situation through their eyes. But as if enjoying himself, Bukowski bathed in the blood and suffering. *Stop!* This was already going too far, so she reined herself in. It's just his style, which judging by his fame, was very popular with both his editors and readers.

Lisa understood that Bukowski loved the camera, and although she wouldn't say that the camera loved him back, he probably just thought that he was not a model, but a journalist, and therefore, a pretty face was completely optional. She also noticed that the operators always shot him on the right, as if in half-profile. Perhaps Bukowski himself asked them to film him like that—that angle, apparently, worked for him the best. Also, if possible, they needed to avoid close-ups, so that the irregularities of his face would remain invisible to the audience.

"Ah, dear, you probably just envy him," she shamed herself, "you write no worse than he does, but he has fame, and you are just a good journalist. Well, enough!" she checked herself again, "as the wise men say online, never criticize yourself. Never!"

Mark really had a very strong and drawing energy, she'd give him that. And she could feel it even through the screen. And that could not be achieved by any methods, he had to be born with this gift. And Mark liked himself on the screen. It looked like he was admiring himself. The right phrases and clever words flew out of his narrow-lipped mouth and filled the airtime.

True, he had recently disappeared from the TV screen, but that was the nature of success. Today you were on the top of a wave, and tomorrow you were not, and this could go on forever.

Lisa skimmed through an impressive list of publications or more like journalistic victories. There was also mentions that her famous colleague would be nominated for the main journalistic award. And she thought that for someone like him getting such recognition was piece of cake.

Perhaps, this was about one of the latest reports that went to print without photographic evidence from the scene. Either it was because of some technical issue or something strange happened to the photographs. Although such prizes were not always awarded for a single publication, there were many nominations, and most often, those were awarded for all the work done by a single journalist.

But without those bloody photos, the text seemed dry and the author's triumph was incomplete.

"So stars also can fail," Lisa noted to herself gloatingly.

The huge revolving glass door at the entrance to the high-rise, which housed many different editorial offices, blinded her with its brilliance and overshadowed the people entering and leaving the building. About 15 minutes had passed, and Mark had not yet appeared. Lisa didn't lay an ambush at the entrance. She just called his office on the internal telephone and asked someone to tell Bukowski that a victim of that terrorist attack at school was waiting for him downstairs. The one with a report without any pictures. And she had some very unpleasant news for him. She specifically didn't ask to have him called to the phone, just for the person to tell him what she said. That way he would not be able to dismiss her, as if she were, say, another crazy person. The entire editorial staff was now aware of the problem, and he would have to react.

"I thought it was you," she heard a voice from behind her.

She turned and saw Mark. He must have used the stairs instead of the elevator.

"I just don't understand. Why all the strange hints? Why didn't you call me on the phone?"

"Be thankful that I didn't say that you tried to kill me."

"What nonsense!"

"Well, of course, it's nonsense!" Lisa burst out laughing. "But you are here, and I have several questions and no time to follow you around. See? It's all very simple."

"What... like right here?"

It looked like Mark was a little confused, but he tried not to show it. Tried and stay collected, competent, one of a kind... In a word, a star!

"We can go upstairs to your office," Lisa suggested.

He hesitated but only for a few seconds. "Let's go for a walk, breathe some fresh air. There is a nice place nearby. We can talk there. Get to know each other properly."

He then took her by the elbow and pulled her along. Through the small steps, they climbed onto the open veranda with the tables covered with blue tablecloths the color of sky and sea. Lisa involuntarily admired the view that opened from the veranda, the vast sky merging with the sea.

"I'm listening," Mark looked at her questioningly.

Without answering, Lisa called the waiter, studied the menu for a long time, then placed her order.

All this time, Bukowski was drumming his fingers on the countertop, casting inquiring looks at her.

The order was brought immediately and Lisa slowly began eating a huge sandwich with ham, lettuce, tomatoes, and mayonnaise, enjoying the meal. She didn't even know she was that hungry. She enjoyed Bukowski's confusion too.

They never actually met until today. Of course, Lisa knew the famous journalist, but it's unlikely he'd ever heard about her. Television made people famous. Lately, however, the Internet had become a much better source, but Lisa worked for a newspaper. Despite all the predictions that print journalism was dying, old well-deserved publications that had their own history remained in demand among their readers. Of course, not quite as numerous recently, but nevertheless, the newspaper fought for them daily in a fierce competition with other media.

"He is clearly worried," noted Lisa. But she already admitted that she had said something stupid, trying to lure him out. And why did he say that he immediately thought that she was looking for him?

Finally, he couldn't stand it anymore. "You wanted to tell me something. I know that you also wrote about that terrorist attack at the school. I know your name, and yes, I read your work."

"Oh," Lisa was genuinely surprised to hear this, "I'm flattered. But actually, I interviewed the victim. It was not a report," Lisa corrected him.

"Yes, yes! You're right. Then she came to you... Did she contact you again?"

Lisa interrupted him. "Tell me what's so interesting about the program that you tried to buy from the crippled coder? Because I refuse to believe that you are just going to rob honest people by withdrawing money from their accounts."

He leaned back in his chair, looked away and raised his hands as if surrendering.

"Easy with the pressure! Sheesh! You won't believe it, but I also want to know what's in that program and why your hacker wanted to sell it to me at such a crazy price."

"My hacker?" Lisa was shocked. "Did he want to sell it to you? So whose program is it? I already know that the cripple and the boy who came to me are working together. But what exactly did he tell you?"

"Yes, wanted me to buy it. Although he was blathering on about justice, but I don't believe in it."

"You don't believe that you can make billions on justice?"

Mark laughed. Unable to restrain herself, she smiled too.

"See, it's funny to you too. But still, I'm curious. Did you meet that girl face to face or was the interview conducted online?"

He leaned toward Lisa, pushing his long chin in her direction. At the same time, his face took on a caricatured appearance. The sharp features and the skin that was too wrinkled for his age, and even his messy shoulder-length hair, prematurely graying, only made things worse. He looked like the witches and hags from fairy tales.

"Are you hoping she still has pictures from that terrorist attack at school?" suddenly it dawned on her. "Your report did come out without them."

"Think. If she's a victim, how can she have any? Where would she get them? This question has been haunting me, but I think..." he looked at Lisa. "What if there simply weren't any to begin with?"

"So I just made them up? Maybe the interview too? Is that what you're saying? Well! They were there. I saw them, she showed them to me, and I sent the video of our conversation to the editor. And when I was preparing that interview, I repeatedly watched and listened to the video, the phone was on it and the pictures too..."

"And then the recording turned out to be damaged exactly where she was showing you the phone and the pictures. All this is very strange."

"But it's not strange that you also lost the pictures for your report. And for some reason, in other publications, the pictures disappeared right before the release. You remember that scandal! We all remember that scandal!"

Lisa threw the sandwich on the plate. It now seemed tasteless and bland. It felt like Bukowski was interrogating her, but originally, she was going to interrogate him. And it was not her fault that the recording was damaged. It just happened... For her interview, the pictures were not necessary. The girl's emotions, the details were enough. With the report, however, everything was different and, it seemed, Bukowski was ready to do a lot to get them.

"Then again, she could show you pictures from any other terrorist attack or from a movie," he continued to insist.

Lisa stubbornly shook her head. "I saw them, and they

matched her story."

"And she picked up the terrorist's phone when she was running away... Is that what she said?"

Mark's phone rang. He spoke briefly and hung up. "It's from the office. I must go. But we didn't finish."

"By the way, she had the same phone as yours."

"She did? This is my favorite brand and case color. True, I often lose them, but always buy the same..." He caught her eye and laughed forcedly. "Yes, of course! And that makes me a suspect in your book!"

Lisa didn't answer.

He leaned back in his chair again and turned away. From the terrace where they were sitting, a beautiful view of the city opened up. The sea in the distance was blue, light clouds floated beyond the horizon, the bright sun was rising higher and higher, making the landscape more distinct, making every detail visible. And Lisa suddenly felt very uncomfortable. Why did Mark bring her here, out in the open? Perfect, clear targets, she suddenly realized. She wanted to suggest that they move from this open place to the closed section of the cafe but resisted the impulse.

"Tell me, and that hacker boy... you still haven't found him? Can you still guess where he might be?"

"No," Lisa answered honestly. "I haven't. And I hoped that you would tell me what was in that program and where I could find the hacker."

"But he came to you, so he must have needed you for some reason."

Lisa nodded vaguely and then shrugged. She shook her head no at the waiter, who had silently approached the table to bring more coffee.

"Are you still looking for him?"

Lisa only grinned, remembering the receptionist calling someone. Surely, Mark left beacons wherever possible, in case someone else was interested in the cripple or in Mark's star person. But as for the man in the subway, she had her doubts. Why would Mark be trying to frighten her?

"Perhaps, he wanted me to tell the world about his program because they are all nuts about the stupid slogan, 'We make the world a better place.' They put it everywhere, in every ad campaign, anywhere at all..."

"Yes, the slogan is good," said Mark. "They just did it to death already..."

"It's making me sick," Lisa was not giving up.

He spread his arms, as if saying, "whatever."

"Then again, who'd be sharing the opportunity to earn billions, unless... he needs a partner," it suddenly came to her. "But... what if he's a genius with megalomania? A young genius! The modern world belongs to young geniuses. It is not for nothing that they are trying to grow them in Silicon Valley and similar places. Children with unformed psyches are trying to rule the world..."

Mark turned toward the sea, squinting from the sun, which was becoming even brighter. He even patted his pockets looking for his sunglasses, but couldn't find them. From her position, even in spite of the blinding sun, Lisa could see a small boat coming in their direction. It wasn't moving at a very high speed, but still was very purposefully coming toward them.

"You're lying, aren't you? I think you know very well what's in that program."

"Yes, I know," he admitted, which was unexpected. "And yes, you guessed it right," he suddenly turned to face her. "He needed a partner. When he showed up, he said that he'd created a program that could destroy photographs from any scene, including terrorist attacks – the nightmare of all reporters, photojournalists, publishers of all mass media. And then he threatened to launch it. At first, I didn't believe him. Would you? After all, this is a violation of every rule..." Mark looked up and held his hands up, as if making the sky his witnesses.

Lisa only nodded, encouraging him to continue.

"At first, I didn't believe it, I simply dismissed him, but that is how it went. My report came out without the photos from the scene. They just disappeared from the database, and yes, not only here. Not a single publication came out with photos then. It doesn't happen. It couldn't be! He could not have access to all the databases. Moreover, at the preparation stage, all the photos were in place, and as soon as it came to releasing them, everything disappeared. A strange glitch, isn't it? And thank God, it wasn't just us. Otherwise, it would have cost me dearly. They would just crucify me for being a lousy amateur, but it all just disappeared from the photojournalists' equipment, just gone in seconds... They couldn't be all connected! Or could they?"

Lisa added. "Some people even believed this was some higher power at work, which didn't want to see people making money on such terrible things..."

But Mark didn't hear her. He spoke, with his long face leaning close, having lost all respectability, just speaking out... Like a man who finally got the opportunity to confess. Out of the corner of her eye, Lisa saw the boat getting closer and closer, but she didn't want to interrupt Mark, she had to hear him out...

"Did you tell your boss?"

He shook his head.

"At first, I didn't believe it and then... Why would I? So he could drag me through the mud? And how could I tell him, if it's just a boy..."

"Did the hacker explain why he did this?"

"You can earn a lot of money by destroying the pictures from everywhere, but selling them later to just one newspaper. And this paper will have exclusive photos. Can you imagine what these circulations are? Can you imagine the sales?! This is a lot of money!"

"Nothing personal... just money... Yes, the new IT generation! They are quick..."

Meanwhile, the boat was getting closer, and Lisa couldn't stand it anymore, so she got up to look at it. It seemed to her that the man on board lifted something resembling a gun. Mark still wasn't seeing anything, lost in his thoughts...

"Did you find him later?"

"No. I told you, I didn't."

"But you're still looking."

"Yes."

"You know, I just thought of something to lure him out."

Lisa didn't take her eyes off the boat, still hoping that it would change course any second...

"By the way, there is an inaccuracy in your interview," Mark was still lost in his thoughts. "At the scene, there was no terrorist shot at point-blank range, as you claimed in your interview. I saw the police report. I know what you're going to say. The girl was in shock and, defending herself from terrible memories, she came up with this version, found you, gave you an interview to strengthen her conviction. That's how the psychologist explained it to me. Perhaps, it was like that, but maybe not..."

And then Lisa finally saw how his face changed, how it became even longer, his mouth opened and a protest appeared in his eyes.

They were already falling to the floor, knocked down by a

sudden force that came out of nowhere when somewhere nearby a blinding cloud of the explosion soared up...

... For some time, they were lying on the ground—Lisa, Mark, and the cafe guard who pushed them to the floor. At the last moment, he noticed the boat and the man with a weapon aimed at them.

Lisa was deafened and blinded by the explosion and couldn't understand what the man in a paramedic's uniform wanted from her. Her head was ringing, her whole body was covered with sticky sweat, and she was quivering.

The boat crashed into the wall of the high coping, finally changing direction a few moments before the explosion. The people who witnessed the incident gathered around them. Each of them was telling their version of what had happened: the boat lost control, the driver was drunk, it was a drunken race... But Lisa clearly saw that the boat was going right at them and the man on board was about to shoot.

"By the way, there is an inaccuracy in your interview. At the scene, there was no terrorist shot at point blank range, as you claimed in your interview."

She ran this phrase through her head the whole time the medics were examining them and the police were asking questions. Lisa refused to go to the hospital, said that she'd rather go to her hotel and asked them to call her a taxi, but she didn't go to the hotel. The taxi driver took her to the station. As soon as she was in the back seat of the car, she found her interview on the phone, flipped to the part about the terrorist shot point-blank.

... She did something that she would never have done in her right mind, but she wasn't thinking then, acting on instinct, not even animal instinct. It was unclear which one. Previously, she would have ridiculed a person who suggested that she might do so. Slowly, very slowly, she was going downstairs, but not to the exit, to him, to this disgusting bastard. She stopped. He took his weapon at the ready, as if shielding himself with it, but she could still smell his body, he reeked... What was that stench? It smelled of sperm, looked like he had already come more than once, it smelled of sweat, pus... And lavender, for some reason, something you'd smell in a cozy home. Perhaps it was his lotion, with which he tried to mask his smells, and this gave her confidence. She stood very close and looked into his eyes, saw his pimples, his barely grown facial hair... Then she leaned to him with her lips, he backed away... his eyes were restless, the mocking smile disappeared. Then she put her hand on his crotch. At first, he twitched and then changed his mind... Well, what could she do to him, this little fragile girl, to him, an alpha male! Besides, it was his day today! His day of greatness!

She squeezed his genitals hard with her fingers, dug her nails and twisted so that he screamed, curled up and dropped the shotgun. She then slapped him on the face with her other hand. Then one more time and once more. While he was trying to deal with the pain and writhed, she managed to lift the sawn-off, step back and shoot him point-blank...

So there was no terrorist killed at point-blank? Mark didn't lie to her, did he? And why would he?

Escaping from one tunnel and flying into another, exploding at the exit with blinding sunlight, the train took her back to the cafe terrace, then rocked her, as if she had already died and entered the tunnel with bright light at the very end.

The smell of lavender flashed brightly in her memory. The victim of the attack said that the terrorist smelled of lavender, of something cozy, homey, and Lisa had recently experienced this smell...

The train was taking her south.

Chapter 11

"I don't believe that you do not know where he is. I want to know what really happened in that school. There was no terrorist killed point-blank."

"I don't understand what you are asking," the cripple backed up with his wheelchair, but Lisa pressed on.

"Don't lie. You already lied to me once!"

The cripple reached for the phone on the table, but Lisa grabbed it. "No, you will not be calling the police. You will not be calling anyone! You were there too, right? Tell me how it really went. There must have been at least two people. It is impossible to make a video and shoot at the same time. Who else was there? Was it your hacker friend who was testing his program and needed some photographs for himself? Did I get it right? Or why? I don't even think you're disabled. You're just pretending. I looked online for information about an incident with the police because of which you became a cripple. I didn't find anything. So, this is a lie! Lisa rudely pulled the cripple out of the chair, and he first gave in, obeying to brute force but then collapsed at her feet.

"No, stop pretending!" She pulled his hand, trying to lift and put him on his feet, but he fell again and looked at her from the floor with eyes full of hatred and pain.

"Come on, hit me! Kick me. Use your legs!"

Lisa suddenly caught herself thinking that she really was prepared to kick him with her feet, and this horrible thought sobered her.

She turned, went to the door, trying to get out into the fresh air and catch her breath, but then she returned, leaned toward the cripple and tried to lift him, put him back in the chair, but his hands pushed her away and his legs remained paralyzed, bent at the knees and turned to one side. It was obvious he couldn't move them.

The thick smell of lavender floated around the room, making the situation even worse. Lisa was dizzy.

He crawled to the chair, and moving his arms awkwardly, like an old woman, began climbing into it. It was really hard, but he almost managed, sat his body down, and his legs remained hanging curled up like a foreign object, like an unnecessary appendage.

Lisa was terribly ashamed. And she had no idea what to do next.

She caught her breath on the street. What was happening to her? Why was she so worried about this case? Unlike Mark, she never got any complaints about the missing photos. She sent a copy of the recording of their conversation to the editor, and the video clearly showed the girl demonstrating these photos on her phone. Yes, her recording was damaged, but there was enough information to believe in their existence. That woman didn't send the pictures she'd promised, and she didn't get in touch anymore. And it wasn't Lisa's fault. But still, she couldn't get rid of this feeling that she was being fooled and that made her restless and angry. If the police didn't find the dead terrorist... could he be alive? And maybe the witness didn't contact her because of this. She somehow found out about this and feared for her life, Lisa thought. Or was there something completely different going on here?

She needed to find a quiet place to think. Lisa didn't want to rent a room in a hotel in this city. She didn't like this city. It gave her anxiety, made her feel like she was being watched from every house on the street, from every passing car.

There was only one thing left to do: go back home. Lisa reached into her pocket behind her phone to see the train schedule, but it wasn't hers, it was the cripple's. She must have put it in her pocket by mistake when she took it from him. Lisa stared blankly at the screen, thinking how to return it to the owner without meeting him, and then, unexpectedly, she found the list of calls and pressed the last one on the list.

Someone answered immediately. A familiar voice hurriedly

said, "Well? Have you thought about it?"

Lisa took the phone from her ear and again stared at the screen. Should she just hang up? But then she wouldn't find out anything and would have to return home with nothing.

Should she reply then? But that meant she knew of their connection and possibly, their plans.

The voice continued impatiently, "Why aren't you saying anything? Hello? Do you hear me?"

"Is this that very 'something' you invented to lure out the hacker?"

At first, it was very quiet, so quiet that she heard him inhale.

"Did I get it right?"

At first, the person on the other end didn't breathe out for several long moments. Then she heard him finally exhale.

"Where did you get this number? What's up with Philip?"

"That's an interesting question," she even grinned at Mark's impudence. "Better you tell me what's your connection to the cripple? And if you want to know whether I killed him, then no, he's perfectly fine, well, save a couple of bruises."

"Did you beat up a cripple?" Mark's voice immediately rose a couple octaves.

"Oh, stop it!" Lisa stopped him. "Enough with the pretend pathos! And the fake resentment! I've heard enough!"

"Wait! You're a journalist, and if you hurt Philip..." Mark tried to seize the initiative.

"Oh, so now you remember about a journalist's duty! Don't even start! I no longer believe in it either, or the higher purpose of journalism. Real journalism has long died. Call it a cliché, but that's how it is."

"Well, yes, of course, we are all predators, hunting for a good story," Mark snapped.

"That you are."

"Let's leave the verbal gymnastics. What are you doing over there?"

Lisa was beginning to feel entertained by Mark's situation, a shark caught on a hook of a simple bamboo fishing rod. And she continued. "So this is your backup plan? You know very well that Philip knows the hacker and may also know how to find him. You really need his program. To get rich, that I understand. But is there something else? I think someone else needs his program. And you need to hurry, because someone has already tried to kill us with that boat, and I don't think I was the target. That boat turned at the last moment, didn't crash into us. This is a warning to you, right? Looks like there are some very serious people behind this, and they are not fucking around..."

There were short beeps in the phone. She again stared at the screen. Her throat was dry. The terrible heat of the southern town, two days without sleep and the disgusting feeling that someone was playing with her were getting to her. The message icon flashed on the phone's screen. Lisa pressed it and another joke appeared.

"It does sound stupid, 'a terrorist killed in a terrorist attack.' It's like an accident at work."

Lisa yelled at the phone, as if those who were sending her these messages could hear her. "That's still not funny!"

She looked around for some cafe, even better if it were a fountain with water so common in southern cities, but found nothing on this sleepy street with shut down windows and fences twined with flowering vines.

The pastoral landscape was disrupted by the appearance of two police officers. They quietly parked at the intersection, got out of the car and slowly approached her, aiming at her with their guns. She was so surprised that she dropped the cripple's phone and it clanged, crashing on the cobblestone pavement.

Chapter 12

They charged her with suspicious behavior. Of course, they did! She was constantly hanging around that cripple's house. She's lucky no one saw her climb the fence. It looked like the police didn't have anything serious on her. Then why target her? Or did she look that crazy?

Lisa took several deep breathes, in and out, trying to calm down.

Why did they need her? Even if they had no grounds to arrest her, they could simply keep her in the police station for some time, which meant she was losing time and she didn't know what Mark was capable of. She needed to go on the offensive right now.

She found her phone in her pocket. The police picked up the crippled boy's phone, logically assuming that this was her phone and calmed down. They didn't even search her. By touch, all the while looking at the police officers, she dialed her editor's number and wrote him a message. Just one word, "Help." Of course, she had the right to an official call, but first she wanted to find out something.

After she had sent the message, without waiting a second longer, Lisa demanded an explanation from the only police officer in the room at that moment. He reluctantly looked up from his phone. Judging by the muffled sounds, he was watching a soccer game. Without turning his head, he asked her to wait a bit longer. The chief of police was going to be there any minute, and he would decide what to do with her.

Lisa got up from her chair, went to the police officer and looked behind the table. He covered his phone with a folder and stared at her.

"Looky at the big bad policeman!" Lisa laughed. "Was that you, by any chance, who made that poor guy a cripple?"

The police officer clearly didn't expect her to accuse him. A wave of emotions swept across his face: indignation, confusion, anger, and a desire to put her into a holding cell or simply strangle her. He was clearly mad at her for distracting him from his game.

"Ah, come on," Lisa waved her hand. "Maybe not you personally, but one of you did it, didn't you?"

"What cripple?" he finally answered.

"Well, the guy, you know. You arrested me by his house, allegedly for suspicious behavior. By the way, what kind of strange wording is that?"

The police officer, a black-haired man with large pores on his oily face, finally managed to get his emotions under control, and his eyes turned from crazy bulging to normal.

"That man whose house you were hanging around?" he repeated her question slowly, clarifying.

Lisa nodded.

He looked at her as if he wanted to say something. Searched for words, probably, fearing that he would sound too rude, but changed his mind. He really wanted to return to his game, but he was already distracted and he was ready to take it out on her. A mocking amusement suddenly appeared in his eyes.

"That guy..." he repeated again, as if thinking.

"Well, yes," Lisa cut him off. "The one who was hit by a police car after he launched his program for tracking corrupt police officers."

"Well yes?" he even stood up. "So we mutilated him?"

Lisa hesitated, not wanting to give up her source. Because he was about to ask her that. The last thing she needed now was for these law enforcement officers to take it out on the waiter.

He was smiling. It was an unpleasant smile. He could hardly restrain himself so as not to burst out laughing. "Did you come up with this just now? Or did someone tell you?"

An explosion of loud screams came from his phone. It looked like something serious was happening during the game, but even this fact didn't distract him from watching how Lisa's face changed. And there was plenty to look at. She was obviously in a pretty pickle. But what if it wasn't true? Lisa remembered how, while escaping from this city on the train, she was trying to find online any information about the handicapped person. But it wasn't working, and she'd dropped the search. Unforgivable for an experienced journalist. Or maybe nothing like that ever happened? What if the waiter actually lied? But why? Sometimes people deliberately dramatized a situation so that it looked more threatening.

Lisa shifted from one foot to another, trying to come up with something believable as fast as she could.

The police officer was now looking down at her, arms crossed over his chest, and what was happening obviously interested him more than some game.

"I understand that an experienced hacker can easily erase any information from the Internet... But there will always be a footprint..."

"So, you are making an unfounded accusation?" he said, triumphantly.

Well, of course, flashed through Lisa's mind. *Now he would accuse me of libel.* If they had nothing serious on her before that, then she just gave them an idea... And this was at a time when she desperately needed to get out of here, when Mark was about to do something most likely radical. She did something very stupid at the worst possible time. What could Mark do? How was he going to lure out the hacker? And suddenly, she understood.

Chapter 13

From the high lancet French window, one could clearly see the curve of the road, mirroring the bend of the mountain river flowing between the green hills, beyond which stood the mountainous peaks. The waters of the river reflected both the rocks and the blue skies, only partially obscured by the snow-white flakes of the clouds. Sometimes it seemed that it was, in fact, smoke swirling from some ice house of a mountain fairy from some kid's tale, living, possibly nearby, and, possibly, at the highest of the peaks.

Ever since he bought this house in the mountains many years ago, he never ceased to be amazed at the constancy and variability of this place. The foliage of the trees and shrubs that blazed in autumn with all shades of purple, mixed with fiery orange and lemon, in winter hid in white furry coats with a blue tint only to flare up again in spring, this time with apple-pink, lilac and snow-white flowers.

Julius was never a romantic. On the contrary, the work of the editor-in-chief of a reputable newspaper with a long history and the head of a large media holding required extreme pragmatism, both before and now in the conditions of fierce competition for readers' attention in the era of the Internet, a young and very pressing competitor.

But looking at this magnificent beauty, he understood every time no matter how many conquerors, real or virtual, came to this land, all of them would eventually subside like dark flood waters and only the eternal would remain. True, lately, global warming had made some adjustments to his confidence, but here it remained the same. Still the same.

Julius walked away from the window, and the lace tulle curtain blocked the view from outside.

"And where is my phone?" he asked, looking around, then repeated the question, already speaking to the smiling woman, his wife, who appeared in the room.

"No, no, and NO!" the woman came up to him and, raising herself on tiptoes to compensate for her short stature, kissed her husband. "We agreed, no calls today. At least one day a year!"

She also ruffled his hair with her hand, then on tiptoes again reached where she could.

"It's your birthday today. That's final."

Julius admired his wife. She was much younger than him, so beautiful with her blue eyes and snow-white skin, light-brown hair and large soft breasts. It was so simple and easy with her. Betty was not a careerwoman. She was just a wife, loving and patient. In a word, a reliable partner for the man who had achieved his success with great effort. He always recognized that there was a large share of her work in his success, domestic, female, designed to protect her husband from household worries, from sleepless nights with the children when they were sick. She was running the house, and to her credit, here he always had a delicious hot meal and a warm bed, no matter what trips he returned from and no matter how exhausted he was. Even now, when there was no need for him to go on these business trips, his position demanded about the same amount of stress as before. And when he fell asleep with her beautiful warm body in his arms, breathing in the smell of her hair scattered over the pillow, Julius felt happy.

His wife always looked at him with loving eyes. His words, his desires, were law. Except today.

"I hid the phone safely. Don't even try looking for it. The children promised to come, so get ready for your night, dress up, and I'll return to the kitchen for now." She sighed pretending to be upset, as if the household chores were too much for her and again stretching on her toes, kissed her husband, this time on the nose.

When the door closed behind her, Julius automatically raised his hand to his nose and wiped it.

It's a good thing that Betty was not a careerwoman. Once she tried journalism, wrote some small articles, but it didn't go further than that, and over time, she even removed the computer from her desk. But then the children, who came back from college, got her hooked on games. She played The Sims, built a large house, cultivated a garden, doing all the womanly things online. Therefore, the laptop went back to its place, but she opened it only when her husband was not at home. Once she even fell asleep with the laptop in bed. Julius was very touched by this sight: his big-breasted beauty-of-a-wife with her hair carelessly braided was snoozing comfortably in their bed with the silver metal laptop on her knees. He looked at the picture on the screen: the hardworking Sims family was building like busy ants. And this peaceful sight touched him. He gently kissed his wife on her flushed cheek and took the laptop back to its place.

Julius loved and respected Betty for everything: for not asking too many questions, for always being ready to support him. And he was touched by her attitude toward people. She helped everyone who needed help. It didn't matter whether they asked her for help or not. She helped both people and animals. He remembered how she was treating a swallow that accidentally flew into the house and was caught by a domestic cat. Together with her children, who were still little back then, they took the swallow from the cat, applied ointment to its wounds and allowed it to sit for a long time on the top of the wardrobe, recovering. They put water and food on the wardrobe under the cat's disapproving looks.

Julius smiled at his memories.

And all this was his wife. His second wife. However, today was not about sad memories. The kids were coming from college today. They always came for their father's birthday.

He went to the fireplace, adjusted the picture of the whole family in an old-fashioned pose—he was sitting in the chair and Betty was standing next to him with her hand on his shoulder and with them were the children, Sasha and Misha. His wife insisted on the photo, arguing that tradition was the foundation of a strong family.

Betty was trying to persuade him to invite his employees tonight, to have a big party, but he was already too old for this and he never loved noisy parties. Although maybe he should gather everyone, especially the young generation. And he should fix this one mistake. He had very talented young people in the office, and he treated them more like he was their father. Maybe because he had his children late and watching them grow was the most wonderful thing in the world. He understood this with age. His youth was journalism, which didn't let him enjoy life. Work, work, and work again always was his passion and his pleasure. Over his life, he had achieved a lot. The newspaper, which he headed, eventually grew into a media holding with many other publications, but still remained his only and favorite beloved brainchild.

Everything crumbled when his first wife left him, taking their child with her. Julius had barely held on. Only the habit of the Spartan lifestyle of a correspondent, which he developed when he was still young, didn't let him spiral into despair, alcohol and drugs. True, that was a dark period, but he managed. As always.

Why did she do that? What was she missing? She said that because of his frequent business trips, she stopped seeing him and wanted to live and not wait to see whether he was going to return. And if so, in what physical and moral state.

He heard rumors that his wife often went to church, prayed all the time, and went to confession with the priest, but he didn't believe it. His dazzlingly beautiful, perky, defiant Noelle went to a priest and told him what? About their relationship? About their sex life? And some old man in a cassock behind the trellised window drooled, listening to the intimate details that you couldn't always voice? Noelle, after all, never minced her words and said what she thought, what she felt. He tried to talk to her about it, to stop her from going there, but only saw a look that suddenly became empty and hostile. Yes, of course, he also understood his guilt in what had happened, but she knew who she was marrying.

He had long forbidden himself to think about it, but sometimes he couldn't control it, and then the melancholy—dull, blind, suffocating—took him over.

He would never forget her words, "You have ceased to be a man. Your work has turned you into a monster, always hungry, ready for anything for a scoop..."

It's just that today was his birthday. A day when anyone is vulnerable. You're ready for gifts and birthday cards, ready to feel things and that's when it overwhelms you.

Chapter 14

The man that burst into the police station looked very much like some creature from fairy tales. Chubby, plump, with a red glossy face, he resembled a donut just taken from the frying pan, only in a police uniform. Nevertheless, when he appeared, Lisa's guard snapped to attention. Two more men came in after him. The donut bore holes in the guard for a few seconds and then asked in an abrupt, bossy voice, "Is that her?" He didn't even nod in her direction or make any gesture, but Lisa knew that he meant her.

"That's right," said the police officer in the voice of a subordinate taken by surprise but who didn't understand what he did wrong.

"Release her immediately!"

The guard's eyebrows went up and his mouth opened, apparently to ask a question. The donut turned around and left just as fast as he had appeared. His two escorts disappeared with him.

The police officer threw a puzzled look at Lisa, closed his mouth since he didn't manage to voice his question, and pursed his lips.

Lisa, who couldn't understand what was happening but was happy to be free again, walked away from the police station. She called her editor, wanting to thank him for the intervention—he was actually cool! She never doubted the connections or the influence he had, but she didn't expect all this to resolve so quickly...

He still wasn't picking up.

Well, okay, Lisa thought, *he's probably angry I was so stupid to get myself into this mess.* Her editor-in-chief did have such a habit of punishing with silence. Now it was more important to stop Mark.

Lisa dialed Mark's phone number, but he didn't answer either. She called him again and again, but nothing happened. It looked like

Mark had already regretted spilling his plan to lure the hacker and now that she called, he was just taking time, hoping... Hoping for what? That she would just let him be?

Lisa called Mark's office and asked them to put him on the phone. She said that it was urgent, but Mark was not there and they refused to tell her where to find him. Lisa barely restrained herself from screaming, "Find him immediately! He's going to do something horrible!" She had to restrain herself because who would've believed her?

At the help desk at the station, she found that she was already late for the last train. Even if she wasn't, where would she even be looking for Mark in this big city? She didn't see the point of going to his place now. Of course, she could return to the cripple and shake him, but she'd already done that. He wouldn't tell her anything. "Stop! No, just stop!" she told herself. She was missing something, something important.

And then Mark unexpectedly picked up. "Were you looking for me? Has something happened? Did you find the hacker?"

Stop again! First, she needed to calm down. Perhaps, he still didn't know that she had figured it out. She just needed to ask leading questions first, but she couldn't restrain her anger anymore and burst out. "You know what? I understand what's happening to you now. Do I have to say it? Or will you just tell me what your plan is, and why you need that crippled boy?"

There was silence on the other end of the line.

"Silence? Ok, then let me guess. You are waiting for the next terrorist attack, hoping that the hacker cannot help but get involved, and in order to catch him, you need another hacker. That cripple is also not a bad one. And they are not friends at all, they are rivals, but they are also possible partners. Did I get it right?"

Mark grunted nervously, and Lisa realized she was on the right track. "And since you may have to wait God knows how long for a new attack, you came up with... Oh my God!" Lisa's eyes shadowed with pain when she realized what he was doing. "You decided to arrange it yourself? No? No, it's not possible."

Mark didn't say anything.

Lisa was waiting for his answer, at least for him to deny it. He could say that she was stupid, that she was paranoid, but Mark wasn't saying anything. And then she continued. "And maybe you were also behind that terrorist attack at school... Nobody would suspect you... and you have exactly the same phone... yes, you said you lose your phones all the time and then you buy the same model... and your phone is the same as that girl's, who survived. She picked it up when she was running away. That's what she told me off the record before I started recording. This information was not in the article. How do you know that? Oh God, Mark, say it wasn't you!"

Lisa thought that Mark was no longer listening. Maybe he just left the phone on, and he... and he... what was he doing now?

"It's not me. For what it's worth, I was not there," finally he answered.

Lisa exhaled. He was there. He was talking. He didn't hang up.

"But you still know more about those events than you let on. Am I right?"

"I have nothing more to say to you."

Lisa was furious. What should she do now? Call the police? Interpol? The UN? And what if she was right? Where would the next attack be? Which country? You could post on social media so that children are not allowed to go to school, but when? A terrorist attack could happen any day. And why wasn't her editor picking up? He picked the worst possible time to teach her a lesson.

Lisa called the chief editor's secretary, Natasha, and to her question when he would be back, she heard Natasha's perplexed answer: "How the hell would I know?"

Lisa even imagined Natasha shrugging. If he turned off his phone, that meant he didn't want to talk to anyone.

"You know this habit of his to suddenly disappear. Of course, I suspect that the right people could find him in any situation. The ones he needs, his people."

At this point, Natasha made a meaningful pause, as if saying that Lisa was also one of his people.

No, Natasha was wrong. Julius always praised her work in their editorial meetings, making others envy her, but Lisa always turned a deaf ear to all the signs that he may have feelings for her. But now the secretary's antics and suggestions made her angry.

Two years ago, Lisa called Julius, a journalist she had always admired and considered her unofficial teacher, and asked him to hire her. She could no longer stay in her town and decided to change both her place of residence and her editorial office. Unexpectedly, this very famous man immediately agreed. Of course, he knew her story, knew everything she had been through. That's how Lisa got into the big, famous media holding company. The job completely captivated her and gave her back her feeling of being needed, of being in demand.

Sometimes, when memories of the past overwhelmed her, she would go to this seaside town just to be alone.

She really needed him now when she found such a story. She couldn't do it all by herself. The situation was too serious, but Lisa wasn't going to give the scoop to someone else. No, she wasn't going to do it when everything was too hot and unpredictable.

The loud signal of the car finally made her return to the real world, and she realized that she was standing on the side of the road and was about to step into the street, although there was no crossing. The driver even slowed down and twisted his finger at his temple. Lisa stepped back, and other drivers and passengers gave her unkind looks from the cars rushing past.

Lisa screamed. "Yes, you all go to hell! I wasn't going to throw myself in front of your cars! I was just thinking! And you can't even imagine what I was thinking about! Maybe the fate of your children is being decided now! Yes, yours!"

Another car swept past, blowing hot exhaust air.

Of course, Lisa had an idea where the editor-in-chief could now be. Most likely, he was in his country house in the mountains. She'd been there once, along with other editorial staff who had come to congratulate him on some anniversary. Usually, her boss hid from people on his birthdays, not at all tolerating the pomposity and solemnity that were traditional for such cases, most often making up some illness or need to restore his health. Natasha was the initiator of that memorable trip. She beguiled the staff into congratulating the boss and throwing him a party. True, only the young employees came, the ones who didn't yet know how much their boss hated such events.

Unexpectedly for all, he met them in full dress in a light ironed shirt and trousers with ironed creases, as if someone had warned him about the surprise. Most likely, one of the employees had called him. But he didn't let the guests go beyond the porch. Here, in the shade of a tall tree, stood a buffet table with champagne, fruit, sandwiches, and cakes. Julius didn't look sick, rather very tired. And then everyone felt somehow embarrassed for pulling the poor man out of bed. In short, there were no friendly hugs or fraternization. Despite the warm welcome and generous refreshments, they all understood then: the boss would never let them into his territory, despite all his friendliness and equality in the office.

Back then, standing on the veranda with a glass of white wine, Lisa casually looked into the room through the transparent tulle curtain and saw what she expected to see: a fireplace and an old armchair by it. There were photographs on the fireplace, probably family pictures and many books. One was open and lay upside down right next to the chair on the carpet, as if Julius had just been reading it and then when the guests arrived, put it aside...

But what if he was now at his country house, and she just went to see him tomorrow? She could take the very first train there. And immediately she somehow felt relieved. She was not alone! She would reach him! And the right decision would be made.

The phone's ringing once again distracted her from her thoughts. They were calling from an unknown number.

Thank goodness! This, of course, was her boss calling from some other phone. Lisa hastily pressed the green button. However, she heard a completely different voice. And that voice made her scream again. "You bastard! Do you know what hell you raised?"

"Do you like it?"

"What? Are you freaking kidding me? Do you know what Mark is going to do to find you?"

"S-so you figured it out? Congratulations!" he interrupted her.

"Don't interrupt me."

"Oh, c-come on, don't yell..."

She even saw in her mind how the hacker boy broke into a smile.

"Did you know that he would do that? What is the point of all this? Stop it right now!"

"Stop it yourself!"

"Are you playing with me? What kind of sick game is this? Is this some hacker's game?"

"And w-what if it is a game?"

Lisa choked she was so outraged. She was searching her bag, searching for the bottle of water she got from the restaurant and trying to speak at the same time. "Stop everything immediately, or I'll..." She choked again and coughed.

"You, w-what? You'll g-go to the police? And who'd b-believe you? J-just a hysterical woman! D-do you know how many such people c-come there?" he was mocking her.

Finally, Lisa managed to get the bottle and opened it, drinking some water. "I'm a journalist."

"And w-where is your evidence? Just phone calls and your assumptions? They will laugh at you! Better get your h-head in the game, reporter! After all, you w-were taught how to w-work out all the options, follow up on all the leads and not go after the brightest and, possibly, most wrong thread. Maybe Mark didn't think about the attack, but you gave him that idea..."

"Who's after Mark? Tell me..."

"G-god, don't you understand?" he interrupted her again.

"No, I don't. And stop interrupting me!"

"Then you're j-just stupid..."

And he hung up.

Lisa again found herself standing on the side of the road.

"Shit. Damn it! God damn it! How could she be so stupid as to pity the kid under the church! Holy Mother Teresa! She felt sorry for him! She was twisting the now empty bottle into some strange shape, but the bottle regained its previous form every time. And it just made her mad. Finally, she threw it right into the rose bush in the flowerbed along the road.

Then again, if not her, then this boy would have found some other journalist, just as compassionate. Or would he? Her head was pounding. It felt as if someone was squeezing her temples with clamps, and she wanted only one thing: to fall on some horizontal surface somewhere and sleep.

God, she was really tired. So much time without sleep and with so little food... She needed to find some place to stay for the night. Otherwise, she could actually step onto the road.

But something was bugging her. *"To work out all the options, follow up on all the leads and not go after the brightest and, possibly, most wrong thread."* She heard these words said by the hacker earlier in exactly this wording, but she couldn't think straight, so she abandoned her attempts to remember exactly where she heard them and simply turned toward the police station.

Chapter 15

The same police officer still sat alone at the desk in a wrinkled and tatty uniform shirt. His head was lowered to one side and supported by one hand with his elbow resting against the desk surface. The other hand dangled limply like it wasn't his.

Must feel good to live in this city, Lisa thought. It looked like she was the only troublemaker here. The holding cells were empty.

This time he was watching TV. Another soccer game was on the large screen.

He idly tore himself away from the screen, turned off the sound and stared at Lisa. "What do you need?"

"I want to apologize for this incident... Well, I did unfoundedly accuse you..."

An amazing, mouth-watering smell was coming from the pizza in Lisa's hands, which she bought at a nearby pizzeria, and tickling his nostrils.

The police officer incredulously looked at the pizza box, then at Lisa and back and finally waved his hand as a sign of reconciliation.

"Come on in. I'll get you some coffee."

Just minutes later, they were sitting in front of each other, chewing the delicious pizza, drinking hot coffee and averting their eyes.

"Why didn't you leave?"

"Well, I just didn't... And you know, I decided not to hide anymore. I really wanted to know this. If no one was harassing Philip, then how did he become a cripple?"

"Oh, it's a sad story, really sad."

He looked at Lisa, as if wondering if she should be trusted, but the good food, a few sips of homemade grappa from the flask and the warm, velvet night outside the window did their job.

"I will tell you a story." Grunting some more for show, he finally decided to tell her. "It didn't happen here. It was a different city. This is a story about some students who raped their teacher."

Lisa put down the half-eaten slice of pizza and stared at him. Without looking up, he moved his head heavily, as if flexing his neck, rubbed his forehead, the back of his head with his large palm, and continued.

"There were four of them. They dragged her into the supply closet. They lifted up her skirt, covered her mouth. Two of them were holding her, the other two were doing the horrible deed. One from behind, one from the front at the same time, then they changed places. It happened several times. Yes, some people are aroused by that even more..." The police officer somehow immediately aged before her eyes.

He repeated, "two were raping her, one from behind, one from the front at the same time, then they changed places, it happened several times..."

Lisa involuntarily covered her mouth with her hand, afraid to scream, but unable to restrain herself, barked, "Enough! Stop repeating it!"

The old police officer shook his head.

Lisa swallowed and smiled wryly at him, as if apologizing for her outburst. "Were they punished?"

"She didn't report it."

"But why?" Lisa jumped up from the chair.

"The bastards who did this horrible thing to her had some really influential parents. She was afraid that she would simply be crucified. After all, she was always very good looking. She wore short skirts, had flashy makeup. Too attractive, too self-confident. Her main drawback was that she succeeded in everything she did. And you know people don't like those types, whose lives are better than theirs."

Lisa licked her dry lips. She remembered Julius' words: *"Never tell loafers or amateurs who they really are—they will make your life hell!"*

And the police officer continued after a short pause. "The school principle, an old, lonely witch, was very unhappy about this and turned the other teachers against her. The principle was mad that a cripple may not be afraid of flashy clothes, may not be afraid to draw attention. Whose side do you think the teachers would take when it is very difficult to find a job?"

He looked up at Lisa, and she couldn't stand his look. She lowered her gaze, admitting he was right.

"That girl just quit. After what happened, she became worse. She used to believe that working with children and being kind to them could change a lot, but she was abused by children, her own students. Yes, her students..."

It seemed he wasn't used to making such a long speech and coughed at the end for want of habit. Then he wiped his eyes, opened the flask and had some more grappa.

Lisa reached for the flask, almost grabbing it from his hands and also took a big swallow that burned her throat.

"You're taking this all too personal! Has something happened to you or your loved ones?" he was surprised at her behavior.

"Nothing personal. It has nothing to do with me!" Lisa insisted. But then she apologized. "Sorry! I was wrong. I shouldn't talk to you like that. Please continue."

The police officer shrugged, but continued. "She moved to our city, lives like a recluse, earns her living herself. It has something to do with computers. I don't know much about that..."

"So Philip is..."

"Actually, it's Philippa. After that incident, she completely changed, wears only men's clothes and all that..."

Lisa was thinking hard. "You said she was hiding who she was. Then how did you know?"

"How did I find out? I had heard this story before, but didn't think that it was her. One time she got a letter. I was driving by. An envelope was lying on the doorstep so I picked it up, wanted to give it to the owner so that it wouldn't get lost."

"Do you know what was in that envelope?"

"Photographs. I couldn't look at them, it was too... Everything was shot in such excruciating detail... Perhaps, they were enjoying the memories for a long time and then found her and wanted to repeat it... I sealed up the envelope as best I could and left it on the doorstep. As I was leaving, I looked into the garbage bin near her house and found some pads with blood. That's when I began suspecting that Philip was a woman. And then, I just put two and two together."

"Did you try to persuade her to report the rapists?"

"I thought about it many times... This was terrible and she's also disabled... But where's the evidence? Since then, me and some of my people at the station have been looking out for her in case they show up. Who else will protect her if not us?"

Lisa listened. She was afraid that a careless remark would frighten away his revelations. She also knew that as soon as the morning came, he would stop talking. Now and only now was the right moment to learn from him as much as possible. Of course, later he would regret telling her and would even deny everything if she required an official confirmation. That's why she needed to continue the conversation. Be persistent but also careful.

"There was a boy, who often visited her. One of our men even saw once through the window how they sat, holding each other, talked for a long time, kissed. We started calling them Romeo and Juliet..."

Lisa's head began spinning from all the possible theories. "And you didn't think that she would want revenge?" Lisa finally said, barely audibly, so quietly that at first, he didn't even hear her question.

Lisa repeated her question and looked him in the face. No, he'd heard her, but didn't answer. The police officer turned to her and she understood everything. He either knew or suspected. And then she spoke slowly and confidently. "She is a criminal and must be tried..."

With an uncertain grunt, he turned to the window, behind which the morning was already mixing the dark colors of the night with the first glimpses of light, although it was still far from dawn. Through the window, she could see the silvery moon path on the sea surface, which had already faded a little, but was still there. A lonely cloud was trying to shield this radiance like a thief, as if wanting to steal it, but it didn't have enough power. The amazing night air blew from the window. The smells of wet leaves and the bark of south-shore trees were beckoning. One of the branches was tapping against the window, obeying the night wind, while the others were rubbing against one another, whispering some story, as if discussing amongst themselves what the police officer had told Lisa. A little longer and all this night magic would just vanish, but for now, the vague rustles and creaks were still reigning, clearly heard in the ensuing silence.

"Listen, what these students did to her is horrible, yes. But if she shot those who abused her, at school, then it's still a crime," Lisa tried to get through to the man. "She must be tried! And if you know about it, then you should speak up."

However, he was in no hurry to confirm her words, just peered into the ghostly landscape outside the window, as if wanting to see the right decision, the only one that could work in this situation. And the tree branch, which had grown too close to the window, tapped harder, almost as loudly as the judge's gavel in the courtroom.

"You are a police officer and you must not hide the truth about a crime... both you and your colleagues, who, as you said, are looking after her... Do they know too?"

He straightened up and then leaned back in his chair, looking into her eyes. "I'm not hiding. I have no evidence. I don't know who killed those people."

He didn't sound relaxed or trustworthy anymore. A stony faced man was now sitting in front of her, and he no longer wanted to be candid. The unknown person in the portrait behind him seemed to be frowning too, and his mouth, framed by a mustache, was ready to make an accusatory speech. Only whom was he going to blame: the rapists or the girl who took revenge on her tormentors?

"And yet, she still needs to be tried," repeated Lisa, "because innocent people could have been among the dead!" her voice trembled with outrage and rose to high notes. This always happened when she couldn't control her emotions. Lisa knew it was wrong, so wrong to do that! There was a court. There was a law. There was a prison and other correctional institutions after all... And justice could only be achieved in that way. What if everyone began taking revenge on their offenders? Then riots would start. People would begin settling scores with others, with those whom they considered criminals, even those whose crimes were not proven. All this already happened in the history of mankind, and nothing good had come of it.

She continued to believe in everything that she was now talking about, despite what happened to herself quite recently.

At that moment, the newscaster appeared on the large TV screen hanging on the wall. She was clearly saying something alarming, requiring everyone's attention. Lisa, who was still boiling with anger, grabbed the remote and turned on the sound.

"... this information has yet to be confirmed. Special services are still checking it, but we've decided to bring it to the attention of the people in our city."

Both Lisa and the police officer jumped at once.

"What, what was she talking about?"

Lisa began channel surfing, trying to find a newscast on other channels, but central television was still running their late-night programs, films about vampires, shows for adults, like who would take off their underpants faster, and all kinds of astrological predictions for the coming day. She threw the remote aside and began searching for information on her phone. She found it almost immediately. Unknown persons had made an announcement that a new terrorist attack would soon happen at a school. They sent information about this to all the media in the country.

The police officer and Lisa looked at each other. It had begun!

However, no such announcement appeared on any channel. It looked like no one believed it was real or considered it worthy of attention. The city news channel was the only one that decided to warn the citizens.

"And thereby sow panic," said Lisa.

And from there, it only got worse: the unknowns who reported the impending terrorist attack announced an auction for the media sources to receive an exclusive on where and when the terrorist attack would occur, and accordingly, only the best bidder would have the material for publication. Plus, as a bonus: a detailed photo report on each fired shot. They even promised to film the episodes that were the most interesting, in their opinion. The price of the lot was offered at a minimum of one euro.

The police officer continued to search for any information on the TV, and he succeeded. After the initial information about the auction appeared on the city news channel, it was as if stagnant water broke through a dam. Both the First Channel and the National Channel and the others, and the commercial ones, condemning and branding both those, were joking in such a cruel way, and those who started this panic, thereby continued to spread terror throughout the country.

News feeds were updated every minute, and insider information soon appeared that some media outlets had already registered for said auction. However, they wished to remain absolutely anonymous. They also wrote that the bids were constantly growing and, in just a short period of time, had reached the hundreds of thousands.

Lisa and her night companion were looking either at the TV screen or at their phones, feeling worse and worse. It seemed that not only the water restrained by the dam was pouring, but also a huge mountain had been disturbed by underground tremors and now boulders, mud streams, and hot lava were flowing onto people's heads.

Lisa tried to call Mark and he answered immediately, screaming into the phone. "It's not me, it's not me, and I don't know who's doing this!"

"Ah, so it's not you?"

"I swear by my mother, it's not me!"

It seemed to Lisa that Mark even crossed himself, so earnestly he said it.

"But your bosses have already registered for the auction, haven't they?"

Mark was silent, breathing heavily into the phone.

"They did, yes? Do you understand that you all gave permission to the terrorists? Do you really need a scoop that bad? Do you really need blood on your pages? But are you also certain that this is her handiwork? Not only did she gun down all those kids at school but... it wasn't enough?!" screamed Lisa. "If you can, stop her!"

The next person whom Lisa called, already walking toward the station, didn't answer. She barely kept herself from throwing the phone on the ground and simply set her boss's number to repeat dialing.

Meanwhile, the city was waking up. The first cars were driving along the clean, washed streets. Mothers in their cozy kitchens were feeding their children and making their lunches for school. The children were drinking their juice, and adults were having their coffees. Everywhere the music of the waking city was being heard...

Would people really take their kids to school today?

Chapter 16

She was rushing the taxi driver all the way, forcing him to drive the last kilometers along the serpentine mountain road. The driver finally snapped, but the huge amount he requested for the urgency calmed him down, and he floored it. Lisa hired him as soon as she realized that she wouldn't be able to withstand several hours on the train, that she would simply go crazy while she waited, and therefore, in the same place, on the station, she took a car. The driver, who happily agreed to such a profitable trip, now regretted his decision. The passenger turned out to be very weird. She almost went ballistic on him when the engine suddenly died halfway, so now he was checking the engine, drawing his head to his shoulders and carefully looking back at the fierce client. He was trying to make it work, but with his whole being, he felt that if the engine didn't work, this crazy woman would simply beat him. He ran his hand over his pocket, hoping to find his phone there in case his worst fears came true and he would have to involve the police.

Having yelled at the driver, who was foolishly fussing over the engine and the nearest lamppost, Lisa began to wave her hands on the road to stop another car, and then, finally, the engine started working. With one leap, she ended up back in the car, and grabbing the poor driver's hand, she pulled him in as well.

They were back on the road. The driver even pulled a cigarette from the pack, intending to relieve his stress with the help of nicotine, but decided not to risk it. However, Lisa herself, in the usual, true, long-forgotten movement, bumped a cigarette from his pack and lit it from his own lighter. She took a drag with pleasure, coughing—it had been long since she'd quit this bad habit—but not today! The driver lowered the window and even waved with one hand, driving the smoke away from her face.

It looked like the storm had passed, and he could just watch the road. And he did this with redoubled attention, thinking to himself that there were actually such bitches out there... She probably had no husband or boyfriend... Who'd even want to be with such a woman, who cares how beautiful...

After enjoying the smoke, Lisa began flipping through the news pages on the phone, hoping to read that the whole auction scandal had ended and that the joker or the pranksters had been found and arrested, as it should have been. And now they would get what they deserved for everything they did. But no, there were more and more alarming messages. At first, parents simply refused to take their children to school. Then, in many cities, people with children began gathering near police stations and government agencies demanding they do something and protect them from the terrorists. The fear for their children drove them out of their homes and made them become more active and aggressive. And this fear, fueled by the unknown, made people angry, ready to catch the bastards and lynch them all by themselves. The spontaneous gatherings threatened to escalate into an open revolt against the authorities that were unable to control the impending disaster. And if these people had even the slightest idea of where to look for those behind this nightmare, no one would be able to stop them. If they only knew where to look.

They tried to calm down the crowd, but no one could say for sure that a shooting wouldn't start somewhere right now. And if not today, then when? It was impossible to put SWAT teams at each school, and yet there were children's sports clubs, all kinds of groups, playgrounds... who knew where the bastards could arrange a massacre. Besides, there was no guarantee that one of those who were now trying to protect people from terrorists wouldn't start shooting... Soon, school bus drivers went on strike. Railway employees, air traffic controllers, bakers, and public utilities workers were about to join them. After all, everyone had children...

Chapter 17

Having asked the driver to stop before reaching the house she needed, Lisa paid and moved along the fence made of gray stones. Around the hill on which the house stood, mountain peaks shone majestically, covered by centuries-old ice, not yet succumbed to the effects of catastrophic climate change on the planet. Altogether, the blue sky and the blinding sun, green pines and the vast expanse that opened before her eyes from this place seemed like a hymn to the endless, beautiful life, but Lisa wasn't seeing it. Hiding in the shade of an old tree, she was watching the house. She could, of course, just enter through the main door. There was little time left. The main news from all the feeds was the message about the growing bid on the exclusive rights to report from the site of the upcoming terrorist attack. Of course, each message ended with assurances from law enforcement officials that the situation was under the control of the relevant services and that the pranksters would soon be found. Nevertheless, the bids were growing rapidly, reaching astronomical figures.

There were more and more people who went to protest at the administrative buildings of the cities and villages throughout the country. The whole country was out on the streets today. The situation was getting even hotter because of the deadline set by the organizers of the auction. They promised it would be over by midnight.

Of course, her editor-in-chief, like everyone else, saw both this message and all the previous ones. Was their newspaper also taking part in the auction? This thought seemed to her just monstrous. *No, not them!* They had an excellent reputation as an old, well-deserved media outlet, and they respected their readers like no others. Julius would never do that! And yet, Lisa wanted to get confirmation as soon as possible that this was really so, that achieving a goal by whatever means necessary wasn't for them. No, they definitely wouldn't have gotten involved in this mess. Or would they? After all, the task of their newspaper, like any other media outlet, was to inform readers. And if the exclusive went to them, who would blame them?

Shadows were moving behind the lace curtain, but it wasn't possible to determine who it was. Perhaps, only the wife or family members were in the house, and her editor was already in the office. But something told Lisa that he was here and, of course, was calling from his secret phones, collecting information, working with his own newspaper correspondents wherever possible.

Crouching low behind the fence, Lisa crept up to the veranda and hid in the bushes.

A wind rose from the side of the road, playing with a scree of dry leaves, tossing them to the sky and throwing them into Lisa's face. She turned away, hiding from the dust. Rain first fell from the sky. Darkness fell quickly and then suddenly a stream of cold rain started pouring. A strong gust of wind threw the unlocked gate open, and it knocked loudly against something.

Lisa took a breath, ran, and climbed under the window, pressing her back against the wall, trying to hide from the rain. For a short time, she succeeded and, catching her breath, looked into the room. Julius was sitting in a chair near the fireplace, next to a table. On the table, there were cups with an elegant blue pattern, a porcelain teapot, and some pastries on a dish. Opposite Julius sat a man whose face she couldn't make out. She could see only the back of his head. The two were drinking tea and talking. Lisa tried to make out something from the conversation, but the sounds became tangled and disappeared in the lace curtain, and the glass also didn't let through any words or even intonations. All she could see was that they were very pleased with the conversation and were laughing at something. And this seemed strange to her because her boss couldn't have been unaware of the main news that the country was living today. Was he really that cynical? This thought offended her. No, her editor couldn't just drink tea and talk about something when children's lives were at stake and nobody knew exactly where the terrorists would strike. This was wrong. This wasn't true!

And then she stopped hiding, straightened up, shook her clothes free of the leaves and dust that had stuck to them while she was hiding in the bushes, went to the door, opened it and went in. With Julius, who was hold a thin porcelain cup in his hand, sat the man who had dragged her into this mess, her old friend, the hacker boy. No sweatshirt, no hood, no frightened look. He looked quite content with his life, even happy...

"Lisa!" her boss said in a loud voice. "How did you get here?" he broke into an even bigger smile. "Come in, come in. Look at the guests I'm having today!" he said, getting up and pulling up another chair to the table. "Well, this is just like a real birthday! This is my son Denis. We haven't seen each other for many years, the circumstances were such that..." Julius's smile faded for a moment, "and now, finally, he's here. Such a surprise!"

Lisa couldn't take her eyes off the hacker, but he was looking at her, moving his lips intensely and only once saying what she'd already heard from him, "Save me!"

Lisa suddenly understood why the hacker's words on the phone were bugging her, *"to work out all the options, follow up on all the leads and not go after the brightest and, possibly, most wrong thread,"* as Julius always taught her, it was his traditional phrase, with which he encouraged young journalists.

She didn't sit down in the chair but continued looking at the hacker, and he stared back at her. Julius finally noticed the tension.

"What is it with you two? Do you know each other?"

He was about to lose all that joyful radiance and good mood.

"Stop with this act already!" Lisa finally snapped. "Somewhere now at this moment, perhaps, they are shooting children, and you are playing games!"

Julius drew himself together. The smile completely disappeared, only confusion remained on his face. "I don't understand. Yes, this is a tragedy, but I cannot stop it... Someone started a terrible game. We are monitoring the situation... But, forgive me, my son came to see me for the first time in years... His mother Noelle and I got a divorced, and she wouldn't let me see him. And then he himself didn't want to meet with me, and suddenly he arrived today... Then again, why am I telling you all this... This is my family. These are my problems..." his voice became harder. "And you, how did you end up here? I don't have guests over for my birthday, and you surely know this..."

The hacker, dressed in a decent navy suit, a light shirt with a tie, and slicked down hair, now looked more like a schoolboy, a high school student—a straight "A" student. A student who was caught cheating. He was looking at her intensely and there was a silent prayer in his eyes, "save me!"

"No," Lisa even stepped back to the door. "I don't believe it!

You came up with all this together. Didn't you? Our paper wins the auction, and we get the exclusive. And my, what an exclusive it is! One can only dream of such material!"

Julius straightened up. "How could you think that? We are not participating in this auction."

At that moment, he resembled a god ready to cast lightning on the heads of the infidels.

"Y-yes, you are," the hacker said quietly. His cup clinked softly against the saucer.

"What do you mean?" Julius looked at his son, not understanding.

"Y-your newspaper is also t-taking part in the auction..." the hacker repeated.

"And I even know who's going to win," Lisa finished.

Julius was looking at his son, at his employee, and his hands suddenly started shaking as if he were a sick old man. For some reason, he picked up the dish with the pastries, as if intending to give it to both Lisa and his son. If only they stopped talking, if only he could go back to the very beginning of this day, to the moment when his grown up, mature son, who was still his child, the child he wanted to have, the child he hadn't seen for years and whom he missed so much, suddenly appeared on the doorstep.

"Y-yes!" the hacker suddenly snapped, turning from a well-mannered boy into the evil rascal Lisa knew. "Yes, it's a p-present for you on your b-birthday, and I made it all happen! Y-your newspaper will win the auction, and you will be the only ones to g-get an exclusive report on the t-terrorist attack."

Julius put the dish with the pastries back where they were. He then wiped his hands on the linen napkin that was lying on the tea table. "I don't understand. I don't understand anything."

And Lisa just looked at her boss, then at his son, trying to understand whether they were playing her or Julius really didn't know anything.

"I didn't ask you about this... We discussed the situation with the members of the editorial board and unanimously decided that we would not take part in it, regardless of whether it was a prank or it was real. But let me just... what do you have to do with all this?"

"You have assistant editors, and they took care of the paper... y-you thought that you were the boss, the almighty, the all-seeing, and you still rule everyone. You b-became old, and you don't see many things and don't understand. I d-don't give a damn about your ethics, but you s-screwed up even here."

Julius seemed petrified. He froze in a hunched pose and now resembled Sisyphus, who had dropped, forever dropped, his stone. And his son continued.

"By the way, another lot w-was announced at the auction, where you c-could cancel the attack, but n-nobody, n-nobody even tried to do this. And don't g-get me started on ethics. Y-you are all jackals. You need some sensation. And y-you t-too, all your life, y-you have been chasing stories all over the w-world, scouring Africa, the East, wherever a f-fire could break out... Y-you left mother and me. I essentially grew up without a father. She left y-you, couldn't stand the c-competition with your s-stupid work. And I have always been a n-nobody to you, even though now you have become an old man and you d-drool – oh, l-look, my son's here!"

The hacker was throwing all this in his father's face, painfully overcoming his speech impediment, but still, every phrase sounded like a slap in the face. The porcelain dish with the cakes was already lying on the floor, only the thick carpet saved it from breaking into a million pieces. He was tapping on the table, and the porcelain cups were making a plaintive sound about to repeat the fate of the dish. The boy's face was glowing with anger that had broken out after being prisoner for so many years.

Lisa didn't know what to do. Julius sent away the house cleaner with one motion of his hand, and Lisa wanted to call the girl again so that she would bring something to calm him down but didn't dare.

"Y-you are so proud of y-your c-children from your second marriage. Oh, Sasha is s-so t-talented and already s-shows promise as a future c-composer. And your s-second, Misha, is s-such an artist, a r-rising star!"

The hacker was speaking out and his words burst out of him like heavy pieces of ice from a frozen river, which suddenly freed itself from captivity under the hot rays of the spring sun. "And h-here I am!

I p-planned and d-did all this! L-look at me! I c-control all the media in the country. If I w-want I c-can make a sensation h-happen on a g-global scale. They're looking for m-me. It d-depends on me whether another s-such event takes place or not! And I d-did it to show how p-petty you j-journalists are, r-ready to s-sell your s-souls for a good s-story, including my father!" His chest heaved, his sweaty face was burning with anger, and sweat was dripping from him.

His father froze like a stone statue, and Lisa simply didn't know what to say, what to do, how to stop and fix it all.

"B-but don't be a-afraid, your r-rep won't s-suffer. No one will know that it was y-your son who arranged all this!"

For a few endless seconds, they were all silent and only the grandfather clock was ticking away, approaching the hour, after which the deadly mechanism would be launched.

"They will find you and put you in jail," Julius was the first to finally break the silence, straightening up and again becoming the chief editor whom Lisa knew and was proud of.

"N-no, not m-me," the hacker waved him aside. "I t-told you, y-your reputation will not be d-damaged. Very s-soon they will c-close in on someone else, and they will arrest that person."

He took out a white handkerchief, sticking out of his breast pocket with its neat corner, and wiped his sweaty face.

"Him or her?" Lisa asked to clarify.

"F-finally, you figured it out. I was disappointed in y-your mental abilities."

"What did she do to you? Why her? It was you who helped her organize that attack, right? She would never have pulled it off alone. And I think, it broke her and finally put her in a wheelchair. And then her exclusive interview with me in our newspaper... was this also a gift to your father? But then you didn't have the guts to open up, or was it just a test attack?"

The answers to so many questions that had been haunting Lisa for these several long days simply rained down on her. She wanted so much to just come up and slap the boy in the face for using her, for playing with her, and she didn't even know whether he was still doing it now.

"He loved her," Julius replied instead of his son, "Loved... I can see that you are also surprised that such a weak old man knows all about you. I have been watching you as best I could. I tried not to lose sight of you, and I know that you loved her and tried to help her after she was assaulted, but you couldn't forgive her for the fact that she was raped. It's you who wanted revenge, not her."

The hacker almost went for his father, barely restraining himself from physical violence.

"Y-yes, I did l-love her! But she went too f-far then. We just wanted to s-scare the rapists, p-put them on their knees and make them b-beg for forgiveness, f-film it and put it online, but then... But then she s-snapped... and now she's v-very dangerous."

"More dangerous than you?" asked Lisa. "You are the one

who's holding an auction as a gift to your dear dad, not her. And innocent people will soon die!"

"There w-wouldn't be any attack if he forgot his s-stupid p-principles... I was relying s-so much on the second lot. I was hoping s-so much that he would just b-buy it, and then they would write about him, a h-hero and that we were still people... And human life is most important f-for us... And all t-that ... That was my p-present! But n-nobody, neither he, nor our valiant united media w-wanted to s-stop the auction!"

"And if they arrest her and put her in prison now, huh? You planted some fake evidence, didn't you, Romeo?"

"She had b-become too unpredictable..."

"Stop this game, cancel it right now!" yelled Lisa.

"No, I w-won't do it! But the second l-lot is open, and you still have time..." The hacker was backing off to the window.

He could jump out the window and disappear like he did before, Lisa thought. And again they wouldn't have any evidence. She didn't know how to stop him if he actually jumped out. It would be like looking for a needle in a haystack.

Suddenly Julius whistled. A huge Saint Bernard burst into the room, breaking the doors. The dog slid on the carpet, noisily shook off its powerful body, ears, hair, muzzle, and, obeying its owner's command, stood before the hacker, ready to tear him apart if he even tried to move.

"No, you won't leave! I won't let you," said Julius.

Through the open doors, the wind burst inside with the dog, tossing the curtains and flooding the room with bright light. The maid began hastily closing the doors and finally disappeared behind them. The curtains settled down. And the big scary dog, having rolled over on its back, was whining and jerking its feet. It was whining with pleasure. The hacker was scratching its belly and saying, "Easy, b-boy, easy. We are f-friends, remember?" He even picked up a cake and offered it to the dog.

Still petting the dog, he turned to his father. "Y-you were watching m-me, and I was w-watching you. I even got your dog to l-like me. And now I will calmly leave, and it won't d-do anything to m-me. L-look at yourself! Y-you don't even know how to manage your dog. But I wonder ... J-just curious... Really r-really curious... Would you call the dog if it were S-Sasha or Misha instead of m-me?"

A minute later, the hacker was gone, and he didn't even jump out the window. He simply left through the door.

In the ensuing silence, there was a message sound.

Lisa took her phone from her pocket, looked at the screen to see another funny joke. "One of the famous generals was asked whether a terrorist should be forgiven. To this he replied, 'God will forgive him. Our task is to make sure they meet.'"

"We'll see," she said to someone, then dialed a number. At the other end, they answered immediately. "Help her."

"Why? She is a criminal and must be punished."

"Do it," she repeated.

"But you said... You were against... "

"No! The SWAT team is already here, and I can't talk to you."

"But you and your men decided to protect her... You yourself said that... And you know the city well..."

"I repeat once again, I can't discuss the details with people outside the force, no matter who you are," he finished the conversation in a dry, official tone.

Lisa wanted to cry with despair, but she was still with her editor-in-chief, her idol. The hunched, gray old man, from whom all life seemed to have been drained at once.

"Who did you call?"

"Not important. You won't approve... Yes, she is a killer. She must be punished... But she is not your daughter, and it was not your daughter who was raped..."

"She must go to jail. Together they must go to jail," Julius said stubbornly, but somehow languidly. "That is the right thing to do."

Lisa's phone rang, and the police officer's familiar voice whispered angrily into the phone. "Would you turn on the damn TV already? I can't talk now."

She grabbed the remote, pressed the button and a picture appeared on the huge screen: an overturned wheelchair on a cliff above the sea, wheels hanging over the precipice, but somehow inexplicably hooked on the root of a dried-up tree. The reporter's voice continued the story.

"... half an hour before midnight, the suspect posted some photographs online detailing her terrible rape and asked the Internet users only one question, 'Would you be able to live with this?'"

The girl's neighbor, returning from work late at night, saw a minibus approach her house and masked men burst into the room. He called the police. However, according to an anonymous source from the police, the tire tracks from a wheelchair on the ground near the back door of the house under the canopy meant that the girl could have left the house before the unknowns arrived. Where the canopy ended, these traces were washed away by heavy rain that erupted that night. It is also unknown whether the people who arrived in the van pursued her. An empty wheelchair was found over a cliff on the outskirts of the city. Since the body was not found, the police are working on two versions: the masked men caught and abducted the girl or she threw herself off a cliff, and the body could be carried away by a very strong current. The search continues."

"Should she go to jail?" Lisa asked Julius.

He didn't answer. Instead, he turned to the window, looking at the magnificent landscape, at the mountains with the white caps of glaciers, at the blue sky washed by the night rain.

Lisa went to the exit, stopped, looked back at her boss. "I'm sorry for ruining your birthday."

Chapter 18

Lisa walked down the street, talking on the phone with Mark. He told her something that she herself suspected. How he screwed up and told his boss about the hacker program and how badly he regretted it later because some very influential people became interested in the program, people who were used to getting what they wanted by any means. He explained how he found out about Philippa, analyzing her interview with Lisa and comparing it with the police report in which there was no terrorist killed point-blank. Then he suspected it was revenge. And from there everything was easy. At the school where the tragedy occurred, he managed to find out about a handicapped teacher who used to teach there and that there were horrible rumors going about her sudden firing. But no one even remembered this—the terrible events crossed out all previous life.

Mark found Philippa and threatened to hand her over to the authorities if she didn't tell him everything. She confessed. Her condition didn't let her just run away. But she didn't know where to look for the hacker and his program. She only knew the number of the burner.

Mark also told her how his boss demanded that he find the hacker at all costs, how these very influential people rushed him and threatened him and then finally caught him on the train. The hacker promised to work with them, but then he fled and now no one knew where he was. Lisa remembered the terrible meatheads, and she shuddered with disgust.

They found the hacker at Lisa's place after her compassionate neighbor, to whom Lisa was like a daughter, called the police. The old man, who'd been pouring out his heart to the boy all night, decided that he should do the right thing, and then he himself was not happy with his excessive vigilance, but what was done was done.

From all this, Lisa drew the right and very disappointing conclusion for herself: they followed her and they never left her alone.

She turned off the phone, put it in her bag, but the sound of an incoming message made her take the phone out again. This was yet another funny joke.

"The Pope is calling on people to stand up to the terrorists. Well, finally the good old crusades are back!"

And suddenly, this seemed funny to Lisa. For the first time in days, she began laughing. She burst out laughing, laughed herself silly, became almost hysterical, doubled over and almost fell to the ground. Passersby looked at her, but she couldn't stop imagining how Julius would be mad at such a joke.

"How can one joke about such things?" he would say. And would definitely add, "we are all human."

Chapter 19

Near the woodshed in the far corner of the courtyard on the wet ground sat a boy in a white shirt, now rather wrinkled. He was crying, smearing tears and snot across his face. The tie that he threw aside was lying twisted like a trampled snake. The crumpled jacket lay nearby. Near the boy, a busty short woman was fussing. She was hugging him, stroking his shoulders, his head, using a lace handkerchief to wipe snot and tears from his face. She tried to make him raise his head by the chin and look into her eyes, but the boy shook her hand away, and his head fell back to his chest. Nearby, the beautiful Saint Bernard was yelping compassionately.

"Let me bring you some tea. Do you want some cakes with it?" the woman asked.

The boy shook his head without looking up.

"Come on, don't beat yourself up over it. Next time, we'll come up with something else. You'll make up anyway..." And she kissed him on the wet, hot cheek.

Chapter 20

Lisa walked along the alley between the rows of graves with monuments and simple tombstones. She hadn't been here at the cemetery in a long time, hadn't come here in a long time, even when she visited her hometown for a while. She'd been walking for a long time, slowly, breathing in the sweet smell of rotten leaves, wiping the rare drops on her face flying from the sky. She stopped by one grave, stood there, then knelt down, placing a small bouquet of flowers on the grass. At first, she wiped away the tears rolling down her face in a stream, and then she stopped, because it was useless. She held the little tombstone and sobbed bitterly, loudly, inconsolably. She stroked the tombstone as one strokes a child's head, pressed against it, as if trying to warm the marble with her body to restore life to the one buried under it. A tall tree with flexible long branches, obeying the rush of wind, wrapped her in its branches, as if consoling her. A light breeze blew over her face on the right and on the left, drying her tears, but they poured and poured...

After having a good cry, she adjusted the bouquet, got up, shook off her clothes and went further along the alley, then turned into another, then another. She went to the grave, fenced in with a wrought-iron fence, with a huge monument. His prototype was captured at full height, his wide shoulders straightened, his beautiful face laughing—a man content with his life.

Lisa walked along the alley between the rows of graves with monuments and simple tombstones. She hadn't been here at the cemetery in a long time, hadn't come here in a long time, even when she visited her hometown for a while. She'd been walking for a long time, slowly, breathing in the sweet smell of rotten leaves, wiping the rare drops on her face flying from the sky. She stopped by one grave, stood there, then knelt down, placing a small bouquet of flowers on the grass. At first, she wiped away the tears rolling down her face in a stream, and then she stopped, because it was useless. She held the little tombstone and sobbed bitterly, loudly, inconsolably. She stroked the tombstone as one strokes a child's head, pressed against it, as if trying to warm the marble with her body to restore life to the one buried under it. A tall tree with flexible long branches, obeying the rush of wind, wrapped her in its branches, as if consoling her. A light breeze blew over her face on the right and on the left, drying her tears, but they poured and poured...

After having a good cry, she adjusted the bouquet, got up, shook off her clothes and went further along the alley, then turned into another, then another. She went to the grave, fenced in with a wrought-iron fence, with a huge monument. His prototype was captured at full height, his wide shoulders straightened, his beautiful face laughing—a man content with his life.

The plaque had one name written on it, "Alexander".

Just Alexander, almost like Alexander the Great.

A beggar quietly approached Lisa from behind and spoke, hoping to get some money. "They say he was a cheerful man, he loved to live large... And women loved him..."

The beggar looked at Lisa's face from the side, hoping to determine what impression his words made, but she was silent.

Having trodden on the spot and realizing that he wouldn't get anything here, the beggar was about to leave, but looked back just in case.

The woman near the grave took a bottle of whiskey from her backpack, unscrewed the cork, and drank straight from the bottle.

The beggar stopped and even threw up his hands. *Damn it, now she will pour the whole contents of the bottle onto the grave...*

He really hated this tradition. Why waste the product? Especially, judging by the bottle, a quality product... She could have left it by the monument, and he would have drunk later in memory of the man. That would be human...

As if hearing his call, the woman closed the bottle.

Well, beautiful! The beggar praised her in his mind, already imagining how he would take the first sip and the strong drink, once in his mouth, would burn slightly, and then would spread over his body with gentle warmth, making him happy. And he stopped. He shouldn't rush, should let her feel sad and leave, but still not be late. There were more than enough competitors here in the cemetery. Therefore, he needed to wait, standing a little to the side but without losing sight of her. It seemed today was going to be a good day, and he would enjoy himself...

And she suddenly swung the bottle and hit it right against the pretty bronze face. The fragments from the bottle scattered in different directions.

"Jesus..." the beggar sprang back as if she had hit him, and then quickly scurried away, fearing that she would actually hit him too.

And the woman only said, "I wish I was the one who killed you!"

Printed in Great Britain
by Amazon

22881939R00178